DEATH PLAYS WITH FIRE

DEATH PLAYS WITH FIRE

A COTSWOLD CRIMES MYSTERY

SHARON LYNN

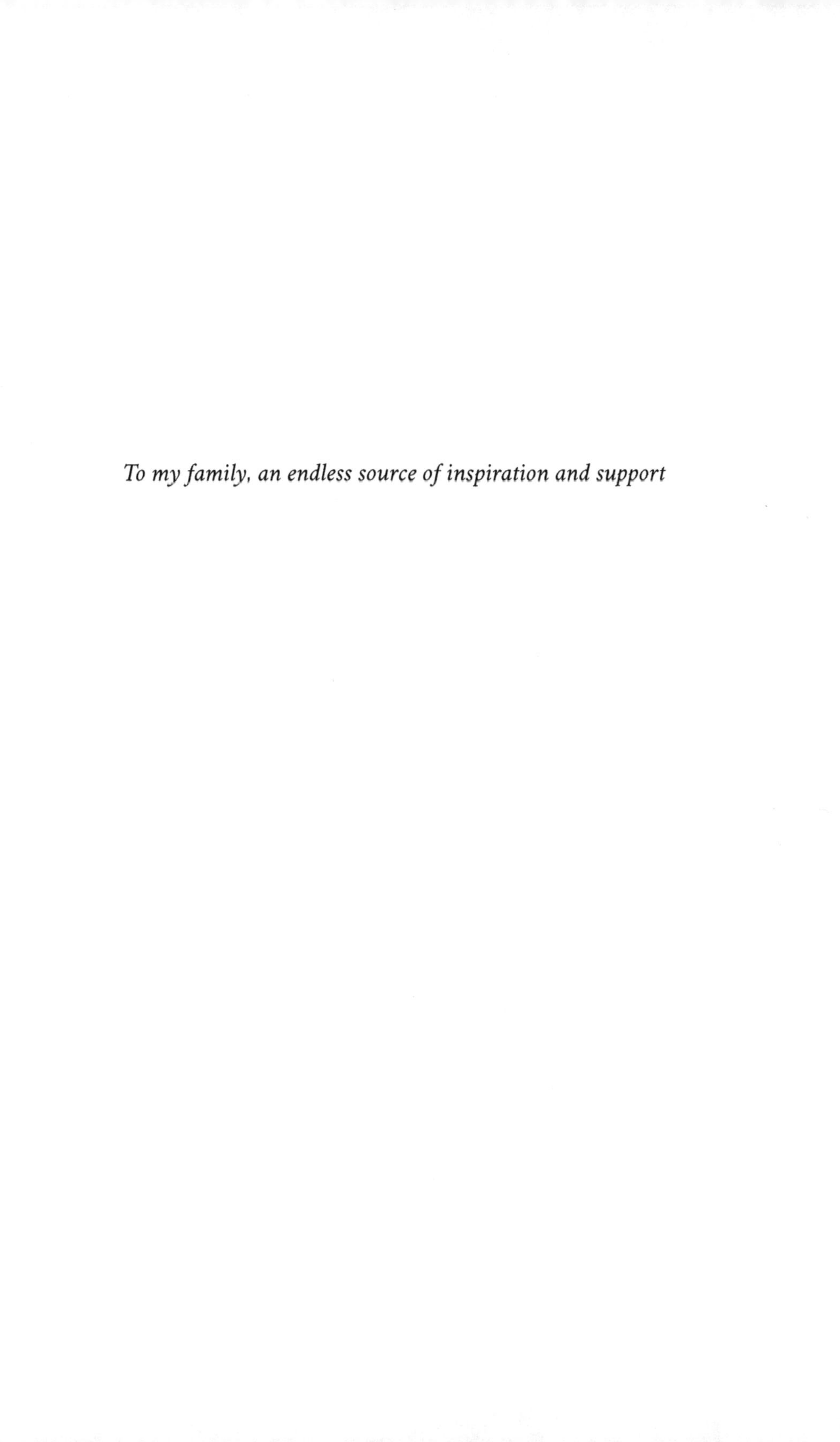

To my family, an endless source of inspiration and support

Praise for Death Plays with Fire

"Fires, daggers, and druids, oh my! This action-packed Cotswold mystery with a colorful cast of suspects burns bright."—Carlene O'Connor, *USA Today* bestselling author of the Irish Village Mystery series

"Madeline McGuire is in the thick of it again. This time in *Death Plays with Fire* at the Chedworth Villa, the Archaeological find of fourth-century Roman occupation in the Cotswolds of England. Of course, it's beautiful, but Maddie soon finds death and destruction that require her energy, intelligence, and unusually high level of curiosity to find her way through it. Sharon Lynn has again crafted an entertaining story that allows her readers to enjoy the vicarious excitement of a wild adventure in the gorgeous country of the Cotswolds."—Emma Dakin, author of *Storms in the Cotswolds: The British Book Tour Mysteries* Book 6

"In *Death Plays with Fire*, Sharon Lynn has penned another entertaining mystery. Maddie McGuire takes us on a tour of the Chedworth Roman Villa while solving a dangerous case. Cozy up with this taut and satisfying read because you won't want to put it down."—Margaret Mizushima, author of the award-winning Timber Creek K-9 Mysteries, including *Gathering Mist*

Chapter One: The First Discovery

An ancient weapon stabbed through a heart, pinning it against the Hunting Lodge door. The organ, charred in spots, oozed blood down the weathered wood.

I stared in horror, the scent of burning flesh circling my nostrils.

"Mon Dieu!" Dion exclaimed. He and the other French intern, Gabriel, backed away, speaking over one another.

Rooted to the spot, my mind rejected emotions, including complete and utter freakout. Pushing them aside in favor of logic, math provided a haven for my thoughts.

With a scientific approach, I examined the organ. Occupying a significant portion of the door, the heart appeared at least twenty inches wide.

The dagger had a blade around five inches long and sunk to the hilt, which meant the heart was at least four inches thick.

Taking in the dimensions, I calculated the atrocity to be closer to the size of a human head rather than a heart.

No way that could fit in a human chest.

"A cow or elk," I whispered, relief flooding through me, weakening my knees. Turning to the French boys, I called, "It's not human."

A brief silence followed by Dion demanding, "How do you know this, Miss Madeline?"

"This" came out sounding like "dis," more like a parody of a French accent, I thought, annoyed. No one called me Madeline except my mother, and only when I was in trouble. I told both Gabriel and Dion to call me Maddie.

We had only been working together at the Chedworth Roman Villa for two days, and already I found the boys' incessant questioning insulting.

Holding on to my annoyance kept panic from crippling me. "Maddie," I corrected, although it wouldn't do any good. "It's too big. It must belong to an animal." Not remembering if England had elk, I kept speculation to a minimum. If I were home in Arizona, elk, cattle, or bears might have provided the sacrifice.

A shiver shook me, causing a stumble. The word "sacrifice" possessed a heightened meaning.

The Chedworth site, ancient Roman ruins nestled in the tree-covered hills of the Cotswolds, created an almost mystical aura—the area just as entrancing as the Baths where I normally worked. The idea of a sacrifice didn't seem out of the question.

"But why then is it nailed to our door?"

He had a point, one that turned my stomach.

A once-over of the abomination got me moving. "I'll get Sam and Simon. Stay here and don't touch anything." Anything to get away.

Gabriel and Dion made distressed sounds at my retreat.

At least, I assumed they were distressed. The pair came from somewhere outside Paris and didn't speak English as much as I would have liked. Although, to be fair, I spoke zero French.

Dwelling on my stubborn decision not to take a language when in high school, I crossed what would have been the fourth-century A.D. Roman villa's central courtyard and over the kitchen area to the National Trust's Visitor Centre.

When the report of our finding formed in my mind, my fortitude crumbled, and I collapsed heavily onto a stone wall. After a few settling breaths, I bypassed the entrance and went to the restroom. Cool water on my face and neck revived me. I took my strawberry blonde hair out of its ponytail holder, raked fingers through it, and pulled it into a ballerina bun.

To get color in my cheeks, I patted my face lightly. Convinced I looked, if not good, at least neutral, I strode into the Visitor Centre. Pulling open the double glass doors, I scanned the cafe and gift shop until I spotted my boss from the Baths, Samantha Nivens, and coworker Simon Pacock.

"What have you found this time?" Simon sneered, looking bored. Despite his expression, I knew the question possessed a wealth of concern for me.

At the same time, Sam asked in her Irish lilt, "What on Earth has happened to ye? Pale as a ghost, you are."

A tear leaked from the corner of my eye.

"Chin up, old girl," Simon chided.

With a mighty sniff, I pulled myself together. "Technically, Dion and Gabriel found it, so it's not my fault."

As if speaking their names made them appear, the two French boys crowded through the door, pushing over one another.

"Le poignard, it is not Roman," Dion announced loudly before checking for tourists lingering in the gift shop or cafe. Fortunately, none did. Elbowing his roommate, he marched toward us and confronted Sam. Thick dark eyebrows drawn over his brown eyes in a scowl, he announced, "We must stop the dig."

Gabriel, the less intense of the two, ran a hand over his spiky light brown hair. "It is a, how you say, a portent."

"The Druids," Dion added, "they want us gone."

"The Druids? You mean a threat, do ye?" Sam asked, her green leprechaun eyes dancing with amusement.

"A warning, perhaps," Simon said, enjoying the situation.

I would have joined their mirth at the ridiculousness of the suggestion if the scent of charred flesh didn't linger in my nose. Sam and Simon needed information about what happened, and the Frenchmen were muddling the facts.

"You were supposed to wait there," I said, immediately regretting it—useless information.

Both boys launched a barrage in my direction. While I didn't understand a word of it, it sounded like berating.

Cowering under the attack, I slumped into a chair. My head sank slowly to the table, and I waited for silence.

A small hand rubbed my back. "What did you find, me girl?" Sam asked gently as Simon hushed the other two.

"A heart, big, cow, stuck to the lodge door. Our entrance." Raising my head, I locked eyes with Simon. "Nailed there. Ancient dagger." The words came out staccato, complete sentences beyond my capacity.

Leaping to her feet, Sam said, "Show me."

Dion held out the dagger.

"You removed it?" I demanded. The ill-advised action rankled me to the point of ranting. "Have you never watched a mystery or read a book in your entire lives? What are they teaching you in France? Everyone knows you're not supposed to touch a crime scene, let alone remove evidence and get your fingerprints all over everything, although it's not a major crime or anything, but you just went ahead and contaminated everything after I told you to stay there and not touch anything!"

During this outburst, Simon stood, moved behind my chair, and placed a hand on my shoulder. For my aristocratic coworker, this action rivaled a fierce bear hug. I stopped talking.

"Mon Dieu," Dion said, which I thought a bit unfair, using the exact phrase he used when confronted by a charred heart on our door.

"Throwing a bit of a wobbly, I'd say," Jill Beaumont, my roommate and fellow student worker at Chedworth, chimed in. Unhelpful in several respects, including the fact that I wasn't sure what she meant. Probably not flattering. Jill's work ethic flew off the charts, but she never considered emotions a valid response to anything.

Rescue came from an unexpected quarter—Gabriel. "You are right, of course, Miss Madeline. We should not 'ave removed the heart. But look."

Gesturing to Dion, who thrust the knife at Simon more aggressively than necessary, Gabriel continued, "The poignard, she is not Roman."

Simon and I both peered at the object as gore dripped from it onto the tiled floor.

My first inspection confirmed Gabriel's conclusion. The dagger's shape, material, and size indicated older than the artifacts from the Chedworth Villa.

Built in the fourth century, the villa housed several exquisite household items, but none as bulky or rough as the knife.

"Celtic." Gabriel pointed. "It is a, as you say, a warning. We should leave dis place." Stress or fear made his accent more pronounced.

Dion nodded emphatically.

"Do be quiet," Simon said, exasperation broadcast in every syllable.

Itching to correct Gabriel's logic, I opened my mouth only to close it again, afraid if I started another rant, I wouldn't be able to stop.

In a rare display of agreement, Jill turned on the two Frenchmen. "Don't be daft. The Celts were gone for centuries when the Romans constructed this villa. As a warning, it's a badly researched one. Just like your conclusion. Aren't you specializing in Roman archaeology?"

Consistently accurate but prone to personal insults, Jill caused Gabriel to shrink in on himself even when towering over her short, squat frame. Dion stepped in front of his countryman, ready to defend him.

Before things got out of hand, Sam returned. "The men made a hames of the scene," she said. "No need to avoid it. Off you lot go, over to the lodge."

As we shuffled out of the Visitor Centre, I hung back, not wanting a reminder of the area. Simon matched my pace, his way of comforting me. Simon and I had been through a lot together, and we formed an unlikely friendship.

"You do seem to be making a habit of this."

"Not my fault," I countered.

"Blaming Dion and Gabriel, are we?"

I huffed. "Well, yeah. As a message, it's to all of us, not just me."

"And I suppose that pleases you no end?"

The accusation couched as a question struck home, and I nodded in agreement. "Yeah, actually. Someone else can be threatened for a change."

Of course, I thought that very thing before and was wrong.

Chapter Two: The Trouble with Vandals

The group gathered around the Hunting Lodge door and debated what to do.

Jill asserted herself as the authority, pushing to the front. "Actually, that heart belongs to a large animal. A bull."

Happy for the confirmation, I chose not to point out that I already said that.

"A bull, yes," Dion agreed with a glower. "A Druid sacrifice."

Turning on him, Jill talked slowly and loudly as if to an obtuse child. "There were no druids here. Do you understand?"

Scowl deepening, Dion let loose a string of French that included curse words even I recognized. Jill ignored him.

Sam looked at me. "Should we call the police? Get your constable to come out?"

The constable in question, Edward Bailey, became the Roman Baths' favorite when he helped guard the museum during what the main office now described as "the unpleasantness." After some ups and downs, he became *my* constable.

"You have a constable?" Gabriel and Jill asked at the same time. Jill seemed skeptical, and Gabriel sounded a little disappointed.

"Detective Constable," I corrected, so proud of Edward for leaping into a new career path. He had several hurdles to overcome before the title became official, but I still liked using it. "And he's with the tri-force Major Crime Investigation Team now. I don't think a slaughtered cow part would count as anything but vandalism."

"I agree," Jill drowned out Sam's agreement in her strident voice.

"That's right fine of ye, lassie," she said, gently but firmly putting Jill in her place. Indicating the Frenchmen, she said, "Since you went to the trouble of taking it down, you might as well dispose of it."

"Wait," I said, still thinking of it as a crime scene. "Shouldn't someone take a picture?"

Murmurs of assent were not accompanied by anyone whipping out their cell. I certainly didn't want those pictures on my phone.

Finally, Jill stepped up and cataloged the heart and the dagger from every angle. Dion fetched a plastic bag from the café and cleared a path to our rooms in the lodge.

"It doesn't make sense," Jill said once we arrived in our two-bunk box living quarters.

The gorgeous exterior of the Victorian Hunting Lodge did not extend to our part of the building. The other half housed the museum and still boasted intricately tiled floors and carved rafters above the display cases. The archaeologist's rooms were utilitarian to the point of monkish.

"I know, right?" I said, which earned me a glare. Ignoring the slight, I soldiered on. "There's no reason for it to be here."

Disagreeing, of course, Jill said, "There's a reason. But why would the druids care?"

Not understanding the ancient priesthood, I wanted to ask her if bulls were sacrificed. But, I didn't want to give her the satisfaction. I had the internet. Answers could wait.

She couldn't. Jill's need to show off her extensive knowledge outweighed her desire to be cryptic. "The druids, as you must have heard even in America, were the priest class of the Celtic people."

Nodding sagely, I picked up my phone to text Edward.

The action made Jill talk louder. "Bulls were sacrificed, but a Druid cooked the heart and drank the soup. He did not nail it to anything as a portent of doom. They presented it to village elders, who then walked over hot coals. If they passed unscathed, the village would have a good year."

"Wait. Cooked?" The stench of the mess still clung to the inside of my nostrils. I gave up the pretense of ignoring her.

She stopped talking.

Honestly? At least I had something specific to research now, so I ignored her in earnest.

I texted Edward, 'Hey.'

'Hey yourself, lassie.'

'So…'

'Do not tell me you found something terrible.'

For most couples, Edward's admonishment would seem extreme. But we met over a severed human ear. Trouble found me far too often.

'Not me, and not human,' I texted back. 'Horrific, though.'

'Call the constabulary.'

Not responding, I opened a webpage on modern druids. At first glance, this did not seem like a group of people who would vandalize a dig site. Healing and nature dominated every line and picture. *Lovely*, I thought.

The only small red flag, more of a pennant, the website triggered for me pinpointed a gathering at the Far Peak Campground for Winter Solstice, one of the eight festivals in the calendar. The campground boasted several oak trees, and the River Coln not far away—both draws for druids.

A quick map check confirmed the area within walking distance of Chedworth at just under four miles.

'Fine,' I finally texted back. 'What's the number?'

Edward provided it, and I turned the task over to Jill.

"Hey, Jill," I said, sounding dismissive. "You don't think we need to call the police, do you? I mean, it's just vandalism."

As expected, Jill did the opposite of what I suggested. "Of course we do. It's probably not important in America, but here in England, we take pride in our environment."

As much as I wanted to point out that my home state of Arizona included the Grand Canyon, one of the Seven Wonders of the World, my desire to have her deal with the police ranked higher.

"Find the number for me, will you?" More of a command than a question, but I pretended to search, then fed her the number Edward gave me.

While she gave her report, more extensive than necessary, I delved further into the nearby Winter Solstice celebration. Ancient druids celebrated the solstice by sitting on hills and waiting for the sun to rise. Not what I would call threatening.

Searching for bulls, sacrifices, and druids, I found, as expected, that Jill had provided me with the correct information. Conclusion? Even if it made sense that modern druids objected to our being here, which they wouldn't, they didn't make threats.

"It is vital that the Chedworth site be free of disruptions. Important discoveries are being made." Jill's tone became more strident.

Odd. We weren't here to make discoveries but to protect the exposed parts of the site. Chedworth's intricately laid mosaics were covered by climate-controlled enclosures with raised walking platforms for viewing. The tiles themselves were on floors supported by pilae, little pillars that allowed heated air to flow underneath. Other mosaics in the courtyard had been uncovered, cataloged, and recovered.

However, the pilae outside needed protection from winter's cold and moisture as the floor covering them no longer existed.

I did, too. My clothes were cotton, designed to allow heat out and cool air in. As days got shorter and the air cooler, I wondered if I would survive a real winter. I regretted my decision to disregard the cold weather gear I acquired during my freshman year in Chicago as too bulky to pack. What I wouldn't give for a proper puffy jacket right about now.

"I understand completely, but it is imperative you arrive today," Jill continued to harangue the local constabulary more intensely than necessary.

'My roommate is abusing the police,' I texted Edward.

'Good. I don't want some handsome constable to show up.'

'Like anyone could replace you.' Absolutely smitten, that's me. Two short months ago, I would have spent hours wishing I could take a response like that back, thinking it too forward. Or that I might send the wrong idea.

Now, I received, 'Right back at ye, lassie,' as a return text and grinned ear to ear.

"If you're quite done focusing on your phone, we should go down to dinner."

It took me a minute to recognize that Jill spoke to me, not into her cell.

"Right," I agreed as she yanked the door open and stomped downstairs. "The French are cooking tonight," I said, although I don't think she heard me. It might be a stereotype, but Dion and Gabriel created delicious dishes.

However, the chaos we encountered when entering the communal dining room did not bode well.

Jill surveyed the scene with a sneer.

With a sniff, I joined her, taken aback. Smoke billowed from the kitchen, and every opened window sucked warm air from the room. The burned stench exploded in my nose, conjuring the bleeding heart with its charred edges.

Emerging from the kitchen, Sam said, "They made a right bags of it, but we're sorted. Fire is out."

"Are they okay?" I asked, concerned.

Summoned by my question, Dion and Gabriel followed Sam, heads bowed sheepishly.

"Desole," Dion said. "Dinner, it is ruined."

"Right, then," Simon's voice proceeded his entrance. "The pub it is. I can take five in the Citroen. Come along." He left before any of us could react.

"Well, obviously, I can't go. The police will want to speak with me," Jill observed.

Someone did need to remain behind to talk with them, but it should probably be Dion or Gabriel. Or me, I admitted to myself, since I found the heart. But I didn't want to stay.

"Good point," I said. "Do you want us to bring you a to-go order?"

Glowering in my direction, she corrected my Americanism to English. "Take away. No. I'll make do." After a few moments, she added, "Thank you."

The disaster chefs conversed in French and seemed to reach a conclusion. "I will stay. Clean the mess. Tell the police I removed the dagger," Dion volunteered.

Nice of him.

"There is no need," Jill said, contradicting my thoughts. "I can handle everything."

True, but why turn down the help cleaning?

"Non. I insist." Dion turned on his heel and headed to the kitchen.

As we neared Simon's sedan, I asked, "Where are we going?"

Trying to gesture my boss to the front seat, Sam said, "Don't be daft. You're a good half-meter taller than me."

A bit of an exaggeration, but Sam's head measured below my shoulder. However, I still wasn't comfortable on the wrong side of the car. As a passenger on the left, I wanted to steer and be across the road. The sensation made me woozy.

Instead of watching the road, I tucked my foot underneath me and turned sideways in my seat.

"Where are we off to?" I asked Simon again.

"Northleach. There's a pub."

The Wheatsheaf Inn, a historic coach house constructed of local stone, appeared unfriendly from the outside. Covered in ivy, it must have been beautiful in the summer and fall; the leaves encased the building in striking color. But with winter approaching, the dead stalks emanated abandonment.

Fortunately, inside, a fire crackled merrily, and the servers welcomed us. Packed to the gills, I worried we wouldn't get a table, but Simon called ahead as soon as he smelled our dinner burning.

Picking our way through an enthusiastic party seated across several tables, we finally arrived at our seats. "Thanks for calling," I said to Simon, failing to pay attention and tripping over someone's coat.

Turning to the owner, I apologized as I bent to drape the garment over a chair. "I'm so sorry. I tripped on your jacket."

A compact man with a mass of blond curls turned. "Robe, actually, but no matter, no matter."

He stood, took the robe, and held it up for inspection. Simple gray burlap but well constructed.

"Robe?" Eloquent, that's me.

"George Lynch," he said, pumping my hand like a water spigot. "Druid, at your service."

"Druid?"

Even though I heard of their celebration nearby, I didn't expect to find druids having a pint at the local.

"Ancient Celtic priests," he explained with a grin. "We all are. Camping at Far Peak, and decided a pint would do us just fine, just fine. And how about you? Local resident, are you?"

"Me? No. I'm from Bath." Then I remembered my accent and figured he must be referring to that. "Arizona, actually, but I'm studying at the Roman Baths Museum and staying nearby."

"Nearby here?" he asked, brow furrowed in confusion.

"No, nearby in Bath on Greenway Lane. They name all their houses in the neighborhood which I absolutely love. Ash Tree Cottage is so picturesque sounding. But we're here, in this pub tonight because we're all on loan to Chedworth Roman Villa to help protect it from winter. You have to pull weeds and put little coats over exposed stone."

I snapped my teeth together to keep from babbling further, but he didn't seem to mind.

"Chedworth Roman Villa, eh? Is that close?"

Nodding, I said, "Yes."

George smiled, which, apparently, was all I needed to kick my mouth into high gear.

"Do druids sacrifice bulls or issue warnings?" The question flew out before I considered how silly I sounded.

George laughed. "The ancients might have, but not us. A friendly lot, we are. Friendly. But I'm new, so let's make sure." With a clap, he hushed his dinner companions and asked about sacrifice before I could stop him and escape.

"No, nothing like that," an elderly woman with silver hair so silky it practically glowed said. "Caesar mentioned the wicker man and human sacrifices, but I personally think he made that up to scare people." With a gracious nod to me, she restarted the conversation among her table mates.

"Thanks." Taking care not to step on anyone else's robe, I got to my friends. They stared.

"What?"

"I don't think ye should be asking around in public," Sam chided gently.

Shaking my head, I agreed. "No, I don't either. It popped out before I could think. My apologies, Sam."

"Maddie." One word from Simon made me feel like a complete and utter idiot.

Which pissed me off. I mean, come on. We needed facts about druids, and we wound up in a room of them. Refraining from sticking my tongue out at him, I asked, "What is a wicker man, and what does it have to do with Caesar? The only thing I've heard of is a bad movie with Nick Cage." I thought for a second. "And Christopher Lee before that."

Gabriel explained, allowing me to ignore Simon's eye roll. "A case made of wicker shaped like a man. People were put inside and le fue. Up in flames, as you say."

"Eww," I responded with a shiver, "disgusting."

"Indeed. As your new friend mentioned, Caesar's drawing is the main source of the druid's performing human sacrifice," Simon added. "Propaganda, most likely."

Ordering commenced, and like me, no one at the table wanted meat. Creamy mussels scented with local cider for everyone, plus a spinach soufflé for sharing. The snap of whole grain mustard cleared the offensive odors of earlier out of my nose.

While my companions debated the merits of pud, which I would never get used to as the term for dessert, I felt a tap on my shoulder.

Turning, I found George the Druid grinning at me. "Some eco-warriors use the druid name in their cause. Warnings, threats, vandalism, violence all in the name of saving an oak. So Muriel tells me she does."

Indicating the silver-haired woman, he confirmed her name. "Muriel's been a member for donkey's years."

"She doesn't look like a warrior," I noted, more to myself than George.

Was someone that dedicated to their cause capable of obtaining a bull's heart, setting it on fire, and nailing it to our door?

With a shake of my head, I said, "But we're not doing anything to threaten trees out at Chedworth. We're preserving a building that's been there for almost 2000 years, but we aren't disturbing anything outside the original grounds."

To be fair, that encompassed several acres, but George didn't need that information. The valley surrounding the villa just had a fresh aerial radar scan. The process digitally strips away trees, and highlights locations of archaeological interest, including impressions in the dirt.

Our team of Student Placement Workers would be Ground Truthing this latest scan. If it shows something, we dig, reveal, and confirm. In most cases, we would replace the ground cover to preserve the find. Sam would work with the National Trust team to identify and pinpoint those areas.

"Miss?"

Lost in my thoughts, I completely ignored George, who stared at me, brows creased in concern.

"I'm so sorry. Spaced. As students, we're getting to expose more of the villa, and I'm super excited. But nothing that would take out a tree," I added quickly.

"I wouldn't suspect you would." George's grin widened when he heard Gabriel pontificating about dessert.

"Is that an Amiens accent I detect?"

Gabriel hopped over to the druid's table in a flash, chatting with George in fluent French.

When I turned to my companions, I found a thick-sided mug filled to the brim with frothy hot chocolate. Eying Simon, I mouthed, "Thank you," but didn't call too much attention to the gesture. Simon hated a fuss, but his kind heart knew exactly what I needed to wipe the earlier troubles from my mind.

Desserts consumed, we gathered our things to go. Gabriel touched my arm. "Stay?"

Shaking my head, I couldn't help but smile at his breezy expression. Scruffy beard and spiky hair emphasized his long nose, but the overall effect exuded a warm friendliness. It was nice to see him having fun. Dion always looked intense and moody.

"Thanks, but I'm pooped. Can you get a ride?"

General assent from the campers assured us that Gabriel would make it back to the Hunting Lodge.

We bundled into Simon's car, and when we returned to the ruins, an unholy screech carried across the grounds.

Chapter Three: The Altercation

The slamming of doors drowned out the voices. We raced across the parking lot, my long legs keeping pace with Simon.

Bursting into the lodge, I stared, dumbfounded.

Jill's short fame stood over a cowering Dion as he tried to melt into the couch. With a voice so shrill we could barely understand her, she scolded her fellow intern for something.

"Do be quiet," Simon admonished while Sam inserted herself between the pair.

Pouring on the Irish accent, she calmed the situation, separated the two, and hushed Jill.

"Maddie, me dearie. Take Jill here up to your rooms, now. There's a good lass."

Not knowing exactly how to accomplish the task, I, too, inserted myself between Jill and Dion and pointed my arm toward the stairs. The attempt to direct her earned a vicious snarl from Jill, but she stomped up toward our room.

Looking at Sam, I hoped for a reprieve, but my boss gestured for me to follow.

"Keep her there," Sam directed.

"Gotcha."

Entering the room, I found Jill pacing, red-faced with fury.

"You okay?" I asked, predicting a negative response.

"Okay?" she shouted. "Okay? Do I look okay? No. I am not okay."

Her body angled toward the door, telegraphing her intention to leave, and

I casually leaned against it. "So, what happened?"

"That idiot Dion contradicted me so many times that the constable hardly bothered to write anything or look anywhere. He didn't even get our names right."

Tamping down the urge to tell her that Dion arrived first on the scene and, therefore, made a better witness, and of course, the constable got their names. I struggled with a response.

"Ah." When in doubt, be vague.

It pushed her over the edge. With a screech, she leaped face-first onto her bunk and had a full-fledged tantrum.

Now, I've been known to lose control, but I don't scream. I count. To myself. Jeez.

Again, at a loss for what to do, I opened the door and snuck out.

In the hallway, I heard voices outside the open window. English accents, male, not aristocratic like Simon, so no one from our team.

Maybe the constable prowled around. Or someone who dropped off Gabriel and decided to tour the grounds. In the middle of the night. In the dark.

Chedworth's location off the beaten track meant no one happened on it by mistake. If Simon hadn't brought me here, I doubt a hired driver could have found it. At one point, we were on what looked for all the world like a cattle track.

Ensuring my shadow didn't fall across the window, I crept toward it, listening.

"It rattled them. That girl's hiding something."

"Treasure," I thought a second man said.

"One more—"

Before I could hear anything else, Jill threw open the door, stalked by me without a word, and entered the bathroom with a slam. The shower water even sounded aggressive when she used it.

Without exception, she was the noisiest person I had ever met.

The voices were gone, leaving me to wonder, "one more" what?

Back downstairs, I found Simon and Sam discussing Dion's account of the police encounter.

"Where did he go?" I asked.

"Is she secure?" Simon asked, followed by, "Right stroppy cow, that one."

Ignoring the last part because I wasn't sure what it meant, I placed my hands on my hips and said, "I didn't tie her up and gag her if that's what you mean."

"One can hope."

"Simon," Sam admonished, but with a grin.

"Gabriel returned. They made espresso and headed to their quarters," Simon answered.

"So what did happen? Jill appeared too angry to speak, which seemed extreme."

"Apparently, she wanted to get the constable alone, and Dion wouldn't leave since he found the heart," Simon explained. "He said that Jill's belligerence drove the constable away."

"An odd one, that girl," Sam commented. "I keep finding her behind the nymphaeum instead of cleaning the moss off the pilae."

"Too dirty for her, I bet," I said. "And I also wager that she yells at you when you find her goofing off."

"Right and right," Sam agreed.

Winter darkness masked the early hour. "Anyone want to play cards?"

Both agreed, and we settled on Black Maria—what I called Hearts— adapted to three players. After trouncing Sam and Simon by running hearts in one game, my confidence got the better of me, and I wound up losing the next.

"Championship round!" I called.

Mid-play, something hit the window.

As Simon investigated, I shuddered like someone walked over my grave.

"What is it?" Sam asked, her voice subdued.

Opening the window, Simon leaned out. "A bird hit the window."

Dread, dark and cold, deepened in my bones. Some say birds are sent to guide you like angels. But in Native American cultures, bird strikes are warning messages from the spirit world.

"Hold on. What's this? I'll be right back." Simon closed the window with a snap that made me jump. Sam followed him out, and they returned with a small brown bird.

"Is it still alive? Can we save her?"

"Quite dead," Simon informed me, setting the creature on our card game.

"Why bring it in?"

"A wren. Some people still kill them for Christmas," Sam said, sounding almost wistful.

"What?" Edgy and flustered, my query came out more harshly than I intended.

Cactus wrens, the state bird of Arizona, were double the size of this little one. I couldn't dream of killing either.

"Do ye not have wren boys, then?" Sam asked me.

"What?" I repeated, still too aggressively.

"For St. Stephen's Day," she said, confusing me all the more. "There's a song and everything."

"Please start at the beginning."

"Me first crush was a wren boy," Sam continued.

Sighing, my head sunk to the table. Until I remembered the dead bird sitting on it, and I jerked upright. "Too far back."

I gave up on Sam and turned to Simon. "Why did you bring it in?"

A tiny tilt of his head invited me to investigate.

Unmistakably lifeless, I apologized to the creature for its early demise. "Sorry, little thing."

When I saw the miniature scroll tied to its leg, I couldn't believe it took me so long. "No way."

"Way," Simon said with a smile. He turned to our boss. "Sam? You have tiny elf hands." The implication clear that Sam should remove the scrap of paper.

"Leprechaun, lad," she corrected.

"How can you be so calm? This is totally messed up! Did someone capture it, add the message, and then it flew into our window by accident? Or did they kill it and throw it at us? Either way, it is totally and completely unacceptable to kill birds because if the former is true, then whomever captured it threw off its aerodynamics by attaching something to its leg, and if the latter is true, well, then, yeah." I ran out of steam.

"Whoever," Simon corrected. "And you eat chicken, don't you?"

This argument was thrown at me every time I chastised a hunter for, well, hunting. I didn't like hunters killing deer, mountain lions, and bears because they were beautiful. Even wild turkeys were fascinating, and they usually outsmarted the hunters. "Those are bred for their fate and to taste good!" My stock response, because hunters wouldn't accept "pretty." "This little one didn't do anything to anyone!"

"Maddie, me girl, what's wrong?"

Pointing at the bird, I declared, "It's a portent of doom." Which sounded silly once it came out of my mouth.

Sam squinted at the note. "Ye may be right there. 'Get out,' it says."

Loud footsteps pounded down the staircase, but uncharacteristically, Dion and Gabriel entered noisily, not Jill.

"We heard Miss Madeline yelling. What is wrong?" Gabriel's soulful eyes found mine.

Mutely, I pointed to the bird.

"A dead wren," Dion said. "But it is not Sunday."

Unable to stand any more cryptic bird remarks, I demanded, "Why is everyone okay killing wrens?"

Simon turned to Sam, and she began. "Three origin stories. The Christian one says that a wren made noise betraying St. Stephen's hiding place to his enemies. That's why it's a Christmas tradition."

Dion and Gabriel nodded, confirming something similar in France, and gestured for Sam to continue.

"800 years later, an Irish army tried to advance on a Viking camp, and the wrens pecked at the drums, awakening the Vikings in time to slaughter the Irish army."

"They sure get a bad rap, don't they?" I glanced at the bird. "Their song is so lovely, though. What's the last story?"

"Pagan," she admitted.

"As in Celtic," Jill said, joining the party. They were gone by the time the villa construction began. It's common knowledge."

How long had she been there listening? It wasn't like her to be quiet. Or sneaky.

As Jill sat on the couch and pulled her knees under her chin, Sam continued. "Aye. The Celts described the wren as the king of birds. There was a contest to see which bird could fly the highest. The clever wren sat on the eagle's back, and it won."

"So why kill it?"

"It symbolizes that past year because it sings in winter. Its death brings the rebirth of the new year."

"It still doesn't make any sense as to why someone wants us to stop our Ground Truthing," I said.

Murmurs of assent, except for Jill, who hugged her knees tighter, a haunted look in her eyes.

Chapter Four: The Wicker Man

I slept like a rock. Awaking muzzy headed, it took me a minute to figure out why. Jill, noisy even in her sleep, abstained from snorting, gasping, and snuffling through the night.

"Did you sleep okay?" I asked before registering her absence. "Ah. That explains it."

Groggily, I stumbled to the communal kitchen for a strong cup of hot tea. But the people cooking breakfast botched it. The stench wafting out a still-open window smelled like the time I got my hair stuck in a blow dryer.

Except, the smoke came from outside, not the kitchen.

Rooted to the floor, I stammered, "He, hel, hello? Is anyone out there?"

Silence.

"Jill? Are you down here?"

Of course not. Because if she occupied a space, Jill raised a ruckus.

Taking a tentative step toward the window, I managed to stay on my feet. Another step and my knees faltered.

Catching myself, I said, "Get it together, McGuire."

Logically, though, there was no reason for a fire outside. Maybe another vandal attack, and hopefully, Jill left to criticize the police.

Except that smell.

Birds, again, perhaps. That would explain the odor. And come on. Stop killing the wrens.

Stiffening my spine, I marched to the door and yanked it open.

And screamed.

A burning wicker man encased a body.

Still screaming, instincts took over, and I ran to the kitchen, grabbed the fire extinguisher, and ran outside.

Heat assaulted my face. Red hot embers snapped, dotting my skin with welts.

"Ahhhhh! Jilllllll! Helpaaaaahhhhhhh!!!!" Incoherent, my trembling fingers pulled the pin. Aiming at the wicker man's feet, I pulled the nozzle. A loud ffpth accompanied the spewing foam, drowning out the fire's crackle and pop.

Spraying back and forth, jabbering Jill's name, I felt an arm around my shoulders, and the weight of the extinguisher lifted away from me.

"Do be quiet," Simon said, pulling me into a comforting hug.

Sam, Dion, and Gabriel rushed to the foamy mess to check on Jill.

But I already knew. No one could have survived that.

Crying into Simon's chest, he shuffled my huddled form into the lodge while Sam spoke to the nine-nine-nine operator.

Leaning on my friend, I felt his grasp on me loosen while he fiddled with his phone. Only Simon would think of texting someone else while offering comfort.

"Who are you texting?" I finally understood why my mom always asked. I hated it when she did, but now I got it.

"Dolly first, then Edward."

Dolly, Simon's fiancé and wealthy aristocratic beauty, ran a spa in nearby Painswick. We shared a terrifying experience that bonded us together like sisters. I hoped to chat with her.

Although, since we were all in Chedworth, she was at the Roman Baths in Bath, volunteering to conduct tours that Simon and I often did.

"Is she busy?" I asked, hoping for a "no."

"Of course she is. However, she'll have a room set aside for you and treatments available. By the time you're ready for dinner, she'll be there."

"Thank you," I said, snuffling into his shoulder. "Edward?" Simon never required full sentences from me.

In response, my phone buzzed.

"Hi," I squeaked, sounding pitiful.

"My bonny lass." The Scottish burr he usually hid at work purred through the line. "The wicker man is yours, then?"

"Not mine."

"You've got MCIT's attention. I dinnae ken if I'll be asked along. If not, I'll come anyway."

"Thank you," I sniffed, grateful. "After they get here, someone will take me to De Valence Medispa."

"Dolly has a room for him," Simon said loud enough for Edward to hear.

"Who could say no to that?"

Voices in the background broke into our conversation. Edward's voice modulated to sound like Simon's. When Edward spoke without his Scottish burr, Simon called it, "Posh accent, no money."

"On my way, sir," he said, and the connection severed.

Simon quirked an eyebrow in question.

I shrugged. "He's going somewhere. I hope it's here."

* * *

Emergency services arrived in earnest at our remote location. Searching the crowd, I spied DI Parikh, who transferred to the MCIT and recommended that Edward do the same.

The downside, however, was that whenever he saw me, a body lurked somewhere nearby. Which is why I wasn't surprised when he shook his head and took a visible breath before heading my way.

"You are making a habit of this, Miss McGuire." The second person to make that observation.

"I don't like it," I said. "It's awful. Really, really, really awful." Blinking seemed beyond me, and I started to shake.

"Bring Miss McGuire a blanket," he ordered with quiet authority.

"I'm glad you're here," I said to Parikh as a constable wrapped a wool blanket around my shoulders.

"The, shall we say, unusual nature of the crime warranted our presence." He surveyed the scene. "I must meet with the evidence team. Someone will be along to take your statement."

Eyes overly large, I scanned the area hoping to spot Edward. No such luck. Instead, I headed to a folding table someone set up with a kettle and paper cups.

"Coffee?" I asked the person pouring water.

"Just ran out," he informed me, then pressed tea in my hands. "A nice cuppa will do you fine."

Taking the brew, I scanned faces, looking for someone friendly. Spying Sam, I gratefully stumbled to her side only to be waylaid by an officer.

"We will be taking your statement now," he said. "Constable Douglass."

"Is—"

"I'll be asking the questions now, miss. Right this way."

Not the best way to get someone to cooperate, but I followed him to a squad car. He leaned against the bumper, notepad in hand.

"Right then. Name and address?"

"Madeline McGuire, Ash Tree Cottage, Greenway Lane, Bath. But I'm from Arizona."

His eyes flicked to my face, then back down at his notepad. "You don't look like a Yank."

Somehow, the tone in his voice made the statement sound like an insult, but I couldn't tell what to take offense at.

Ominous clouds moved into the valley on a cold wind. The blanket around my shoulders billowed and snapped, and I hunched against the car.

"Can we—"

"Please, miss. No more questions." This, like I'd been jabbering incessantly for hours.

"Right," he repeated. "If we could just get on with this."

Wanting to give him the benefit of the doubt, I bit back a retort and waited.

"Why did you touch the murder scene?"

Honestly? Hardly a question. More of an accusation.

"I didn't." Petulance got the better of me. He would need to be nicer if he wanted good information.

"It was disturbed."

I shrugged.

"Right. Let's ask an easier one, shall we? What did you do when you saw the scene."

To be fair, a better question. "As wicker man burned with Jill inside, I ran to the kitchen to get a fire extinguisher. I used it to put out the fire."

"And how did you recognize the victim as…" he checked his notes for effect. He just wrote it down seconds ago. "Jill?"

"Because she wasn't in our room. Hadn't been there all night. I guess I assumed."

With a derisive snort, he continued. "Why didn't you notice she left earlier?"

"Because I was asleep."

"Then how do you know she was gone?"

"Because if she were there, she would have generated noise."

"Are you sure it isn't because you knew she would be missing?"

"What?" I snapped.

"Answer the question, please."

"No. It was rude."

"Now listen, miss. I've had just about enough of you—"

"Oh no, you have not. Did you find your roommate on fire this morning? I bet not. And let me tell you, it is not anything you want to ever experience, even if you're not overly fond of said roommate." Anger fueled my outburst, creating heat in my body. I bundled the blanket up and contemplated shoving it at Constable Douglass.

"So you admit your dislike of the victim." Douglass pounced on this information like he'd just solved the murder.

I gaped like a codfish.

"Could you not bully my girlfriend? She's seen more dead bodies than you." Edward's admonishment of his fellow constable filled me toe to head with relief, then with giddy happiness, followed quickly by tears welling in my eyes.

Squeezing them tight, along with my fists, I counted to ten to keep from crying in front of the mean officer.

"Hey," I said. Cool, that's me. "Are you on the case, as they say?"

"Oh, hello, Bailey," Douglass said to Edward. "Feisty," he commented with a nod in my direction.

Wisely refraining from comment on my personality, Edward said, "I've got it from here."

"Good luck," Douglass said to Edward, snapping his notepad shut.

"How dare he?" I demanded, stamping my foot. The feisty reaction registered, and I put the blanket down to hug him instead. "Never mind. Can we go someplace warmer to take my statement?"

"I cannae take it myself since you're my lassie, but once you're settled, I'll sit with you and Douglass."

"He's very mean."

"Wants to make detective before me."

Edward's title remained Police Constable, but he was training to be a Detective Constable.

"You have more experience."

"Because of you." Edward grinned. "He's brash but thorough," he continued, referring to Douglass. "Give him a chance."

"Fine."

Laughing, Edward said, "That is the exact expression I pictured when you texted me the word 'fine.'"

"Resigned annoyance?"

"That's it!"

"Well, in America, it's crazy to talk to the police without a lawyer. No matter what."

"Do you think that's maybe propaganda started by lawyers?"

"I heard it from a criminal justice teacher." I shrugged. "Okay, I'll talk with Constable Meany."

"Are you sure, now?" Edward's eyes danced with merriment.

"And I'll behave."

Edward sent a text, and Douglass returned with renewed vigor. "DI Parikh says you do an automatic writing trance to jog your memory. I'd like to see it."

I sighed.

Audibly.

"It's not like I'm conducting a seance. It's stream-of-consciousness, which everyone can do. Just write whatever comes into your brain, and don't edit or stop."

Douglass looked slightly disappointed, which made me like him a bit more.

A shout from across the compound drew Edward's attention. Turning to me, he asked, "Y'alright?" He scampered off at my nod.

"Can you do it out loud?"

Shrugging again, I said, "I never tried."

Recording device in hand, Douglass suggested we try.

Eyes closed, I put my elbow on the table and rested my forehead on my palm. Without prompting, I started with waking up. "Quiet in the room. Blissfully quiet. Jill makes more noise than any human anywhere, even when she's asleep, so yeah. Great night's sleep. That's when I noticed she wasn't in the room, but it's not like we keep tabs on each other. Well, Jill might. Busybody. Except for the night before when we found the dead wren with a scrap of paper. Where did she disappear to then? She might be the wren killer. Never much one for wildlife, and the little wrens have such a beautiful song. I love them and can't believe anyone would want to hurt one. Jill didn't come in when everyone else did, which is suspicious in my book, especially considering how she photographed every little detail of the heart and Celtic dagger, getting her fingerprints all over everything. And insisting she stay behind to talk to the police when she wasn't the one who had found it. She wanted all the glory. Or attention or something."

As I continued to babble, Douglass whispered, "Wicker man."

"Wicker man. Right." Concentration broken, I opened my eyes. "What about the wicker man?"

"I think this will do for now," Douglass said, looking supremely pleased.

As he walked away, I tried to recall everything I said and groaned. It sounded very much like I didn't like Jill. At all.

I texted Edward. 'I think I'm Douglass's number one suspect.'

Chapter Five: Sherlock Holmes

Wondering how long the villa would be closed off by the police, I found Sam and asked.

"The DCI assures me that the lodge won't be open for a fair while. But we can get on with our work as long as we don't cross the police tape."

"Honestly?" I couldn't believe it. "I thought we'd have to give up for the season."

"The site needs protecting no matter what, and since we're doing that, we may as well confirm the aerial findings." She grinned at my expression of glee. "You look like you've found the pot of gold."

"The last two days aside, this experience taught me so much about Roman life and architecture. Brilliant engineers. Chedworth is so well preserved it's like stepping back in time. The Baths are amazing, but seeing how a family lives adds a different dimension."

Also, as much as I wanted to be home for Christmas, no one mentioned extending my internship into next semester. Everyone seemed happy with my work. Dr. Daniels, the archaeologist heading the dig at the Baths, finally recognized me and remembered my name. But these next few weeks might be my last in England, and I needed every ounce of experience I could get.

Movement by the hunting lodge caught my eye. The wicker man, free of its body, collapsed in a smoldering heap.

Blood drained from my head, and I swayed unsteadily.

"Don't you faint on me, Maddie," Sam barked in an Irish brogue that brooked no arguments.

Instead, I doubled over and rid my stomach of its contents.

Sam patted my back. "That's better," her voice gentle. "You're far too tall for me to catch you if you fall."

After composing myself, I straightened. "Sorry. I've gotten better at compartmentalizing my emotions." I peeked at the lodge. "Then things sneak up on me, and I'm not prepared."

Putting her arm around my waist, easier for her petite frame than my shoulders, she guided me away from the murder scene and toward the Visitor Centre.

"There'll be no work today, so why don't you take your wee self to the medispa? Dolly has room for the whole team."

Emotions sideswiped me as she walked away to locate a ride, and I sobbed, body shaking until a local officer cleared his throat.

With a gasping inhale, I noted his uncomfortable expression and fought to contain my outburst.

"Sorry," I said, swiping at my face with my sleeve.

"De Valence Medispa, miss?"

"Yes, thank you," I sniffed and hung a smile on my face. "How did you get stuck with driving duties?" I asked, trying to lighten the mood.

"I volunteered, I did. All this is too much for me. Things like this don't happen around here."

I heard that a lot. Disaster found me and clung like glue, in every idyllic spot I explored in the Cotswolds.

Falling into a strained silence, he delivered me to Dolly's manor house, half of which housed an eco-friendly med spa.

Once her uncle stepped away from management duties, Dolly embraced everything local for the spa, from honey to employees, and set about to create a carbon-neutral environment. In her spare time, she still volunteered at the Roman Baths Museum, conducting tours, especially when Simon and I were working elsewhere.

Pulling into the semi-circular drive, the officer seemed surprised when a valet appeared out of nowhere.

A valet. To collect my stuff, none of which I had. All my travel clothes were at the Hunting Lodge and off-limits.

"Can I get my clothes from Chedworth?" I asked the officer as the valet opened the door.

Before the constable could reply, the valet offered, "Lady Gwendolyn has stocked your room with a wardrobe and toiletries."

"Wow," I breathed. "That's amazing." Thanking everyone multiple times, I zombie-walked into the rosemary-scented lobby and instantly relaxed.

"If you like, miss, Dora here will take you straight to a massage."

Dora, a girl about my age and smaller than Sam, shuttled me to a treatment room and worked magic on my muscles. After that, Dora helped me to my room, where I melted into the bed for a brief nap.

I awoke disoriented but relaxed when I registered my surroundings. Tapping the white box on the nightstand, I clicked through a menu until a lavender mist emitted.

The menu on the magic box changed since the last time I occupied a room here, and surprisingly, it included a Wi-Fi password. Formerly forbidden tech, they now offered a robust connection.

"Awesome," I said, connecting my phone to a chat program to call my best friend in Arizona.

Tori Gonzales picked up immediately. "You didn't calculate the time difference, did you?"

"Uh."

"That's what I thought. What did you find?"

The advantage of childhood friends is that that backstory isn't necessary.

"Body in a burning wicker man," I said, hearing the whimper in my voice.

After oodles of comfort and cajoling, Tori got down to business. "So, gross."

"Agreed."

"Who was this person?"

Swallowing hard, I said, "Jill, my roommate for the Chedworth clean up."

"Uh-oh."

"I know, right? It's bad enough when I find a body I don't know. Now I'm Constable Meany's lead suspect."

With a giggle, she asked, "Is that really his name?"

"No, Douglass. But he bullied his way through my interview, and I wound up sounding like I hated Jill."

"How did he manage that?"

I paused, thinking. *How did he manage that?*

Sighing, I admitted to myself that he didn't. I did. "Well, he just asked me to tell him about her, and everything I said sounded negative."

After an epic effort not to roll her eyes failed, Tori steered the conversation in another direction. "Have you checked what Sherlock Holmes has to say?"

"What?"

"Come on. Holmes has been steadfast—offering clues that we usually misinterpret."

Laughing, I explained that all my things were back at the lodge, and I didn't have a computer.

"There must be a complete works around there somewhere. But, in the meantime…"

Keyboard clicks accompanied her murmured search criteria.

"Add druids," I suggested, reviewing the Holmes stories I could remember and coming up blank for anything related to fire.

"Of course," Tori said. "The wicker man."

"Why have you heard about that, and I haven't?"

"Believe it or not, I do learn stuff in my major."

Her devout abuela offered to pay for Tori's apartment if she majored in Religious Studies, which is more of a major than an occupation. The degree proved more fun than I thought, as Tori often roped me into her research projects.

"The thing is," I said, "there were no druids here. The Romans chased the Celtic tribes off the land three centuries before. So there is no reason for the druids to protest us."

"Okay, yeah, odd. Maybe it's an age-old Christian versus pagan thing?"

Shaking my head, I said, "Not really. One of the fascinating things about this villa is that originally, they built a nymphaeum —"

"A pool to honor nymphs—"

"But at some point, they turned it into a place of Christian worship. The Greek letters X and R, chi and rho, were carved into the entry to the pool."

"The first two letters of Christ," Tori added, showing off.

"Exactly. But later, villa owners took the stone out, turned it over, and used it to build something else, returning power to the nymphs."

"I feel a final paper coming on."

"I would actually read it."

"What we have here, then, is a confusion of religions at many levels over many centuries."

Gasping, I said, "One of the novels."

"What novels?"

I rolled my eyes at her. "What we're talking about. Doyle. He wrote four Holmes novels, and one had to do with Mormons, which he wildly misinterpreted."

A brief pause ensued while Tori typed.

"'A Study in Scarlet,'" she reported.

"That's the one!"

"I'm trying to divine your thought process here. Mormons, Druids, Christians, Romans. What's the connection?"

With a shrug, I said, "There probably isn't one. But I'm going to read the book again anyway to give my brain something else to think about."

"Good plan."

As always, after chatting with Tori, life looked rosier. Between that, the massage, and the lavender-scented air, my stomach actually settled. A healthy spa dinner in a quiet dining room where fluffy robes were expected sounded appealing.

Donning the pale lemon-colored silk pajamas that Dolly found for me, I sighed in relief. Everything fit. I tried wearing Dolly's clothes once, and it looked like I Hulked-out in them, as she is a good seven inches shorter than my five-foot-nine-inch frame. The pale yellow complimented my strawberry blonde hair, now pulled into a ballerina bun.

Covering the PJs with a fluffy white robe and adding fluffy slippers to complete the ensemble, I headed downstairs.

The dining room's tables were mostly full, but the ambient sound floated away pleasantly. Warm overhead lights lit each table highlighting food, while subtle blue created calm throughout the space.

With no message from Edward when he might arrive, I chose a table by a wall, sat, and closed my eyes, allowing the homey smells of cooking to wash over me. When I opened them, a server appeared with a glass with deep amber liquid over sparkling ice.

"Is that," I began, my mouth going dry, "iced tea?"

"Yes, miss," he replied, clearly pleased at my reaction. "Lady Gwendolyn herself set the menu."

His uniform, complete with the De Valence family crest of blue stripes on a field of white surrounded by red birds, made him appear older. Once he spoke, I realized he must be a teen from Painswick as a part of Dolly's plan to employ only local villagers.

"What's your name?"

Blushing, he answered, "Gilbert. I just started."

"You're doing great."

A grin split his face, exposing an endearing gap in his front teeth. "Back in a mo'. Uh, sorry. I will return shortly."

When Gilbert brought my food, my disbelief continued. A chicken enchilada with smoky red sauce sat next to Spanish rice and beans. The scent of chilis spiraled from the plate to my nose, grabbed hold of my brain, and took me hostage.

I stared.

I may have drooled.

"Is it alright?"

Shaking my head, I responded, "No. It's better. It is ambrosia."

Gilbert's head tilted.

"Thank you. Thank the chef. Thank everyone," I said, pulling the plate toward me and tasting the first spicy, melt-in-your-mouth bite. The balance between rich smoke and the acidity of jalapeño complemented an uncommon sweetness.

Digging my fork through the interior of the enchilada, I discovered bright orange cubes. Sweet potato accompanied the chicken, with a hint of garam masala in the mix. All in all, it tasted more East Indian than Mexican, but the spicy meal satisfied a nagging homesickness that had hounded me since discovering Jill.

Sated and calm, I pushed back from the table and headed toward the elevators when a loud discussion by the main door captured my attention. One of the voices sounded familiar.

Edward stood with his hands around one side of a small box, and the valet who had helped me earlier clutched the other end. Neither seemed willing to let go, but both were too polite to say so.

"What's up?" I asked.

"A package," the gray-haired valet reported, yanking the box into his hands and presenting it to me at the exact time Edward said, "He won't let me inspect the box."

Cold dread shivered up my spine. "Let's open it together."

As Edward removed the lid of the box, the doors from the East wing opened, and Dolly emerged, looking elegant in rose sweatpants and a matching top.

"Maddie!"

"Dolly!"

We embraced, and she commented with a dry wit that would make Simon proud, "Found a bit of trouble, did you?"

"A bit," I gestured to the box, "and I think more has found me."

"Thank you," I said to the valet, but the man had disappeared as miraculously as he had appeared when my car arrived. I knew Dolly disabled most of the cameras on her property, so I concluded the man could turn invisible on command.

Arm in arm, Dolly and I peered over Edward's shoulder. A small brown bird lay stiffly in the box. With gloved hands, Edward removed a scroll from around its leg and unfurled it.

Glancing up at us, he reported, "It says, 'Stay away.'"

Chapter Six: Coffee, Need Coffee

Dolly squeezed me as Edward bagged and tagged the paper and box, then photographed the bird.

When he finished, he asked, "What do you think?"

"Terrifying," Dolly said. "Absolutely terrifying. The dead wren should symbolize the New Year, not be used as a warning."

With a sigh, I enunciated loudly, "No. The wren should be left alone to sing its beautiful song in the winter." *Jeez.*

With a critical gaze in my direction, Edward asked Dolly, "Would the kitchen have something akin to a caramel coffee?"

"One macchiato coming up."

Once Dolly scampered into the medispa, Edward dropped his professional demeanor, wrapped his arms around me, and whispered Scottish terms of endearment in my ears.

A few tears leaked out of my eyes, but I got under control by the time the lady of the manor returned with my coffee.

A tentative sip danced on my tongue with sweetness, masking a rich, slightly bitter bite with hints of chocolate. The taste took me back to high school, having coffee with my mom, safe and threat-free.

"Good?" Dolly asked.

"Like everything you do, it is perfect. Thank you."

As the coffee restored my equilibrium, I pondered Edward's question. What did I think of this warning?

He eyed me, nodded, and pulled out a notepad.

Sometimes, thoughts telegraphed across my face like neon signs in a cartoon. And by sometimes, I mean always.

"Okay, yeah," I said, organizing my thoughts. "Clearly, something is happening at Chedworth that we don't understand."

Unhelpfully, Dolly and Edward nodded, waiting for me to continue.

"Okay," I said. "Did Chedworth have a secret, and Jill got in the way, or were the warnings aimed at Jill? And if so, what did she find?"

"And why did she hide it?" Edward added the question to his list.

"And who wanted to know enough to kill her?" Dolly asked, eyes wide.

"Point," Edward and I said simultaneously.

Ignoring our grins, Dolly continued. "Has anything of great value ever been discovered there?"

Another good point that I pondered before responding. "From a historical standpoint, the entire site is priceless. The pieces in the museum, likewise. The insight into everyday Roman life that Chedworth provides is astounding. Everything from plumbing to hairpins tells us how these people lived."

My friends stared, and I realized I lectured rather than answered.

"Nope, no treasure," I stated.

Something about my statement triggered a memory. The two men outside the window who weren't part of the dig team said the word 'treasure.'

"What?" Edward asked, accurately reading my 'I've remembered something' expression.

"The night before Jill," I paused, taking a scalding gulp of my coffee, "before the wicker man, I thought I heard someone outside my window. And they may have said the word 'treasure,' but I can't be sure."

Unable to meet Edward's eyes, I could feel them boring into me. "Did you tell Douglass this?"

I shook my head. "I didn't remember until just now."

"You should call him."

"He'll think I'm making it up to cover up my guilt," I said, still refusing to look at him.

"Why ever would he think that?" Dolly said as Edward leaned into my field of view.

"It's important," he said.

"Then you tell him." I turned to Dolly. "Because he thinks I somehow gained the knowledge to create a wicker man and coax my roommate into it just because she snored, that's why."

"I say," she said, placing a perfectly manicured finger on her cheek. "Where did the wicker man come from?"

My head whipped toward her. "Good question. The gift shop sure doesn't sell them."

As I chuckled at my lame joke, I touched Edward's hand. "Can you stay, or do you have to take the bird somewhere?"

Turning to contemplate the box in the evidence bag, he said, "As I'm here, and the threat is directed at you, I can protect you."

My eyebrows went up, and he smiled.

"It's settled then," Dolly said before I began a tirade about being able to protect myself. "Do you need dinner?"

When Edward shook his head no, Dolly turned to the spa lobby. "Mack, would you be so kind as to take Detective Constable Bailey's things to his room?"

The stout gray-haired man Edward had struggled with earlier appeared and silently took Edward's rucksack while pointedly ignoring the evidence bags.

A jolt of horror shook me as I looked at the little bird and its cardboard box, the similarity too close to Jill's burning prison. "Poor Jill," I squeaked, holding back tears.

"She died of a stab wound from the back through the heart from something long, like a hunting knife. Death would have been instant. She dinnae suffer, lassie."

The news provided some comfort as my mind refused to contemplate burning to death.

"Then why the wicker man?"

"Dire warning?" Edward suggested with a shrug.

"Rather effective, actually," Dolly said.

"But directed at who and why?" I insisted. "It couldn't be the druids. They're just camping for the Winter Solstice."

A stillness settled over Edward that I associated with him controlling an outburst.

"Druids?" To his credit, he said it calmly, which shouldn't surprise me at this point.

"I'm sure I mentioned them before."

Eyebrows up, Edward indicated I should continue.

"We met them at the pub in Northleach. They're camping," I repeated.

Edward's expression hadn't changed as he took notes. I knew the next question before he asked.

"I got two names. George, a newcomer to the group, whose last name started with an L. Leach or Lynch or something. A jolly guy with lots of blond hair. And then Muriel, the high priestess. She had long silver hair that practically glowed. Beautiful."

With a sigh, Edward said, "You're not going to like this, but between the bird and the druids, you need to talk to Douglass again."

"Do I have to?" The query sounded whiny even to my ears. "Can't I call DI Parikh? He doesn't think I'm guilty."

But Edward's expression told me no. "Give Douglass a chance."

I may have growled. Quietly, though, because it wasn't Edward's fault.

"Do you want me to call him for ye?" he asked, his Scottish burr comforting me.

My turn to sigh. "No. He would probably think I'm using my wily charms to bamboozle you into thinking I'm innocent."

"Aren't ye then?" he asked, then kissed me on the forehead.

I responded with a more forward kiss, which caused his voice to rumble in his chest.

Until Dolly politely cleared her throat, and we broke apart.

Grinning, I pulled my cell out of my fluffy robe pocket and called the number he gave me.

"Douglass."

With some effort, I bit back the urge to say, "McGuire," and instead told him about the threat delivered to the spa.

"I suppose Bailey's there with you," he said, with little to no concern for my safety.

"As a matter of fact, yes, he is."

"Right then. I'll speak to him."

As much as I wanted to hand the task of speaking to Douglass to someone else, I refused to be dismissed.

"In a moment," I said, contempt oozing off every syllable. Edward laid a calming hand on my shoulder. "I also remembered something from last night."

A grunt indicated I should continue. "There was a group of druids camping nearby. But they're all about communing with nature."

This news earned silence until Douglass asked, "Far Peak?"

"Yes, I believe that's what George said."

"George?"

"One of the members. Followers. Campers." The correct term eluded me, so I tossed out a few.

"Which is it?" Douglass demanded.

"How should I know?"

"Don't you study archaeology?"

Try as I might, I couldn't contain my ire any longer. "Well, yessir, I sure do. And you know what that means? It means I'm super good at Roman architecture—ancient Roman, like 2000 years ago. It doesn't mean that I've learned jack-squat about living people who follow a Celtic religion and are camping down the road. You're the policeman. You figure it out."

And I hung up.

Edward and Dolly stared at me.

"He annoyed me," I explained.

"Clearly," Edward said as he pulled a ringing phone out. "Constable Bailey," he said, a polite note in his voice, unlike some constables.

"Ah, well, yes," he continued, all traces of his Scottish accent gone. "I've found honey often works better."

As he spoke, Dolly pulled me aside. "I don't like that the wren found you so easily. Absolutely terrible."

"Agreed. But I can't go to the lodge."

"Why don't we pack you off to Comer Manor? I'm sure Lady Vivian would love to see you."

I twisted a lock of hair around my finger. Simon's aunt, Dowager Countess of Comer, intimidated me a bit.

Okay, a lot.

"I don't want to be a bother."

"Rubbish. Dora will gather the clothes and toiletries, and Simon will pick you up tickety-boo. Get a wiggle on and change."

I tilted my head and asked, "Are you using every obscure British slang you can think of?"

Throwing her sheaf of silky blonde hair over her shoulder, Dolly flashed a brilliant smile and said, "Absolutely."

When I first met her, I underestimated Dolly, an error I would never repeat.

In the face of such confidence, I had no choice. "Fine."

"You've been saying that a lot," Edward commented.

"It's code for 'leave me alone.'"

"We know," Dolly and Edward said after nodding at each other.

Outnumbered, I trundled to my room and changed into clothes more fitting for meeting a lady.

By the time I returned to the front door, Simon had arrived, car idling, heater on.

As I sat, he quirked an eye in my direction.

"It's not my fault," I repeated.

"Of course it isn't."

It's important to understand that most of what Simon says means the opposite.

"You and Sam were with me the whole time. The French boys found the warning first. Jill spoke to the police." My voice caught, and I swallowed a couple of times before asking, "How could it possibly be my fault?"

"The Frenchmen wanted to abandon the site right away. You and Jill were all for staying on," he said as he navigated the winding road that took us to Comer Manor.

A wave of nausea hit me. "Could you not put me and Jill together like that?" The thought of being next on someone's list of wicker man victims plowed straight into my gut.

"Ah, yes. I see your point."

"Besides, no one is sending you threats."

"They wouldn't dare. I'm a lord."

With a bark of laughter, I punched him lightly on the arm. His status, while accurate as the current Earl of Comer, always struck both of us as ridiculous. He and his aunt Vivian had apartments in Bath, but she spent far more time at the manor house, especially now that Simon and I figured out how to pay for the upkeep.

However, while the idea of a caste system was completely alien to my way of thinking, whenever the aristocracy expected and received respect, it surprised me.

Hawthorn, the manor butler, answered the door. "Lovely to see you again, Miss Maddie. Lady Vivian will meet you in the drawing room."

After exchanging pleasantries with butler and lady alike, I settled into a deep wing-backed chair in front of a roaring fire. A sense of contentment settled over me.

Until the doorbell rang.

Chapter Seven: Edible Gold

I knew from experience that one never ignores a doorbell in England. People took the effort to find a front door in the country and wouldn't be put off by a lack of answering.

It rang again.

Sitting up, I turned to the drawing room door, where the lady of the manor perched behind her Hepplewhite desk. Unperturbed, she continued to read her magazine.

Momentarily, Hawthorn appeared, informing us that Constable Douglass had arrived and wished for an audience.

I scanned the room, hoping for an exit, but I was stuck unless I wanted to hop out the mullioned windows.

"Show him in," Lady Vivian said, and I sighed.

Barely two steps into the room, Douglass started in on me. "Why did you feel it necessary to flee the scene of a crime, Ms. McGuire?"

Before I could respond, Lady Vivian stood and inserted herself between us.

"Where are my manners?" she asked, clearly disapproving of Douglass's behavior. "You must be tired after such a long drive. Would you care for coffee or tea?"

"Ma'am," Douglass began.

"Actually, a small thing really, but it's 'your ladyship,'" Vivian interrupted. "I'll just ring Hawthorn."

Spluttering, Douglass made his annoyance clear.

Some revere the aristocracy. Edward always modified his accent and stood straighter in their presence, including with our friends Simon and Dolly.

However, it appeared that Douglass fell in the opposite camp of those who thought titles were useless. As an American, I used to agree, but seeing how much Dolly did for her village changed my opinion.

Before Douglass could resume his interrogation, Hawthorn entered, and an overlong discussion of refreshments ensued.

In the face of unrelenting politeness, Douglass lost steam, giving me the opportunity to plan for his attack.

"Do you have any idea how they found me so quickly?" I thought the question diffused the situation nicely.

I was wrong.

"The most obvious reason would be that the guilty party planted the bird in order to appear innocent."

As in, I planted it because Douglass thought I was guilty. Again, the Dowager Duchess came to my defense.

"Shall I play mother? Sugar? Milk?"

The words sounded the height of gracious, but as she said them, she shoved the tea cart rather aggressively between us and over Douglass's foot.

"Watch it!" he barked before realizing to whom he spoke. "I don't need any tea or coffee. Thank you."

As he got more flustered, his voice took on a slightly nasal tone, and I wondered if he hailed from Manchester, like my doppelgänger friend Lily in Bath.

"What I need is for you to c—"

"Are you from Manchester?" I interrupted.

"What?"

"My friend Lily is from there, and she sounds a bit like you. She says her rowdy brother likes it, but she prefers the quiet of Bath."

"Regency shopping center, that is," Douglass muttered.

"I beg your pardon?" Offended on behalf of my adopted city, I geared up for a rant about its status as a World Heritage Site. Before I could launch, he relented.

"I'm sorry for the mither," Douglass turned this to Lady Vivian. "Yes, tea would be lovely. May I sit?"

Nothing charmed Simon's aunt more than good manners. She nodded him toward one of the twin couches that bordered an elegant Persian rug, then shuttled me to sit facing him.

Her velvet blue eyes bore into me for a moment, and the message settled into me: be polite.

Holding back another sigh, I sat straight and asked, "What can I help with, Constable Douglass?"

Eyes narrowed he scrutinized me before taking a more civilized approach to our interview.

"When did you find the bird?"

"At the De Valence Medispa, the valet, Mack, wanted to bring a box addressed to me to my room. Constable Bailey arrived about then and insisted he search the box first. I found them and the box at the same time. I didn't touch any of it. Constable Bailey opened with gloves and bagged everything as evidence."

The door opened, and Simon joined us.

As Douglass opened his mouth, probably to object, Lady Vivian said, "Good, Simon, you're here."

Settling in next to me, he waved his hand at his guest. "Pray, continue."

The interruption brought an angry flush to Douglass's cheek, so I started talking before he could take it out on me.

"As the officer and I discussed the meaning, I mentioned that it didn't make sense to have Druid warnings. The ancients left the Chedworth area three centuries before the Romans built there. In addition, as I mentioned earlier, those druids camping at Far Peak were very friendly."

Douglass scribbled notes, even though I knew Edward told him this information after I hung up on him.

"I met two in the Northleach pub."

"Wheatsheaf," Simon provided.

"Yeah, that. George was new to the group. He pointed out Muriel, who was in charge."

I smiled. Friendly. Helpful even.

He scowled.

"Again, why did you leave?"

"What do you mean?" I knew what he meant but couldn't believe his insensitivity.

"You received a vital clue in a murder investigation, and you left the scene."

Leaning forward and making intense eye contact, I said, "So I didn't get murdered."

With a snap of his notebook, Douglass leaned away from me, still frowning.

However, I wasn't done. "The police presence advised me to leave the location as I was found so quickly." Emphasizing every word, I said, "I do not wish to be barbecued."

Rather than saying anything nice, like a normal human, he huffed and warned me to stay put until he said I could leave.

I waited until he left before mimicking in a nasally voice, "Stay here until I say so." I double-checked he'd left before adding, "Twit."

At that moment, I remembered Lady Vivian's presence and turned to her, ready to apologize.

"Quite right," she said with a nod. Standing, she straightened her pale pink cardigan and beckoned me to follow her. "Most unpleasant young man. Why isn't your constable here?"

"Mostly because he is my constable. Conflict of interest or something."

"Ridiculous. They can't think you're a suspect."

Unfortunately, Douglass thought precisely that.

As I followed her strides, Simon caught up and pointed out various improvements and repairs to Comer Manor.

"We were able to find a glazier who repaired the mullion windows without damaging the Grade I original work. They are far less drafty, and the heating bill has dropped significantly."

Lady Vivian patted an unassuming door. "This room is where Hawthorn and I brew our special compost. Strictly off-limits."

I threw a questioning glance at Simon. "Carbon monoxide levels," he explained quietly.

"This way," his aunt said, hurrying us through the kitchen.

At odds with the rest of the house's decor, the kitchen boasted several upgrades: new tile countertops, gorgeous wooden cabinets, and an industrial oven and stove. We hustled through and stepped outside into a greenhouse that smelled like heaven.

"Lavender," I said, taking in deep breaths while surveying the vast addition.

Simon looked pleased. Simon never looked pleased.

"What?" I asked.

Ignoring my question, he explained, "Lavendins, actually. English lavender is from the Mediterranean and doesn't do well in the damp and cold. The greenhouse provides protection, of course, but this hybrid is better. We provide the De Valence Medispa and the new day spa here in our village. We're hoping to expand production to provide more of the Cotswolds with Comer Lavender."

Something about his cat-like expression made me wonder, "But these little purple flowers here wouldn't have paid for a glazier for the whole manor, would they?"

"Quite," Lady Vivian agreed.

Neither offered additional information, but experience told me not to ask. As Earl of Comer, Simon inherited the manor house from his parents, who died when he was young. Much as I wanted to hear the story, he would clam up if I asked direct questions, so I didn't have more details about his childhood.

He had shared with me that since their deaths were unexpected, the trust they set up for him strictly forbade funds for house repair, and upkeep became strained. Hawthorn and his wife were their only full-time staff members, but his nephew, Rupert, helped out as much as an eight-year-old could.

When Dolly took over the medispa, she wanted only locally, sustainably sourced ingredients for their products. I suggested Simon use their extensive garden and greenhouse system to help them both. Apparently, he took the suggestion to heart, but something else happened.

Wandering through the doors to the next greenhouse, I saw basil, parsley, oregano, chives, mint, thyme, and rosemary. "This is amazing! How many restaurants do you provide?"

"Six, in addition to Dolly's." Pride radiated from him.

Still, his enigmatic expression persisted as he glanced at his aunt, who guarded a door to another garden.

"Strictest of confidence," she warned me before unlocking. "I gave up my prize orchids for this."

Contradicting her words, gorgeous striped orchids dotted the tables between rows and rows of lovely purple flowers. They looked like the crocuses that bloomed all over Chicago in the spring.

Arching an eyebrow at Simon, I mutely asked for an explanation.

"Buried treasure," he said, grinning.

Turning to Lady Vivian, I asked formally, "Why are they under lock and key?"

With a sniff, she explained enigmatically, "We've had difficulties with theft before. Rather unpleasant, actually."

'Unpleasant' covered everything from rudeness to murder in Lady Vivian's mind, so I didn't want details. However, no one answered my question.

"So, what are they?"

"Red gold," Simon offered uselessly.

"Dude." When Simon got obtuse, a good old Americanism usually shook him out of it.

"Fine," he said, and I wondered if I picked up the word from him. "Saffron."

Blinking, I took in the information. I knew it was a spice that colored paella. "Gold because of the color," I said, attempting to appear incurious and knowledgeable, a surefire way to get Simon talking.

"A twenty-eight-gram vial will fetch between sixty and one-hundred-and-twenty pounds."

After quickly calculating the exchange and conversion rates to seventy-five to one hundred and fifty dollars per ounce, I said, "Whoa, honestly?" Simon's Cheshire Cat grin made sense. "That is treasure."

The word recalled the voices outside the lodge window. They spoke about treasure. I couldn't remember if I told Douglass.

The sinking dread in my stomach made me realize I hadn't.

Chapter Eight: The Lost Wicker Man

When the police cleared us to return to Chedworth, Simon attempted being cheery, probably to keep me from bolting. Cheery didn't suit Simon well, and the jolly attitude as we approached the scene of my roommate's murder poked at my nerves.

"Just, just, stop. 'K?"

Not offended, he shrugged. "Practicing human skills for my upcoming nuptials."

Barking a laugh, I smiled before punching him lightly in the arm. "Thanks."

Grateful that I couldn't see the remains of the wicker man from the parking lot, I followed Simon to our makeshift team office, set up in a spare room behind the gift shop.

We found Sam moving boxes and looking harried. She said, "Simon, good you're here."

My eyes went wide as I assumed a poker face. Her usual smiling Irish greeting abandoned her.

"Settle yourself down, Maddie, you're not in trouble."

Relieved, I managed, "Oh, good."

Nodding toward a piece of cloth at the end of the table, she turned back to Simon, who held up a hand to stop her. Wordlessly, he began reorganizing the office.

"You're a godsend, you are," Sam said, her impish grim in place.

After my first couple of weeks at the Roman Baths Museum, Sam took a leave of absence, and Simon took charge. First, he rearranged the office and then updated the filing system. When she returned, Sam confessed that her downfall as an administrator was organization, which Simon excelled at.

Recalling my reaction to what I wrongly assumed was Simon's interference at the time, I examined the fabric Sam directed me toward. A short note from Edward said, 'To keep you warm when I'm not there.'

I unfolded a cream and tantartan-patternedscarf made of Scottish wool. Draping it around my neck, warmth flooded through me, and I longed to get outside to work.

As I texted my thanks to Edward, Sam pulled on her coat before we left Simon.

The Frenchmen were already hard at work picking weeds and scrubbing moss off the nymphaeum. Without Jill to support our numbers, winterizing the site before snow fell wasn't guaranteed. Temperatures were already dipping.

"Start by brushing moss off the rest of the pilae and securing the covers," Sam directed.

To my surprise, she joined me.

"Why is so much of the site gone?" she asked, and I realized that the archaeology lectures that Sam started at the Baths were not stopping just because we were away.

The question reminded me of how my education lacked over two full years of schooling. Landing the internship at the Baths as a sophomore instead of as a senior undergraduate student caused trouble in more than one way.

Instead of apologizing for my lack of education, I examined the Chedworth Villa. When James Farrer, uncle to the estate's lord, discovered the ruins in 1864, he knew enough to protect what he could. Capstones, like little roofs, covered every exposed wall, preserving the outline of the villa.

All of this Sam knew that I knew and didn't address the question.

A gust of wind whipped across the valley, masking my sigh. Stopping work, I folded the wool scarf in half and replaced it around my neck, now with twice the protection.

Which got me thinking. The storms in this area brought snow and freezing rain. Back home in Tempe, heat and sun expanded anything metal, causing cracks and deterioration. Clay did okay, though. The conditions were opposite here, and I formulated my reasoning.

"Obviously, looting of building materials that happened everywhere," I began. Rocks at Avebury, the largest stone circle in Britain, were taken and used for walls or fences. "But, since we're here covering things, my guess is that rain or snow got into the stones, froze, and expanded, which made everything crumble."

"Right you are, Maddie, me girl." Sam moved to another pilae before asking, "What have you seen in the collection that interests you?"

Bright green slime trickled into my glove, and I formed my answer as I removed the glove and wiped the cold ooze on the dead grass.

The museum displayed many fine pieces, from hairpins to a boldly carved balustrade, but many more artifacts were cataloged.

"Flue tiles?" I knew fireplaces had flues, but our house back home only had a fire pit in the backyard, so I wasn't familiar with how they worked.

"Did you never open a flue in a chimney?"

I shook my head, then shouted, "No," over a sudden howl of wind.

"Never?"

"We get 300 days of sunshine a year."

Sam's wistful expression made me think I'd lost her to a daydream. It took a moment before she snapped back.

"Right then. The box flue tiles were hollow rectangles made of clay and set into walls. Solid on two sides, with slots on the others, they allowed fire from the hypocaust to travel up, spreading warmth for cozy rooms."

"Sounds perfect," I said as another glop of freezing moss plopped onto my wrist, the only exposed skin of my body.

Teeth chattering, I moved to the next pilae, freeing it from plant life and giving it a warm jacket for the season. I envied it a bit.

"What else?" she asked as she deftly cleaned and protected another pillar.

As my fingers locked up with cold, I blurted out the first thing that came to mind. "The padlock? I've only seen the pieces. How would the rest fit together? How would it work?"

"An excellent question, and something I've been working on. Have you been to the Mary Rose Museum?"

Shaking my head no, I admitted to not having traveled out of the Cotswolds after landing at Heathrow.

"Amazin' site. Underwater for four centuries before they raised her. Any artifacts with parts missing were reproduced in acrylic."

"I love that idea," I said, able to picture a part of a rusted cross completed with a translucent material. "Very cool," I said lamely, my mental capacity waning as I slowly froze.

As feeling left my fingers and toes, I longed to ask Sam when we could take a break, when I got a reprieve from George the Druid. Strolling across the grass from the parking lot, his thick curls danced with every step.

Not one to miss an opportunity to move, I attempted to bound toward him but only succeeded in stumbling over my rapidly numbing feet.

"Hi!" I called with a wave, dislodging a stray glob on my glove, which flew into my hair.

"There's a familiar face I didn't expect to see, I didn't," he said, approaching me. "Madeline, yes?"

"Maddie," I said with a smile. "What brings you to Chedworth? May I offer you a tour?" Anything to get away from cleaning slime.

"That sounds delightful, that does," he said, but his face clouded over before I could launch into a spiel.

"What's wrong?"

His head bobbed, blond curls dancing. "Well, it seems we had a theft, and we heard about a bit of a bother here as well. Muriel sent me to check on our wicker man."

A whole new kind of cold seeped into my bones.

"Your wicker…" I couldn't bring myself to finish.

"Wicker man, yes. It seems it went missing. We were going to use it as a bonfire to keep us toasty during the Solstice vigil. Took donkey's years to build, it did."

The word "bonfire" triggered a physical reaction that I fought hard to control. With little grace, I fled George's company in favor of the bathroom, where I called Edward.

"The camping druids had a wicker man that got stolen," I told him with no preamble.

"At Far Peak. That's too close." Edward paused for a moment, probably struggling between his cop and boyfriend roles. Fortunately, boyfriend won. "Must have been quite a shock. Y'alright?"

Having once told him I had no idea how to respond to "y'alright?" he tended to use it when I was particularly stressed. "Yeah. I freaked a little at being reminded of Jill, but I'm okay. I'll hang up and call Douglass," I told him before he asked me to.

After he reassured me a few times, I smiled and disconnected.

Leaving the bathroom, I dialed Constable Douglass.

"Douglass."

The acerbic voice put me on edge instantly, but I vowed to stay calm for Edward's sake.

Rounding the corner, I discovered a distressed George.

"Are you doing alright, Maddie? Saw a ghost, did you?"

Pointing at my phone to indicate my conversation with someone else, he stepped back.

"The wicker man may have come from the druids camping a Far Peak. They're missing one," I said, hoping that a straightforward report would make him happy.

It didn't.

"How do you know that?" he said, more as an accusation than a question.

After counting to five and taking a deep breath, I answered, "George, the one I told you about, heard something happened, and he came up to ask."

"How did he hear that?"

Instead of responding to something I couldn't possibly be aware of, I ground teeth together. "Do you want to speak to him?"

"No need."

Confused, I said, "Okay, well, I thought you should have the info."

"Ms. McGuire," he said, sounding very much like my mother about to administer a lecture, "you have no authority to discuss this case with anyone, including Bailey—"

"I didn't—"

"And especially not as gossip with random passersby."

"He wasn't—"

"Remember you are still a person of interest, and therefore, you have a responsibility to keep quiet. I have the situation under control here at Far Peak, and I would thank you, to leave me to it," he interrupted before disconnecting.

Glaring at the phone, I said, "You could have opened with that. Twit."

"Is everything quite alright?" George asked, causing me to jump as I'd forgotten his presence.

"Apparently, the police are talking with your fellow campers."

"Excellent news! That means I'm off the hook, as you Americans would say, you would. Muriel will have everything under control." He beamed at me. "I guess I can have that tour after all."

Putting my conversation with Constable Grumpy-face behind me, I took George around the villa, using my tour guide skills acquired at the Roman Baths.

The perfect tourist, George listened attentively and asked interesting questions.

"What about that area under the floor?" he asked at the far end of the enclosure, which covered the mosaics.

"Note that the floor is the same level as the dining room we looked at first. The pilae support the floor all the way down so that the fires could warm every room. Because this floor is broken, you can see how it all fits together."

Continuing outside, I shivered with cold as we looked at the nymphaeum and the mostly covered outdoor floor pillars.

With a sigh, I stamped my feet to encourage warmth and said, "Thanks for letting me babble at you about Roman archaeology. I love it. But I need to finish protecting these." I extended my hand over the area where Sam worked.

"I can tell you do, Maddie; yes I can. You're the person who will have all the answers."

We shook hands, and he wandered toward the parking lot with a jolly farewell.

I miss conducting tours, I thought.

Another pang of insecurity about my future gripped me as I returned to work. Lady Vivian could undoubtedly get my student visa extended. But neither she, Simon, nor Sam had mentioned the desire to do so.

Dr. Daniels could also make me a member of his team, allowing me to change my visa status, but I hadn't heard anything from him either. Also, I wasn't sure if my taking off to Chedworth would impress him or not. Yes, it showed commitment to the field of work, but it took me away from sifting dirt for him.

A violent gust of wind stripped the bag I partially secured from my hand, and I ran after it clumsily, unable to feel my freezing toes. The bag caught on the wall surrounding the nymphaeum, and I snatched it before it could plop into the water.

Blowing snow fell in huge fluffy flakes as I returned to the worksite. Fighting with the bag in the wind distracted me from my future. I gave it a final tug before moving on to the next pillar and noting they were all covered.

Frost and snow dotted the tops, protected just in time.

The sense of accomplishment dimmed as my subconscious whispered, *And what about Edward? What happens if you leave?*

Starting his new career as a detective with MCIT, Edward didn't need distractions about my fear of leaving. He needed my support, so he made detective before that twit Douglass.

The conversation I had with the constable still annoyed me. Despite doing everything right, he still considered me a person of interest, which I figured meant something like hostile witness and not suspect.

Didn't it?

Chapter Nine: Blood in the Snow

Having successfully put all silly notions of being a suspect from my mind, my subconscious treated me to a nightmare version of Douglass with terrifyingly long arms chasing me down an endless corridor.

In no shape to encounter Lady Vivian for breakfast, I texted Simon to bring me food to his car.

Still dark, I hadn't bothered to open my curtains, so the view out the door stole my breath. Overnight, the snow and wind transformed the landscape into a winter fairyland. Every white mound and drift invited a running jump. I refrained, unable to remember what lurked under the surface.

Amazingly, no snow clogged the driveway. Rupert, the enterprising nephew of Simon's butler Hawthorn, shoveled away.

"Hello, Rupert!"

With a hop, he turned, face beaming. Waving excitedly, he called, "Brilliant, innit?" and returned to work.

Watching the shovel fill and toss looked more satisfying than I imagined, and I longed to try it myself.

Until a gust of wind bit into my cheeks. Teeth chattering, I got into the car.

Fortunately, I didn't have to wait long before Simon slid in and handed me a sausage roll and tea in a De Valence Medispa travel mug.

Attempting not to drool, I inhaled the scents of peppery fennel and pork. "Mmmmm, thanks. This is cool," I said, indicating the wooden mug with the De Valence crest etched into the side.

"Indeed," Simon agreed. "Local chap makes them. Dolly plans on opening a gift shop soon full of wares from the vendors she uses. It'll be up to the council, of course."

"Great idea."

"Of course it is. All her decisions are."

I assumed he counted her decision to marry him among those ideas, but I still had my doubts. Knowing Simon's preferences veered in another direction didn't dissuade Dolly, but I found the choice to marry for the sake of the aristocracy and not love an odd one.

Simon never asked why I did the things I did, so we rode in companionable silence until I finished eating.

"Nightmares," I explained eventually.

"'I see."

More silence.

Finally, I asked, "Any ideas?"

"About Jill or the druids?"

"Both."

He spared a quick peek at me as we pulled into the parking lot, which he insisted on calling a car park. Like the cars go there to play.

"The campers seem friendly enough."

I launched into the small opening. "Right? George came by yesterday, all distressed because of their stolen wicker man. Which explains where it came from, so that's good. But who would have known about both the camping druids and Jill? And what was she up to?"

"As I've mentioned before, her behavior struck me as too aggressive for the dig. Chedworth is a treasure, to be sure, but not a source of secrecy."

"Maybe she found something that connected the druids to the site," I pondered. Evidence pointed to the Druids having been chased out centuries before the Romans moved in, but they didn't write anything down, so pinpointing the Druids' whereabouts proved difficult. "What if she discovered something showing a resurgence of the religion in the fourth century? A new cult rising. That would be a secret worth protecting as it would make her career."

Icy wind rushed across the clearing as he hurried toward the Visitor Centre.

"Bonjour!" Gabriel shouted from where he and Dion worked, removing muck from the nymphaeum pond. Although the ground glistened with inches of fresh snow, the pool did not freeze, so cleaning the nymphaeum continued.

"Good morning!" I greeted them, noting their puffy jackets. "I need new clothes," I complained to Simon.

"Indeed," Simon said, opening the door for me.

Warmth enveloped me as we entered, and relief tingled to my fingertips from getting to work indoors. The Frenchmen already covered the only outside place that had not yet been cleaned and covered.

Hanging my jacket next to Sam's, I rubbed my hands together in anticipation of a desk job. Would wonders never cease? Usually, I couldn't wait to get out in the field, but the second I encountered bad weather, sign me up to do paperwork.

"Where do I start?" I asked Sam.

Pointing at a green puffy jacket on the hook, she said, "I borrowed a jacket for ye. Matches mine, it does."

Sweet of her, but it indicated something I didn't want to hear.

"Uh."

"I'll need for you to replace Gabriel and Dion at the nymphaeum."

"Why me?" I whined.

At this, she pulled me aside, speaking quickly and quietly. "Jill dug around back there, and it's unsettling that the French volunteered in this weather. It's an awful job, but I'd rather have you discovering Jill's secret than them."

On one hand, aww, she had faith in my skills! On the other, it increased the target already on my back. Birds and notes were one thing, but being imprisoned in a wicker man was another.

"Okay," I sighed, sounding grouchy. I smiled at Sam and offered a brief thumbs-up.

As I picked up the jacket, I remembered my history lesson from the previous day. "Oh, hey," I said, stalling, "you never finished telling me about the padlock."

"Interrupted by the druid. It warmed my heart that you dropped into tour guide so quickly." She paused, went to her computer, and displayed the padlock image. "We have a couple of springs, end bars, and a bolt."

"Right," I agreed, hoping the weather would warm up while I distracted her. "Iron and very rusted. I can't figure out how it would come together." The lock looked more like a hair pick with missing teeth than anything else.

"Behold," she said after tapping a few keys.

A 3-D rendering of the padlock appeared—the existing parts were solid, and what would have been the remainder displayed as a wireframe.

"Whoa, that's awesome," I said. Seeing the completed piece allowed me to examine it from every angle. "Effective, but easy to pick."

"I have a friend with a 3-D printer. I'll send him the file and see if we can get a working model to play with."

"Honestly? Thank you!"

Sam laughed and handed me the borrowed coat.

Pulling on the puffy green jacket, I threw an envious glare at Simon and trudged into the cold.

Gabriel jumped to his feet and greeted me at the pool entrance. "Miss Madeline! How are you this glorious morning?"

"Grumpy," I admitted as he scrutinized my appearance, including taking my shoulders and turning me around. "Hey," I complained, stumbling.

"What is this, this thing you are wearing? You look like a green, what is it called, a marshmallow. A green marshmallow." He nodded, satisfied at his description.

"Thanks," I said, stepping around him to get Dion's attention.

Glowering, Dion stood, wiping dirt from his gloves.

"Sam wants you inside. I'm stuck out here."

"Ah, that explains the marshmallow. But really, we are fine with the, the, the, grunt work, as you say."

"That's kind of you," I said. Weird, but nice. Stepping back, I waved them toward the office. "Sam needs to show you how to read the maps and match them to the radar scan as part of your training."

Dion threw down his trowel and stomped past me.

Gabriel lingered. "I could stay here with you," he said, his voice soft and alluring. A thrill passed through me, and I considered the offer longer than I should have. Confidence paired with his easy manner, made him appealing, easy to be around. Sparkling eyes didn't hurt either.

The wolfish grin that took over Gabriel's expression reminded me not to trust him.

"Thanks, but no. Sam needs you inside."

After Gabriel joined his friend, I knelt on the pad Sam provided and started after weeds, thinking. Gabriel's charisma, for lack of a better word, put me off my guard when I needed to focus. Sam sent me here today to keep them from discovering anything Jill may have found.

If the French knew Jill uncovered something important, then the two were prime suspects in her murder. The thought chilled me more than the gust of wind that twisted my ponytail in knots.

"Stay frosty, McGuire," I said, trying a new phrase and finding it completely and utterly lacking in motivation. Instead, I stood, danced around for a minute, and then focused on the site, not the clean-up.

Pennycress, the weed that sprouted between the tiles, dotted the nymphaeum walls, but one section gleamed, completely cleared. Examining it, I found a loose tile that came up quickly in my hand.

I dug a little—nothing underneath but dirt.

Why would Jill have removed a tile and not reported it? To keep the site intact, it should have been secured with period identical mortar.

Having learned exactly nothing, I sighed. The rest of the pennycress wouldn't pick itself.

After filling a bag, I bent to clear moss off the pool's edge just as the sun peaked out from the clouds. A glint sparkled in the water for a second, and I leaned over to get a better angle. A coin, maybe. Wondering if tourists used the ancient pool as a wishing well, I leaned closer.

"Miss Madeline."

Dion's stern voice sounded so close behind me that I yelped, my hand slipping from the edge and plunging into the water.

Terrified that he would push me under, I scrambled backward, batting away Dion's hands.

"Mon Dieu!" he shouted, followed by a string of French that I happily didn't understand.

With every flail, I lost more control, my arms sinking further into the water. As soon as I stabilized, fear of being pushed in caused me to spasm, and my face inched toward the surface.

"Let me help you," he insisted.

It didn't sound like a phrase a killer would use.

I relaxed, and with Dion's help, I got to my feet without being murdered.

"Sorry," I said lamely. "You scared me."

"Lunch," he said, glaring at me while pointing toward the centre.

My attempt at a smile did nothing to brighten his mood.

Water dripped from my jacket sleeves. Pulling my hands deeper in, I shook the ends of the arms, flinging droplets everywhere.

Dion muttered something under his breath that sounded suspiciously like eejit.

A little British slang rubbing off on him, I thought with a grin.

Since we no longer had access to our kitchen, the Cafe at the Visitor Centre prepped extra sandwiches for our team. Although tasty, I missed Dion's cooking.

"When will we be able to get back in the lodge?" I asked, not sure of the answer I wanted. Proximity to work and a kitchen counted for a lot, but threats and violence weighed more.

Sam's shrug, the perfect response, meant I didn't need to think about it. Instead, I leaned in her direction and asked about the coins in the fountain and the loose tile.

Patting my shoulder, she rose, grabbed her jacket, and slipped out the back entrance.

Simon, Gabriel, and I helped with the cleanup and straightening of the gift shop before resuming work.

"Ta very much," the friendly lady manning the counter that day called to us.

I waved, feeling bad that I hadn't learned her name yet. As the boys continued out, I doubled back to ask.

By the time I returned, she'd left.

"Tomorrow," I promised to go to the empty cafe and gift shop.

With a shrug, I left by the front door, which lay closer to the nymphaeum. As I turned toward the pool, I saw a green clump on the ground—almost like a green marshmallow.

"Sam," I gasped, recognizing her matching coat. "Sam!" I yelled as I ran, just in case she found something and not…

I didn't want to think about how inert her form looked.

"Sam!" I tried to get her attention again, but she didn't move as I neared.

With her arm dangling in the cool water, blood pooled around Sam's head, dripping into the nymphaeum.

Lunging down, I felt for a pulse in her neck. Pounding strong.

"Thank God. Hang in there, Sam."

Not knowing what else to do, I pulled her arm out of the water and then looked at the wound on the back of her head, which still oozed.

Unwinding the beautiful scarf Edward gave me, I used it to staunch the bleeding. Once I tied the muffler tightly, I patted Sam everywhere, ensuring no knife protruded. Jill had been knifed to death.

"Nothing. Good." I gently tapped her cheek as I called to her but didn't get a response.

I normally didn't bring my phone to the grounds, but I stuck it in my back pocket after texting Simon this morning.

Hitting his number, I typed, 'Sam's been hurt.'

No response came, and I wondered if he got the message when I heard, "Maddie!"

Standing, I jumped up and down to get his attention.

"Report," he said in a way that made me not want to, but I dismissed my childish reaction.

"I came out and saw her lying here. Head wound. Her pulse is strong, but she hasn't woken up."

At that moment, her eyes fluttered. "Maddie?" she asked as her hand reached for mine.

"I'm here, Sam. What happened?"

But her eyes closed again.

"Police and ambulance are on their way," Simon said, sitting on the icy stones beside us.

We waited with her until the EMTs took over, cooing soothingly as they did so.

"She'll be alright, love. Don't you worry."

Flatly ignoring their advice, I fretted and paced until the police came in to talk to us. Instead of a local constable, however, Douglass strolled in.

"We asked Ms. Niven who did this," he said with no preamble. "And she said only one word.

His eyes drilled into mine as we waited for the revelation.

"Maddie."

Chapter Ten: Bath

Douglass's expression of triumph at his accusation almost made me stamp my foot. Not wanting to be accused of stroppiness, if that was even a thing, I clenched my fists and jaw and counted to ten in my head. Holding my breath didn't help, so I exhaled and added another five-count.

Turning the Visitor Centre into a makeshift police station, Douglass took us each to a separate room, and in my case, made me sit there. Forever.

When he finally entered, I said, "Sam said my name because she needed my help. I found her and stopped the bleeding."

"Bailey will have a thing or two to say bout how you treat his gifts," Douglass said, ignoring my logic and trying to bait me.

Another count to five before I responded. "Yes," I managed a smile that probably looked like a sneer, "he will be pleased with my ingenuity."

"Not at seventy quid a pop, he won't," he muttered.

Wow. Scottish wool is pricey, I thought. "Anyway," I said loudly, getting us back on track. "Sam left early from lunch. After we finished clearing dishes, we returned to work and found her by the pool."

"All of you?"

Thinking, I realized that, no, not all of us—just me. I said as much.

"And again, you disturbed the scene of a crime."

After discarding the impulse to kick him in the shin, I explained, "No. I dressed a wound of a hurt person to stop her from bleeding." Tilting my head to the side, I asked, "What crime? Didn't she slip and fall?"

Instead of answering, he picked up an evidence bag containing a familiar-looking tile, now stained red. "Fingerprints on this should reveal something," he said.

Heart sinking, I told him I moved the stone earlier, so we needed to eliminate mine.

Douglass smirked. "And why weren't you with your workmates after lunch?"

"I was!" I practically shouted, so pleased to have an alibi. "We helped the cafe staff clean up, and then the counter lady thanked us, and I realized I didn't learn her name…" I petered out, remembering that I left Gabriel and Simon to go and talk to her.

"You didn't know her name?" he prompted.

"Well, no. And I felt bad for not having learned it, so I went back in to ask her."

"And?"

"And, what?"

He sighed.

I rolled my eyes at my predicament and said, "She'd left."

"So she can't confirm that you were inside."

"No." My heart sank more.

"How about the gift shop clerk?"

I could tell from his expression that he already knew the answer.

Shaking my head, I said, "No, she left, too."

"You're telling me then," his shark-like grin widened as he spoke, "that no one saw you for over ten minutes. Plenty of time for you to whack Ms. Niven over the head."

"That makes no sense. Why would I hit her and then help her?"

"You tell me."

My need to always do well on quizzes almost forced an answer out of my mouth before I strangled it. Unhelpfully, I could think of a reason for that behavior. Hit her, take what she found, and then bind the wound to cover my tracks. Or because I had what I needed. Either way, my rescue attempt didn't prove my innocence.

"It doesn't make any sense," I repeated while squashing a guilty expression.

"Wait here."

Like I had a choice.

Since Douglass hadn't taken my phone away, I texted Edward. 'Sam attacked by the nymphaeum. Douglass thinks I did it. Don't let him arrest me. 'K?'

'K,' came his immediate response. 'Chatting with Parikh now.'

No words of comfort, nothing about overreacting, no further texts.

Worrisome. *Or is it 'worrying?'* I'd ask my mom.

After what seemed like forever, Douglass's displeased voice flooded through the closed door. "What do you—...Bailey—...You can't ignore—"

He must have disconnected before the inarticulate scream erupted from his throat. Slamming open the door, he confronted me, red-faced and panting.

"Hi," I said with a smile, enjoying his discomfort.

"Listen here, you."

His intensity sobered my mood. Like he hated me with every fiber of his being, he searched for a way to dispose of me.

"You've been in this country for one semester and have seen more bodies than most police officers do in a career in these parts. You may have fooled DI Parikh, but there is something wrong about that."

"I almost got killed, too," I retorted, taken aback. "It's not my fault." A phrase I said far too often.

"So you say."

Before I could defend myself, he continued. "There is a car waiting to take you to Bath. You may resume your work at the museum, but you are not to travel anywhere under any circumstance. You are not officially under caution, but let me be clear about this. I am cautioning you."

The way he delivered this speech stopped the breath in my chest. Every part of me turned cold, unlike anything I experienced outside.

"Now get out."

Any remaining bravado abandoned me, and after grabbing my purse, I ran to the car.

The same constable who had taken me to Dolly's waited, heater on.

"Greenway Lane in Bath?" he asked.

"Yes, please." My voice sounded small and weak. "Ash Tree Cottage."

Unable to muster small talk, I tucked my legs into my chest and listened to the chatter on his radio. The countryside, grey and devoid of leaves, appeared abandoned, the snow cold and hopeless.

As we climbed into Bath, traffic offered an odd comfort, no longer alone in an isolated area. The stunning Regency architecture carved in butter-colored limestone cast its spell on me, but weaker this time, not strong enough to ward off my fear that I might not make it out of this predicament unscathed.

The weathered white gate set into the stone wall surrounding the Priestlys' home greeted me. Roger and Meryl rented out a studio room on the top floor to a college student every year. In a stroke of luck, I got it for the length of my internship at the Roman Baths.

However, when I opened the gate into the massive garden that gave way to the valley below, cold darkness stared at me. Not a single light shone from the three-story house, built into the side of a hill.

Of course, why would it? Meryl and Roger could be anywhere from a community activity to a quick cruise. Why leave on a light, for a girl far away in the countryside?

Wishing I'd called ahead, I picked my way down the paving stones and by the ash tree that dominated the area to the front door, which I stared at, shivering.

My things were still in the lodge.

When I got out of the car, the constable who drove me gave me a small bag. Using my phone flashlight, I looked in and fought back tears of relief to find the house keys.

The bulky key screeched with rust when I turned it, and the French door to the boot room clanked like the ghost in *A Christmas Carol.* Spooked, I rushed through to the main door, opened it, and switched on the lights.

The living room burst into color, not from the chandelier, but from a massive Christmas tree in the corner between the window and fireplace.

"Oh my," I breathed, the pine scent enveloping me. "A real tree?"

Scampering toward it, my worries fled momentarily. I touched the soft boughs and noted the water around the base. Real trees were available in Tempe, but the desert air turned them into kindling. Plus, my mom liked the fact that the fake one came pre-lit.

"You," I stroked the tree as I spoke, "are magical."

Thoughts of my mom, alone at Christmas, brought too many emotions to the surface for me to sort through. Sinking to the floor, I cried. Confusion, fear, Christmas, Douglass, my visa, my future, Edward—all too much.

After a good release, I washed my face in the kitchen sink and texted the Priestlys that I had come home to find the beautiful tree.

'It will be lovely to see you! I came to the church office with Roger today. We'll be home for dinner, and you can tell us all about it,' Meryl responded.

Dinner? I hadn't gotten used to being so far north on the globe. As the winter solstice neared, daylight hours dwindled unlike anything in Arizona. At the dig, we tended to work sunup to sundown and didn't pay much attention to the clock. I'd been getting away with relatively short workdays and not realizing it.

Not wanting to bug Edward, while he worked an important case, I texted Lily, who took the lunch shift at The Pump Room, an elegant restaurant attached to the Baths.

'Wotcha doing home?' Lily responded.

'Long story.'

'Always is with you. Boater?'

'Yes, please!'

Although slippery, the walk down the hill to the Pultney Bridge pub allowed me to shake off my gloom. Ennui, I corrected, my mother's voice insisting I increase my vocabulary.

Sparing a grin for my mom, I entered The Boater and found Lily flirting with the bartender.

"Your friend's here," he told her, nodding in my direction.

"Wicked," she said, beaming at him. "Cheers."

Lily and I looked quite similar, except for my height and her blue eyes vs. my green, so people tended to lump us together. I appreciated it since it made me feel more like a local.

"You remember Donny?" Lily asked, indicating the young bartender. With his flop of dark brown hair covering one eye, he reminded me of a character from Lady and the Tramp.

After hugging her, I said, "Of course, Donny. How are you?"

"Y'alright?" he responded, holding up a half-pint mug.

"Zumwalt Porter." From a local brewery, I liked the chocolate and malty notes. And, yes, okay, the fact that their logo included a bunny.

"Why are you back? Did you find another body?"

Lily's excitement, at odds with her quiet nature, grew from vicariously experiencing my adventures. With my every mishap, her decision to live a peaceful life in Bath was validated.

As I opened my mouth to answer, another barkeep approached. Middle to late aged, with steel gray hair in a crew cut, he boomed a jolly laugh in reaction to Lily's question.

"What's all this then, Lily?"

"Mac! Alright cock? This is my friend from America, Maddie."

"How do you do, Miss Maddie?" he asked formally but with a broad smile.

"I'm good. Mac?"

"Yes indeed! What brings you all the way to our fair city?"

Sipping my beer, I filled him in on growing up in Arizona, attending university in Chicago, and landing the internship at the Roman Baths. He listened attentively but without being nosy. The perfect bartender.

After our chat, I guided Lily to a quiet corner by the mural of Bath and related my story. Her eyes grew wide with horror. I often spared her the more gruesome details, but right now, I needed to get it out of my head, from discovering the charred heart, the wicker man, Sam's attack, and Douglass accusing me.

"That's a right mess, it is. If you want my opinion?" She paused, her question genuine.

I nodded.

"This Douglass person doesn't care about you at all. He just wants you to look guilty to get Edward in trouble."

Gazing into nothing, I weighed the idea. "You might be right."

Preening, she sat straighter and explained, "We learned about transference at work. If we look nice, and the food looks nice, the customer will think it tastes nice before they try it."

"So everyone looks down at Edward for having the American girlfriend accused of attacking her boss."

"And murder," Lily added unhelpfully.

"Yeah, that." I gulped my porter. "So, what do I do?"

"No idea. You're the brains."

It didn't feel like it right then.

We chatted until she finished her tea, and she walked me to Roger's church so that I could catch a ride home.

Finding the Priestlys in the car park, I scrunched into the back seat of their Mini Cooper while Meryl invited me to go to the Christmas markets with her the next day.

"Sounds lovely," I said without much enthusiasm.

I mean, yes, it did sound lovely, and I'd never been to a Christmas Market. Tempe had an arts and crafts festival every December, but the weather usually showed off at seventy to eighty degrees, and no one roasted chestnuts or sold wreaths of actual holly. My mom would go crazy for an actual market, but she wouldn't be here.

We made a fast dinner of cheese toasties on Meryl's delicious seed bread, which turned out to be grilled cheese sandwiches.

Both Priestlys possessed an uncanny sense of when to approach a subject. They waited until we were washing dishes before asking why I returned early.

My story was abbreviated. I only reviewed the details of finding Sam, the part I needed most to process.

"Oh, you poor dear," Meryl said, sweeping me into a hug.

Allowing myself to be mothered soothed my jangled nerves until Roger asked, "Will this affect your internship, do you think?"

After recounting the madness of the past few days twice, I managed to put thoughts of my future aside.

Until now. Willing my chin to stop trembling, I muttered something vague and shrugged.

"Roger, don't be so callous. Can't you tell she's shattered?"

"Yes, of course, my dear. You're right, as always."

Except, they both looked at me with shifting eyes.

"It's just that," Meryl began.

"We always have a tenant," Roger finished, fidgeting with a pound coin.

"And, of course, we would love to have you, well, forever, quite frankly."

"But we do need to know if you'll be here next term to let the flat."

A tear trickled over my cheek, as I looked from one to the other.

"Oh dear," Meryl said, hugging me again. "But we can wait, can't we, Roger?"

"Of course, Yes. No problem at all. Take your time. You're always welcome." The coin traveled nervously through his fingers, reminding me of something.

"I'll let you know as soon as I hear anything. I promise."

"But you've thought of something," Meryl said, examining my face.

"I did. Before Sam's attack, I thought I saw an object glinting in the nymphaeum, like a marble or coin."

"Do you think that's why someone hit her?"

I thought about it. "I told her, which is why she went out during lunch, but no one knew that."

"So only you and she knew about the glint in the water?"

Nodding, my chest began to tighten as dread took hold.

Tall and silver-haired, Roger's serene presence exuded calm. Quietly, he asked, "Are you sure they meant to hit her?"

Sam's and my physical appearances were strikingly different.

Unless we were in matching green puffy jackets.

Chapter Eleven: Roddy's Treasure

Heading to what I referred to as my own private princess tower on the top floor of the Priestlys' house, I contemplated that Sam and I had matching coats. Her short, bright red hair couldn't be mistaken for my long, strawberry-blonde ponytail. But to someone in a hurry, the jacket and any hint of red would be good enough to identify as me.

I called Tori.

"Am I your one phone call?" she asked, grinning.

"Closer than you'd hope."

"Constable Meany still after you?"

"Oh yeah. I think Edward and DI Parikh stopped him from arresting me, but he told me I was under caution from him if not the police."

"OMG, Maddie. What did you do to piss him off?"

Letting out a long puff of air, I explained everything and relayed Lily's theory.

Tori's slow nod meant she agreed, but she added to it. "The thing is, he has a point about you and the bodies."

My eyebrows knit together and raised in consternation.

"Don't give me that look," Tori said. "If he can prove you're a criminal mastermind, he gets one up not only on Edward but also the DI and DCI."

"You're forgetting I almost died, too."

"Par for a criminal mastermind."

"Stop saying that."

"Evil genius?"

Narrowing my eyes, I growled before saying, "And I have no motivation. I didn't benefit one whit from those previous encounters."

"Oh yes, you did!" Tori exclaimed, warming to the idea of my guilt. "Who is friends with a dowager duchess, an honest-to-goodness lord, a lady, can stay at a posh resort with no cost—"

"Tori! Whose side are you on, anyway?"

"I'm just saying. It's like one of those mysteries where the guy makes a girl fall in love with him so he can kill her and take her money. Except you're the guy."

"Those are Agatha Christy plots, not Sherlock Holmes."

"True, but maybe you should read those instead this time." Her gaze fell away from the camera as she typed. "*Death on the Nile*, obviously, and oooo try *Endless Night*."

"I'll try a little Holmes and some Poirot," I said as Tori continued to type.

"*Endless Night* is a novel, but 'The Case of the Caretaker' is a short story with Miss Marple. Do that."

"Sounds a little dark for Miss Marple, but I'll give it a try." Pausing, my eyes traveled up, thinking. "It won't make me look like I'm doing research, will it?"

Tori nodded. "Yes. Yes, it will. Do it anyway."

"Fine. I'm going to bed."

"Before then," Tori batted her beautiful brown eyes and tilted her head, knowing it made her look like a Mexican work of art. "Are you headed near the Abbey anytime soon?"

I'd been Tori's research assistant, for many of her Religious Studies classes. Father Michael, Deacon at the Bath Abbey, proved a great resource in addition to Reverend Priestly.

"Not another nursery rhyme," I pleaded as she had ruined enough of my childhood.

"Nope. Solstice info this time. Remember how stone workers carved the Green Man icons into cathedrals? Could you find out if they did anything for the solstice?"

"I'm guessing you've already found the answer."

"Well, yes, of course. Yule logs, mistletoe, bells, all pagan. But I can't find anything about stonework."

"Meryl is taking me to the Christmas Market, so I'll stop in and visit with Father Michael."

"You're the best!"

"Think of a way to save me, would you please?" I begged.

"Love you oodles!"

Putting her dire logic aside, my mood lightened after our chat. But not enough to keep me from tossing and turning all night and oversleeping in the morning.

Far too late, I got up. Having missed breakfast, I made a French press coffee, mumbled greetings to Meryl, and mug in hand, wandered out to the garden to visit Roderick the Rabbit.

"Hey, bunny," I called, wrapping my sweater tighter around me. The walled garden afforded protection from the wind, but snow crept over my shoes.

Long black and white ears stood up like beacons, and I stepped over the little fence to his enclosure. "How are you, Roddy?"

Hopping toward me, he wiggled his nose in greeting.

I bent over to pet his silky fur, thick and fluffy for the winter.

"Hello there, Maddie," a male voice called. James, Edward's troubled younger brother, opened the gate and sauntered in uninvited.

"Hi, James," I said, lifting Roddy to create a barrier between us.

"Edward asked me to stop by and check on you."

Edward's intention to reform his larceny-prone younger brother often clashed with James' actions. His charm was different from Gabriel's easy manner. James' bad boy looks and gang-related past made his smile irresistible to just about everyone susceptible to danger.

Except me, who found him annoying.

"I have a hard time accepting that," I said, refusing to be drawn in.

"Okay, so maybe I volunteered." That smile. That Scottish burr. I had to admit I understood the appeal.

My glare faltered as he upped the wattage of his grin.

"Alright, I give. Why?"

"Lunch?"

My annoyance with him broke as he sounded so much like Winnie the Pooh. But I didn't let up. "I happen to know you're a very good cook."

"I dinnae have any food. My wee brother ran off before buying anything."

When I moved in, the Priestlys made it clear that all my meals were to be taken in my studio at the top of the house. I had a small fridge, hotplate, and microwave. Since then, they had invited me to breakfast, lunch, and dinner every day, treating me like family.

Which sometimes extended to Edward. But not to Edward's brother.

"You cannot expect my landlords to feed you. It's," I paused, searching for the perfect word, "impertinent."

Reinforcing my point, I set Roddy down and stood between him and the house.

The boot room door opened, and Meryl called, "James? Is that you? Are you hungry?"

The million-watt smile flashed to her, and she ushered him into the house. "A ray of sunshine on a winter day you are, Mrs. Priestly."

Meryl giggled.

Fighting to not roll my eyes as it made me look like a middle-schooler, I returned to Roddy to discover him nibbling.

"What have you got there?" I asked him.

By way of answer, he pushed a scrubby carrot toward me, then resumed nibbling. There are few things cuter on earth than watching a bunny eat. However, I wasn't positive that carrots were a normal part of his diet, Bugs Bunny not being the best source of information.

Picking up Roddy and the carrot, I went inside to find James sitting on the kitchen counter while Meryl cooked. They chatted like old friends, a manipulative skill of James and a gracious attribute of Meryl.

A rich tomato scent perfumed with basil and something else wafted in my direction.

"Hello, Maddie dear. I thought I'd whack together some tomato soup for our guest."

I looked at James in disbelief, and he winked at me. *Cheeky*, I thought for the first time ever. What a perfect sentiment for boys like James.

"Are carrots good for rabbits?" I asked, holding up Roddy's two-inch treat.

Meryl moved closer, examining the little vegetable. "It must have fallen out of the compost heap when we moved it to the bin."

"Twenty-four carrot gold to a rabbit," James quipped, and I cursed myself for not thinking of it first.

"Quite the treasure," Meryl agreed.

Everything circled back to treasure. Or my mind highlighted the word as important, and I wished I could figure out why.

When the object in the fountain glinted, could that have been treasure? Instead of discovering a connection to druids, Jill might have found something physical, worth more than its archaeological value.

If so, it wouldn't make any sense that the druids punished her, though.

Except, they didn't. The druids nearby were not crusaders but campers who lost their wicker man.

On the other hand, maybe George didn't understand as much about the druids as he thought. Could the ethereal Muriel have a different agenda?

"Maddie, it looks like you're watching a tennis match. What are you thinking?"

Meryl's voice cut into my thoughts.

"Huh? Oh, yeah. Sorry." I sniffed as she ladled soup into bowls. "Tomato, basil, and something else I can't name. What's your secret ingredient?"

"Try it," she said with a broad smile.

After blowing on my spoonful of soup, I tasted it, savoring the deliciousness. Acidic tomatoes balanced with herby basil hit my palate first, followed by a sweet but almost mushroom flavor. I reported my analysis as James and I scooped more soup into our mouths.

"Saffron!" Meryl said, pleased with our reactions.

Knowing how much the stuff cost, I almost blurted out not to waste it on us. Muting my response, I said, "But it's so expensive. You shouldn't have used it on me."

"Rubbish. You're both worth it."

James blushed and looked away, not used to compliments. Or he manipulated us like a master, making everyone want to take care of him. I honestly couldn't tell.

"No, really," I insisted. "Simon is growing it, and they sell it by the gram."

"Like drugs," James added, which earned a withering scowl from me and a slight frown from Meryl. He had the grace to look ashamed and began gathering and washing our dishes.

"One of our more well-off parishioners gave it to me. She bought it to make paella, but her husband found the flavor too bitter. Apparently, it's marmite. I love it."

Marmite, a spread for toast made of yeast extract, had nothing to do with saffron.

"Uh, marmite?"

"Oh, sorry, dear. You either love it or hate it."

Nodding, I filed this phrase away to try in front of Lily and gauge her reaction. Of my friends, she tuned in most with random English phraseology.

Meryl put the soup in a container and gave it to James, along with a loaf of her bread. Insisting we drive to the markets she also drove James to the train station where he could walk to where Edward's boat currently sat. With no permanent moorings in Bath, the boat had to be moved every three days.

As we waved farewell, I asked, "Do you think he will reform?"

"That's up to him, not us. All we can do is offer support."

My mom also lectured about the importance of support, and another pang of homesickness took me. Maybe I should go home and not worry about extending my stay. Mom would take care of me. And Dad, too. If I went back to Chicago for school, where my warm clothes were.

Except, of course, Douglass told me not to travel.

"I have just the thing to wipe that forlorn expression from your face," Meryl said kindly. Taking my arm, she led me to the Christmas Market.

Tempe had a Festival of the Arts twice a year, so I thought I knew what to expect. I was wrong.

As we neared, scents of brownies, pancakes, and plum pudding mingled with natural botanical Christmas wreaths. Yes, there were the typical homemade goat's milk soaps, cutting boards, and soy candles, but also several artisan gins, handmade papers, and homemade curry sauces. Stall after stall displayed new delights, and Meryl's prediction of lightening my mood came true after my first bite of brownie. I grinned like a kid in a candy shop.

Focusing on food for Edward, I put together a basket that would allow for easy storage on his narrow boat but give him plenty of options for quick and flavorful meals. I also grabbed some souvenirs to give to friends and family back home.

With a bag of gifts each, Meryl and I parted ways for a while. Taking in the winter sights and Christmasy scents, I bounced my way to Bath Abbey to do research for Tori that she didn't need me to do. Somewhere in my mind, I suspected she sent me there because my mood improved after my visits.

After the magic of the Christmas Market, I couldn't imagine how my mood could get better unless my boss appeared by magic and offered to extend my internship indefinitely.

Entering through the gift shop, I waved at the clerk and asked after Father Michael. As I opened the door, my eyes automatically traveled up to the fan-vaulted ceiling. Laid out like a field of daisies, it soared to the heavens, lifting my spirits.

Father Michael found me, mouth agape, staring with my head back.

"Maddie, a pleasure to see you. Still impressed?" he asked, indicating the ceiling.

"Yeah. I don't think I could ever get used to it. Do you?"

He shook his head. "Sometimes I forget to look up, but then the Lord reminds me where I am. Have you a research question for me?"

Grinning, I said, "Once my friend found out about you, she won't do an assignment without a quote."

Stumbling through the complex question Tori posed, Father Michael nodded slowly, his finger on his chin.

"She's right about the Yule log, mistletoe, and bells, of course. Wreaths and holly have pagan roots as well. But as far as stonework..."

His voice trailed off as he pulled a cell phone from his vestment pocket. The action seemed so incongruous with the garment that I almost gasped.

"There is the Newgrange Tri-Spiral," he said, tapping.

"Newgrange?"

"Yes, in Ireland. And it's megalithic, not a church."

Pausing, he checked my face for understanding. I didn't know Newgrange, but I could show off about the term megalithic.

"Prehistoric and made with huge rocks. Like Stonehenge."

Smiling, he continued, "Even with evidence to the contrary, the tri-spiral is often attributed to the ancient Celts."

He showed me a picture on his phone.

"Oh, a triskelion," I said, recognizing the shape.

"Yes. It's as close as we'll get for your friend's paper, and you don't find them in British churches. One or two in France, I believe." He added, "Interesting query."

Snapping his fingers, he turned. "Not solstice, but this may suffice, and I believe you will find it of interest as well."

We entered the door to the bell tower, but rather than ascending, he took me over to one of the small windows. Placing his hand on the wall, he asked, "What do you see?"

Once my eyes adjusted to the dark, I could make out a circle about five inches across with six petals inside, almost like a sand dollar.

"What is it?" I asked, my eyes glued to the pattern.

"Some say it's to mark the spot where a medieval bishop consecrates a church building with holy oil. But more often than not, those spots are marked with crosses. My belief is that they are apotropaic symbols."

"Symbols? There is more than one?" I asked.

"Indeed. We have several of these compass designs, all by windows. But sometimes you'll see a Solomon's knot."

Swallowing my pride, I asked, "What does apotropaic mean?"

"From the Greek, apo means "away," and tropaic "turn." They are protection symbols."

We moved back into the sanctuary, and I asked, "Isn't the whole church a protection symbol?"

He laughed and said, "Well, yes. However, we have our hunky-punks that scare off evil."

"Hunky-punks?" Every time I think I'm getting the hang of this country, I'm reminded that I'm not.

Another chuckle. "Gargoyles and grotesques."

"Those I've heard of."

"The term hunky-punk seems unique to the Somerset area. I'm quite fond of it."

"I can see why." I smiled. "So, how is the compass a protection from evil?"

"Demons, according to medieval citizens, are fascinated by lines. They can't look at one without following it to its end."

"And these designs, like Celtic knots, have no beginning or end," I said.

"Exactly. The demons start to follow the line and get trapped in it."

Grinning, I said, "Thank you. I learn something new whenever we chat."

"My pleasure. I hope someday to meet this friend of yours."

"She's awesome."

"How is your Roman Villa?" he asked as I approached the exit.

"The religious symbols change from Roman to Christian and then back again," I said, hoping to impart new information to him.

"Just the thing to spark a holy war," he said as I departed the sanctuary.

Chapter Twelve: Miss Marple

Playing over Father Michael's final words, I emerged to a swirl of snow and shoppers flooding to the hot chocolate stalls or into tea shops for sustenance. Huddled over my bag to protect the contents, I made my way toward the church to meet Meryl.

When I got to the Mini, I plopped into the front seat and burst into tears. Meryl turned the heater down a notch, undid her seatbelt, and held me.

"Miss your mother, do you?" she asked with insight I didn't think possible.

Taking her proffered tissue, I sniffed and dried my eyes. "How did you know?"

"My daughter called, also in tears. She's in France but is gutted about missing the Christmas Market."

"Yeah. My mom would love this."

"Check the time zones and give her a call when you get home."

The bell at the Abbey rang six o'clock p.m., well after midnight in Arizona. My call would have to wait.

Not in the mood for dinner, I climbed the stairs to my top-floor room and stared out the window at nothing. The garden lights stayed off this time of year, as no one but Roddy enjoyed the weather. The Priestlys erected a tent over the rabbit's enclosure to keep the snow out of his hutch, but allowed him freedom to hop.

With a melodramatic sigh, I opened the e-book of "The Case of the Caretaker" and read. Wrinkling my nose at the end, I took notes to discuss with Tori, who, using ESP, called me.

"Hey, it's the middle of the night there."

"Like you ever worried about that."

"Yes, but I want credit for being polite." Grinning, I lifted the notebook to the camera. "I took notes."

"Ooooo, good for you! But I have a deadline. What did your Abbey source tell you?"

After relating the triskelion, hunky-punk, and apotropaic news to Tori, she said, "I didn't find anything about apotropaic designs. Thank you, and thank Father Michael for me!"

"He wants to meet you. Thinks your research questions are brilliant."

"Well, to be fair, they are."

I chose not to respond and instead said, "Have you read the Miss Marple?"

"Yep. You?"

"Yeah. So, here are my questions. Am I the devilishly handsome Harry in this scenario?"

"If we're going with my 'Douglass thinks you're guilty theory,' yes."

"Which would make Douglass—"

"Miss Marple," we said together.

"Right, because she's just lying in bed," I said, glancing at my notes.

"Not collecting evidence."

"Just using wild suppositions about young men's preferences."

"And assuming guilt without a care for anyone."

I sighed. "Well, she was right."

"Of course she was. She's Miss Marple. But look at her level of confidence. She thinks she perceives human nature inside and out."

"You sound like my mom talking about Shakespeare."

Tori smiled. "English authors with a high understanding of motivation. There's a connection."

"Okay, so we have a parallel. How does this help me? Anything I do to ingratiate myself to Douglass will only make him suspect me more."

"Forewarned is forearmed," she said uselessly.

Thrusting my jaw at the screen, she added, "And don't scowl at me," before I could express my disbelief.

"What do I do?" I demanded.

Tilting her head to the side, she narrowed her eyes and said, "What do you think?"

"Now you sound even more like my mom."

"A comparison to the brilliant and beautiful Heather McGuire is never a bad thing."

"Fine. I will lay low, tread lightly, and try to be invisible."

"A great plan, but hard when you find bodies. Try to avoid that."

"Yeah, thanks."

"And don't rant."

"I don't—"

"Thanks again for the info! You're the best!"

And the connection went dark.

"Rant. Please. Since when do I rant? I mean, sometimes I may ramble—"

A message came through, interrupting my thoughts.

'Stop ranting,' Tori texted.

* * *

The following day, sunshine flooded my room, indicating I overslept. However, my head cleared, and I could think better than any time the previous two days.

I planned to lay low, do the job I came here for, and hope Douglass found the murderer without my intervention. If threatened to stay away, I would stay away—easy.

After dressing, I hurried down the stairs, snatched a piece of toast Meryl left out for me, and picked my way through melting snow to the Roman Baths.

By-passing the domed Georgian architecture entry that housed the ticketing lines to the museum, I plowed into the Oversight Office. I assumed it would be empty as I left most of the team behind at Chedworth.

I was wrong.

Lady Vivian perched elegantly behind the desk, her eyes narrowed, her mouth downturned.

84

"Your ladyship," I stammered, "I didn't think anyone would be here."

"Clearly, as indicated by your unceremonious entrance."

"My apologies. Since I came home, I thought I would help out at the dig or do tours." I added unenthusiastically, "Or filing."

"I may be misinformed," she said in a way that indicated she was never misinformed, "but I believe Ms. Niven is back at Chedworth and expecting you there."

"Wait, what? How come no one told me?" Once out of my mouth, the question sounded a lot more immature than I hoped.

"I mean—"

The door opened into my back, causing a small scream to strangle the rest of my words.

"What, what?" Dr. Daniels said.

Head of the archaeology team exposing a newly discovered room far below street level, Dr. Daniels had the power to change my future. One word from him, and I'd have my visa for as long as I wanted.

"Ah, it's you, uh, Miss Mmm?"

I spoke up, leaping at the chance not to be confused with Lily and his lunch order. "Miss McGuire. Or Maddie," I stuck out my hand for a shake, which he accepted absent-mindedly. "How wonderful to see you, Dr. Daniels."

"Aren't you supposed to be at the villa? A great opportunity, volunteering for the Student Worker program, what?"

Pleased? With me? I might have hopped once or twice. "Sir, yessir. I'm on my way back right now."

Not that I knew how to do that. Certainly, the police wouldn't send a car. Taxis cost a fortune, but if it pleased Dr. Daniels by going to Chedworth, I would spend it. And probably wind up asking my dad to reimburse me, but still.

"Good. That's good," he said, turning to go.

"Did you need something?" Lady Vivian said in mild exasperation.

Relief replaced momentary panic when I saw her gaze directed at Dr. Daniels.

"What? Ah, yes. Quite right," he said, moving to close the door.

As I stopped it to escape, Lady Vivian turned her velvet blue eyes to me. "Rivers will be at your disposal for your return. Shall I call him to your home in the morning?"

"Yes, please. And thank you!"

Lady Vivian's chauffeur, Rivers, was a compact and affable man who drove like Mr. Toad from *The Wind and the Willows*. Still, I would get to Chedworth in record time.

"And before you go today," Lady Vivian said as I tried to retreat, "please check on the new Romans. Make sure everything is tiptop." Her pink nails extended a piece of paper toward me. "And deliver this message to Mr. Armstrong, emphasizing that we prefer not to play secretary in the Oversight Office."

I sort of half-curtsied like a maid in a black-and-white movie and ran through the exhibits and down to the Great Bath. The new Romans, as Lady Vivian referred to them, were guides dressed in Roman clothing who lingered around the displays looking authentic. They added texture, provided facts, and made the museum come alive.

Rudy and Fiona sat on a bench by the Great Bath, chatting with a group of school-aged children who looked enthralled. I got close enough to eavesdrop on the information they provided.

When finished with a technical explanation of the great arch across the Bath from our location, Fiona looked at me wide-eyed. Smiling, I gave her a thumbs up, and she visibly relaxed. "You're doing great," I whispered as I snuck away to find Drake Armstrong.

Following a line of giggling middle-school girls, I found him striking an impressive pose by the eastern baths. Dressed as a centurion, he stood near a door to the saunas and changing rooms. Projections of the rooms being used played over the area, giving Drake the appearance of a guard at the entrance.

Never breaking character, he stood stoically as little girls took selfies with him.

I waved the paper to catch his eye.

"Now, return whence you came," he intoned portentously, pointing an impressive arm toward the Great Baths.

Until that moment, I hadn't realized that he probably made up his name.

Once the kids were out of earshot, his voice lightened with excitement. "Did they call?"

Keeping the paper out of his reach, I conveyed Lady Vivian's displeasure at taking a message.

"I know, I know, but I don't have any place to hide a phone in this," he said, gesturing to the short leather straps and leg greaves.

"The point is that you don't take phone calls while at work. At all." I admit to channeling Lady Vivian at that moment. Since I constantly had my phone, I felt sorry for the guy.

"But I'm waiting for a role," he said, his voice getting whiny.

Wordlessly, I handed him the message.

"Brilliant!" he practically shouted.

"Get the part?"

"Marc Anthony in Julius Caesar. We open at the Theater Royal Bath in three weeks."

"Congratulations, Drake. Will you stay on here?" None of my business, but I knew Sam would need the info so she could start recruiting.

"Yes, yes. Helps me stay in character."

"O, pardon me, thou bleeding piece of earth?" I asked, using one of Marc Antony's lines from the play.

Not one iota of acknowledgment that I recited Shakespeare from memory. Instead, he started muttering the rest of the speech with a crescendo at "Woe to the hand that shed this costly blood!"

"Break a leg," I called, having done enough theater to know better than to wish him luck.

Wanting nothing more than to head straight back to Chedworth, I couldn't. I needed clothing in case the police hadn't released the lodge yet.

As I hiked back to Bear Flats and Greenway Lane, the wind picked up, bringing clouds. To take my mind off the chill, I called my mom.

"Hello, beautiful girl!" she sang. "How are you this glorious day?"

No matter what, no matter how annoyed or unhappy, her voice always made me smile. Not that I would confess that to her.

"Don't tell me. The sun is shining, and it's seventy-five degrees?" A gust of wind punctuated my question. I scurried, hunched against the onslaught.

"Only seventy," she said. "I can finally wear my new knee-high boots. But I'm sure you didn't call to discuss the peculiarities of inclement weather."

No one who lived outside the southern United States would consider seventy degrees "inclement," but I let it go.

"My brain is in a jumble." Whenever I needed to vent, my mom remained quiet, so I pressed on. "I have tickets for January 15. But then I hoped to extend my visa and keep working for the Baths, or Dr. Daniels. But we went to the Christmas Market yesterday, and…" I trailed off, a tear leaking down my cheek until the wind whipped it away.

"And you miss home?"

Not technically home, as she sold my childhood house, the second I moved to Chicago for school, but yeah, I missed swimming in a solar-heated pool while listening to Christmas music.

"I don't want you to be alone," I said, trying to sound mature and unselfish.

"My sweet girl. I would smother you with attention if you came home early, but do not do so on my account. Rita and I are quite up to our necks at the current moment."

"Mom, you're not in trouble again, are you?"

When I first went away to college, a serial killer focused his attention on my mom.

"No. A student is acting erratically, is all. Don't send Tori and her mother over with another cat."

"How is Oberon?" The cat in question, an oversized, goofy Maine coon, must have heard us talking about him as a yowl erupted in the background.

My mom's laughter traveled across the world and filled my heart. "The cat will mew, and the dog will have his day."

"Wait, I remember that one." If she could answer a question with a Shakespeare quote, she would. "Hamlet, maybe?" A guess, but since it was her favorite play, I risked it.

"Full marks! Act V." A knock distracted her. "I must be off. You will be brilliant, as ever, and arrive at the perfect conclusion."

She hung up before I could tell her about the wicker man or Jill.

Shrugging, I put my head down and rushed up the hill to Ash Tree Cottage.

I gave a quick shout to Meryl about my impending departure, and I pounded upstairs to pack.

"Oi," a familiar male voice said, coming in after me.

"Edward!" Not to be sappy, but I flew into his arms and didn't let go until the tears stopped.

"I mean, uh, hey. 'Sup?"

Laughing, he kissed my forehead. "Day off. I stopped by to see Sam. She's fine and not happy with Douglass."

"Good." I kissed his cheek. "I loved the Christmas Market, but I'm not used to snow for the holidays." Another kiss, and I tilted my head to the side. "Why are you here? Why didn't you call?"

His crooked grin appeared.

"What?"

"Surprise?" he offered, knowing how much I disliked them.

I shook my head.

"Okay. It is a present, so not actually a surprise, but it involves swimming, so get your stuff."

"Swimming?" An over-chlorinated indoor pool with screaming children would not make me happy. Still, Edward's thoughtfulness couldn't be ignored.

Inexplicably, I had brought two bikinis with me to England. Well, one counted as a one-piece missing most of the fabric. For a public pool, it would do.

"Do I need a towel?"

He shook his head no.

Packed and unenthusiastic, I followed him down and out.

Rather than his gleaming motorcycle, a SmartCar awaited us. Edward told me once it belonged to a friend of his mum. However, I'd never met this friend, and I wondered why. He could be secretive, but I should meet his friends, now that I knew about his brother, his past in Edinburgh, and where he lived.

As we approached the city center, I expected to blow by to a new area, so I broached the subject.

"Who exactly is this friend who owns this car?"

Instead of answering, he parked near the back of the Baths in the middle of the town's shopping district.

"Not my friend. His mum."

Bewildered as to where we were going, I let it drop. Walking slowly, I tried to figure out our destination.

The Gainsborough rose behind The Cross Bath, a recently restored Regency-era pool, and I quickened my step, sure the hotel was our destination. A fancy place would have a sizable indoor pool.

Before I got far, Edward stopped, causing me to pivot around him and face the opposite direction. Thermae Spa, an aqua blue door with white lettering, declared.

"Spa, like massages?"

Grinning as he opened the door, he funneled us through the line where we picked up scanning bracelets and towels, refusing to respond to my questions.

Humid and warm but without an overly strong chemical scent, I still didn't know what to expect. I pressed my plastic bauble to a scanner and the gates opened to a unisex locker room.

Panicked, I turned to Edward. "I don't get my own bathroom?"

"Bathroom, yes. And changing room, yes."

Pressing the bracelet to a tiny dressing room, he unlocked it and waited while I did the same. Once inside, I changed and donned the terry cloth robe provided, along with the plastic flip-flops.

A mirror would have been helpful, but I twisted my hair into a ballerina bun and patted around for stray hairs. It seemed okay.

"Leave your clothes in the wee room," Edward called.

I did so and emerged to find him in a matching robe.

"Ready?"

Shrugging, I said, "I guess."

An elevator announced three stories up and one down with names like The New Royal Bath, The Wellness Suite, and Rooftop Pool. Edward pushed the button for the roof.

Still unsure, I followed him down a hallway and out into the winter chill.

Wafts of steam rose from a giant square pool, obscuring the stunning view of the Abbey, the hillside, and the Gainsborough Hotel.

A waterfall disgorged from a pipe into the pool, drowning out the chatter of other guests.

"Hot springs, same as the Romans used."

I finally got it. Not just a regular pool but a bath spa experience like everyone from the Romans to Jane Austen enjoyed.

"Oh," I exhaled, overwhelmed. Edward found the one thing that made me feel at home and love being in England even more. "Thank you."

"You dinnae try it yet, lassie."

After hanging up our robes, I stepped into the water. Warm, welcoming, soft.

Hurrying down the four stairs, I launched into the pool, unexpectedly buoyed. Taking bouncing steps, I jumped and floated to the edge, where I could see the surrounding hills.

"This is amazing!" I said, grinning at Edward. "I feel so floaty."

Eyes narrowed, Edward asked, "Can you not swim?"

"Of course I can. This water is different, though."

Summoning my tour guide persona, I explained, "The natural hot springs have over forty-two minerals. It's like bathing in vitamins."

With quick strokes, I covered the length of the pool to the other side, near the hotel with its giant crest of Bath—bear and lion holding the shield of water.

"It's effortless," I said as he caught up with me. "The water is holding me up."

Launching myself at him, I wrapped him in a hug.

"Thank you. So much."

Cleansing in mineral-rich water restored my mood, equilibrium, and excitement about returning to the dig.

No matter what I found next.

Chapter Thirteen: A Glint in the Water

Still not used to waking up in the dark, I pawed unceremoniously at my alarm until it stopped. The sun would lighten the sky by 8:00, but we needed to be on our way by then.

"Ten more minutes," I pleaded.

No one answered. The problem with adulting is that you have only yourself to answer to. "Fine."

Fumbling in low lamplight, I packed. Since my carry-on was still at Chedworth, I crammed things into a hiking backpack that folded into a small pocket when empty.

Creeping downstairs to avoid waking the Priestlys, I yelped when a shadowy figure emerged from the dining room and entered the foyer.

"So sorry, dear," Meryl said, pushing the button to turn on the light and handing me a sack. "I thought you would need sustenance."

The sturdy bag contained two sandwiches wrapped in cellophane accompanied by a thermos.

"Builder's," she assured me.

A good, strong tea with milk would make a perfect travel companion.

"You're a genius," I said, once again marveling at my luck landing in their rented room.

I hugged Meryl and then scampered out the front door, through the boot room, and up the garden path to the gate. Outside, Rivers waited on the street, sipping from a coffee flask of his own.

"Good morning, miss," he greeted me.

"Hello, Rivers. Thank you so much for taking me out to the dig site."

I clipped on my seatbelt and wrapped my arms around my goodies before he made a U-turn over the sidewalk on one side and the icy berm on the other, accelerating at breakneck speed.

"No problem, miss," he said in a calm voice, contrasting his frantic breaking. "Always happy to help."

Once on the highway, his speed matched the posted rate, and I opened my thermos. A sip of creamy, rich tea warmed the back of my throat and radiated to my fingers and toes.

"Ahh," I sighed contentedly.

At this point, Rivers accelerated around a semi-truck, and I sloshed hot liquid on my shirt.

"These lorries take up too much room. Need better drivers they do."

Unable to formulate an appropriate response, I carefully replaced the lid on my tea and securely stowed it away.

Holding my rapidly cooling shirt collar away from my skin, I watched the scenery zoom by. The cleared road dried, but the hills still sparkled under a blanket of white, emphasizing the leafless trees.

Once off the highway, the rutted country lanes made drinking tea impossible. Turning at the small, unassuming wooden sign, we entered the Villa's car park.

Sam and Simon rushed out, which, in Simon's case, presented as long, languid strides of seeming indifference.

I leaped out of the car, tamped down the queasiness in my stomach, and hugged Sam.

"A sight for sore eyes, ye are," Sam said, pouring on her Irish accent.

"You too! Are you okay? Should you be back at work so soon? You're sure you don't have a concussion. The doctors checked for that, right?"

As she fielded my questions and worries, Simon rolled his eyes.

"Hey," I said and punched him fondly on the arm.

"Indeed," he responded.

"How did you get me cleared for work?" I asked, grateful.

"That jackeen Douglass couldn't tell a clue if it bit him," Sam spat. A jackeen must be bad. "I said your name to check on you. Our wee jackets match, and someone could have been after you. But no, he had to throw you off-site like so much rubbish."

"Not to mention the inconvenience to the site," Simon said.

I glanced at him, and he jerked his head toward the nymphaeum where police tape criss-crossed the entrance.

"Lit up like a Christmas tree," Sam said, following our gazes. "To be fair, Dion did try to sneak under at one point."

On cue, the Frenchmen appeared at the entrance to the gift shop, so we headed toward them.

"What excuse did he use?" I whispered to Sam, knowing Simon's answer wouldn't be informative.

"Said he wanted to protect the pool before more snow came."

"Helpful, that," Simon said, indicating how little he thought of the idea.

"It is good you have returned," Dion said in an uncharacteristically friendly comment. Which he spoiled by adding, "We are getting behind."

Gabriel tilted his head and smiled, looking at me through long, thick eyelashes. "I am happy to see you," he said, a little more quietly than necessary, creating an intimate mood.

"Me too," I whispered back before I could stop myself.

Their short sleeves indicated the Frenchmen were still on ground truthing duties, comparing radar images to existing pictures and pinpointing areas to explore further. Much as I wanted to help decode the images in the warmth of the office area, I ached to try and locate the coin that had caught my attention before.

Herding me away from Gabriel, Sam said, "I can't remember seeing anything before my attack. Memory lapse or the brute got to me before I could look."

"Let's go together and search. Protection in numbers."

The police tape didn't pose much of a barrier, coming down with a couple of tugs.

"Should we have left it, do ye think?" Sam asked.

As I stuffed the balled-up tape into my pocket, I said, "They'll put it back if they want it up. We can say the wind took it."

Answering my comment, a gust blew across us, turning my damp shirt collar into an icy, stiff wedge.

Already cold and uncomfortable, I got on my knees in the snow and put my nose close to the still water.

"Why doesn't it freeze?" I asked, looking at her.

Sam blinked at me. "I never thought of that. It's fed by a spring, so there may be too much agitation to allow crystallization?"

"I'll buy that," I said, inching closer to the water that reflected the gray sky. "I don't see anything," I said, unable to discern anything other than the dark stone under the surface. "It's all just…"

A glint caught my eye as I twisted my head to talk to Sam. Shifting back and forth, an object definitely sparkled if I didn't look directly.

"There," I said, memorizing the location.

Standing, I pointed as Sam dropped to her knees. Mimicking my head movements, she grunted, shifted, and went stock still.

"Is that what ye saw, then?"

I nodded, although her eyes were still glued to the pond. "Run and get Simon, quick as you can."

"Nope. Safety in numbers, remember?"

Instead, I turned toward the Visitor Centre, stuck two fingers in my mouth, and whistled like a fan at a high school football game.

A gasp sounded from nearby.

"Who's there?" I shouted as a pheasant shot into the air.

Dion and Gabriel appeared near the pond wall, rejecting orders to stay inside and compare photos. Had they been waiting for one of us to leave so that they could bash the other on the head?

Before I could think about their unexpected position further, Dion launched into a tirade.

"What is this 'orrible sound you are making while I try to photograph? Unacceptable, this noise. You Americans, you 'ave no appreciation for the nature. The faisan, the, the, pheasant, 'e flew away."

Bird watching? The French were bird-watching. Okay. To their credit, the pheasants were stunning with their chestnut brown bodies and iridescent green heads.

Ignoring a variety of responses from incredulous to impressed, I said, "Go to the centre and get the cameras, grid paper, the gripper, and Simon."

"What have you found?" Gabriel asked.

"Now," Sam called from her position on the ground.

Everyone returned at once, eager to work. As always, Simon organized everything for efficiency while Sam double-checked our work for accuracy.

We recreated the crisscross pattern with twine, mirroring the existing grid map.

Gabriel's drawing skills rivaled Dolly's, and I wondered if he had a similar job of drawing artifacts back in France.

Pinpointing the exact location of the glint, we noted it in multiple places before Simon reached in with a gripper.

With exquisite care, he wiggled and tugged at the object while the rest of us held our breath. As the object came loose, more could be seen. Gold beams twinkled under the waves in the water.

The extraction complete, Simon brought the gleaming coin out of the water and dropped it into the pH-neutral cloth Sam laid out for him.

"Is it Roman?" I blurted out, unable to keep quiet any longer.

"An aureus," Sam said, sounding awed.

Wracking my brain, I cursed myself for not being further along in my archaeology degree. "As in, Emperor Aurelian?"

When I got the internship at the Roman Baths, I studied every emperor from Claudius, who sent the Romans into Britain in 44 A.D., through the next three centuries until they withdrew.

I got the name but couldn't remember anything about him.

"Yes," Simon agreed. "He reigned only five years and never visited near here."

"270 to 275 A.D.," Sam confirmed. "But it isn't inconceivable that the wealthy occupants of Chedworth had a coin or two."

"Or one of their visitors," Simon added. "The mosaics indicate they loved to entertain.

"Is it normal for emperors to have gold coins?" Museums usually displayed

Bronze.

Sam and Simon nodded, and I marveled at how well the two worked together.

"Yes, although with such a short reign, not many would have been minted in gold. This is worth quite a lot."

With a no-nonsense nod, Sam said, "Right. You two," she pointed at the Frenchmen, "call the Douglass and find out when we can get back into the lodge. We'll need to be close."

Once they were out of earshot, she said, "I do not trust them enough to tell them where we store the coin."

Holding onto the treasure delicately, Sam led us to the Visitor Centre where we used a simple lockbox, which we then locked in the cafe's safe. "It'll have to do for now. Simon, call the Cultural Heritage Curator at the National Trust. They'll send someone out right away."

As far as hiding places went, it lacked discretion. I mean, where else would it be?

"That is way too obvious," I said. "And easy to get to."

With a wink, Sam agreed.

"Don't you think…" I let the question trail off, figuring Sam had a plan.

Gabriel returned, announcing we could use the Hunting Lodge again, and we trundled over, chattering excitedly.

"How did you see that?" Gabriel asked me, eyes glowing.

As much as I wanted to give an impressive answer, I admitted, "Clumsiness, mostly. I slipped and got too close to the water."

"Magnifique," he said, scanning me, a half-smile playing on his lips.

After gazing at him for a little too long, I said, "Right-o then," and marched away to catch up with Simon.

In response to his quirked eyebrow, I said, "Just, just, I don't know, hush," as I brushed past him and entered the lodge.

Odd smells permeated the main workroom, and I fought hard not to identify them. Even so, a flash of the burning wicker man entered my mind, and I had to pinch my nose closed for a moment.

Dion showed up with the pile of radar images and the plan for securing the site for winter.

"Haven't we finished that?" I asked, pointing to the winterizing documents.

"It needs to be checked again," he said, his accent dripping with such disdain that it sounded like I had suggested eating a kitten.

Before I could muster an appropriate response, he continued, "And we must hurry."

All of a sudden, Dion transformed into Mr. Efficiency. Weird, considering how little he and Gabriel accomplished. A cursory peek at the truthing documents showed their lack of progress.

I wondered if, like me, they were not as far along in their archaeology program as they said. Unlike me, however, their education seemed woefully lacking.

"Imposters," I muttered with an incredible feeling of superiority until the scent of burned wood sideswiped me.

What if the Frenchmen weren't who they said they were?

Chapter Fourteen: The Tourists

With a shake, I put paranoid thoughts aside and asked Sam what she wanted me to do.

"Scour the wee pond and map everything. It's been done, but the coin came from somewhere. Maybe there are more."

Out in the cold again. Awesome. "Once more into the breach," I quoted from Shakespeare's Henry V.

"We happy few, we band of brothers," Simon added from a different act.

Unwarranted surprise must have telegraphed across my face because Simon added, "Quite the hero, our King Henry the Fifth. Defeated the French."

Because my Mom taught Shakespeare, I knew a lot more plays than most people my age, but I never thought of their historical significance. Having been in England for a few months, I began to understand that animosity toward the French mingled with national pride. Henry the Fifth defeated them, and against incredible odds.

"Yeah, about that. Do you want to band with me and keep me safe?"

Without a word, Simon re-zipped his jacket and helped me gather materials.

Outside, I pointed to the loose tile and asked Simon's opinion. With great care, he photographed and then examined both sides of the stone and the ground underneath with a magnifier app on his phone.

The dirt appeared soft, and he used a brush to move it aside.

"Nothing here," he declared after meticulous digging. "But Jill may have been using it as a hiding place. Note the height difference between the earth underneath this tile and those surrounding it."

I did, seeing what he meant. Jill could have hollowed out the area to hide coins or documentation.

"I hadn't noticed that," I admitted.

With a shrug, he expanded the search area and set me to work behind the wall that separated the nymphaeum from the woods.

"Honestly?" I whined. While, yes, I recognized an amazing opportunity to actually dig, the wind rushed through the forest like a frozen freight train. "It's like, ten degrees colder back there."

A tilt of his head, and I corrected to, "Four degrees Celsius. And I'm going, I'm going."

Unlike the manicured grounds of the villa, snow drifts from the constant wind piled on the far side of the nymphaeum. However, it showed signs of trampling. About to call Simon, I stopped myself, remembering Dion's pheasant photography session.

Stepping in the depressions they made, only small amounts of snow fell into my shoes, chilling my ankles.

"It's cold back here," I reminded Simon, who ignored me.

Further along the curve of the wall, the drift changed again, as if someone had swept it away from the wall. Using my phone to shine a light on the area, I found scrape marks around three bricks at the base near the dirt.

No way Jill would have made such a mess of it. Someone could have seen her, removed her from the picture, and then come after what she discovered.

Opening my mouth to tell Simon as much, the grating air brakes of a tour bus drowned out my voice.

When the doors opened, a flood of tourists erupted onto our peaceful site. Diesel fumes hung over the crowd, amplifying their cheerful chatter.

Noting Sam's appearance, Simon and I exchanged glances and joined her to head off the crowd.

"Welcome to Chedworth," she said.

The bus driver answered, "We ain't never had no welcome committee before."

"Today is your lucky day. I'm Samantha Niven, and my team of experts and student workers will happily guide you through the site. Does anyone speak French?"

Heads shook, and one person asked, "Gaelic?"

"Are ye Irish, then?" Sam responded and they fell into a happy conversation with several tour members following.

Wondering how Sam recognized Irish Gaelic from Scottish, I raised my hand and said, "Full disclosure, I have an American accent."

Several more tourists gathered around me, including a group of Japanese who didn't speak any English and probably only responded because I gestured to follow me.

Simon summoned the rest of the group, some of whom looked familiar. Craning my neck, I tried to remember where I'd seen them, but they moved away too quickly.

An expectant sea of faces gazed at me, so I started my tour, using the same route I'd taken when showing George the Druid around.

One person, however, is different than several. They asked questions about things I already explained, they stopped for pictures, and my wet socks kept me from getting warm. The unexpected guiding left me exhausted.

Teeth chattering, I waved to Simon, who stood sentry at the nymphaeum, as I headed into the lodge and upstairs. Everything sat where I left it, but the room emitted a creepy invaded aura. The police would have gone through everything and removed Jill's belongings. Much as I had longed to return, I now wished I could leave.

With no other available rooms, I rearranged this one to give it a new look. After changing my socks, I pushed the desk under the window and set the beds into an L instead of parallel. The change made the room cozier, if a little off-balance.

Next, I took the clothes in my bag and hung everything in the closet, using the top shelf for small items.

Anticipating the need, I pulled a soy candle from the Bath Christmas Market out of my travel backpack and lit it. Cinnamon and pine filled the space, driving away demons.

With everything in its place, I couldn't shake the feeling of something wrong. Looking through the closet and laundry, I discovered one of my shirts was missing. A blue gingham, and it's one of my favorites.

"Why would the police take a shirt?" I wondered out loud, then shook my head. "They wouldn't." Nine inches taller and much thinner than my former roommate, my clothes wouldn't have been confused with hers.

Opening the door, I headed out to ask if anyone found it in the dryer.

The hallway smelled like cleaning solution, so I opened the window at the end, hoping to draw my candle scent into the common area and flush out the bad air.

As I stepped onto the stairway, I heard voices outside.

"We have to hurry," a male with a London accent said.

"I tore up the letter. We'll be fine," a second male responded.

Sitting on the top stair, I listened more intently. I'd heard those voices before, the night before Jill's death.

"After the letter, the phone calls will start."

"Two more days."

"The girl needs handling."

The lodge's front door banged open, and I stifled a yelp. Simon stomped up the stairs.

"What a waste of a perfectly good afternoon."

Holding my finger to my lips to shush him, I waited for the voices to resume, but they didn't.

"Maddie?" Simon called as if he couldn't see me.

I crawled back to my room, so my head didn't appear in the hallway window, then shouted, "What?"

"That smells rather nice. Don't have a spare, do you?"

With a smile, I grabbed the candle and headed downstairs, quietly closing the hallway window along the way.

The candle brought a little cheer into the dining room and workspace.

True to form, Simon didn't ask why I shushed him. After I checked the windows and made sure Dion and Gabriel hadn't returned, I told him what I had heard.

"Do you think it's important?"

"Not really, except for two things. I think I heard those same voices the night the wren hit the window. I also recognized some of the people in your group. Could you place anyone?"

Simon closed his eyes, a crease between his brows. "There were three people I recognized," he said, looking at me. "The Wheatsheaf Pub?"

"Maybe. Where else could we have seen anyone? Locals or maybe druids? How can we find out where the tour bus came from?"

"The full buses usually originate in London."

"So how would locals get on?" I wondered.

"Maybe a stop in town? It is worth looking into," Simon agreed but offered no suggestions on how to do it.

Wishing I'd taken a picture of the bus, I tried to remember details. "Green" came to mind. Not much help.

Back in my room, I used my phone data to search tour companies. The bus driver sounded like he'd been to Chedworth before. The image tab brought up several possibilities, but none looked right.

Seriously wanting to give up, my mother's voice popped into my head. *"Anything worth doing is worth doing well."*

"But I'm tired," I reasoned. The deafening silence in my mind drove me to continue.

Finally, a small company boasting bespoke tours in luxury coaches displayed an image that matched the one in my mind.

"And it stops in Northleach. Perfecto."

However, I didn't grasp the significance of the find other than it would be perfectly normal for anyone, druid or local, to be at Chedworth.

Relaying the information to Simon after dinner only produced more questions.

"Back to my original question," he said.

"Do I think it's important?" I reiterated. "I don't know. You?"

Simon shrugged with a refined elegance.

"Not helpful," I said.

Another shrug, "How would they have information about the gold?"

"Jill blabbed," I said without much conviction. Jill's many faults didn't include gossip. "Or someone overheard her telling a partner or colleague. Maybe a college professor." Thinking of my many encounters with Jeffery the Reporter, I added, "Or the press?"

Another noncommittal but elegant gesture from Simon.

I growled.

When the rest of the team joined us, we devised plans for mapping the nymphaeum in hopes of recovering more of the aureus coins.

More exciting than tourists, I put conjecture from my mind and allowed myself to wallow in the excitement of our discovery. After texting Edward a picture of the coin, I drifted off.

* * *

The following day, an unpleasant voice oozed into my dreams.

"How can you be sure Ms. McGuire didn't plant this herself?"

Douglass.

How could a morning be more unpleasant than, to begin with, a visit from our least favorite constable?

Unfortunately, I found out.

Chapter Fifteen: A Small Token of Terror

Rolling out of bed, I tore through morning ablutions, as my mother referred to them, threw my hair in a ponytail, and dressed in as many layers as possible.

Douglass and Sam stood toe to toe, seething at each other, when I rushed downstairs. The image of my tiny boss holding off the constable would have been funny if I hadn't figured they were talking about me.

"What is it this time?" I asked.

That's when the scent hit me. Something woody, charred, and smoky wafted in the room—not unpleasant but disquieting.

On one of the tables, beside an evidence bag, lurked a miniature wicker man with a burned piece of cloth poking out—blue gingham cloth.

"Is that my shirt?" I blurted out before thinking, a habit that needed squashing.

"That, Ms. McGuire, is my question," Douglass said with a sneer, reminding me of the Grinch.

Giving up on subtlety, I plowed ahead. "Well, yeah. I mean, I noticed one of my shirts was missing. I thought maybe you guys took it, confusing it with Jill's personal effects."

Sam indicated I should hush, but I wasn't done yet. "I liked that shirt. My mom got it for me at the Biltmore."

The Phoenix shopping center boasted some of the finest stores in the area, none of which she could afford as a single mom. But for my seventeenth birthday, she drove me there for lunch and one item of clothing.

A tear threatened to leak out of the corner of my eye, so before it could, I took the offensive. "How did it get there?" I demanded of Douglass.

"Another of my questions."

"Fine. I don't have a clue."

Unsatisfied with my response, he wasted our morning with statements and implications about my involvement.

"Why did you not report the missing garment?" Douglass demanded.

Channeling Tori's advice, I regretted my initial outburst and remained meek. Ish. Neutral, at least.

"I thought the police mistook it for one of Jill's. Or maybe I left it in the dryer." Suppressing the urge to point out, that a missing blouse didn't require a call to the cops, I remained friendly.

"Do try not to scowl, Ms. McGuire."

Sighing, I said, "I'm not scowling. I'm concentrating. A lot of weird things happened, and I don't understand why the wicker man is aimed at me, and I very much want you to find out what's going on. Okay?"

Instead of responding to my distress, he rolled his eyes—like a middle-schooler. The expression came across as annoying, as my mother always said. Huh. Good to know.

Once released from Douglass's incessant questions, I went straight to work on the nymphaeum, using the plan we mapped out the previous evening. Ignoring Simon, who started before me, I muttered dire warnings about Douglass and uppity constables.

"Do be quiet," Simon said. "You sound like a madwoman."

"Huh? Oh. Yeah. Sorry."

The silence, however, worked my nerves. Without ire to drive me, my teeth chattered, and a shudder formed in my chest. Fear more than cold produced the reaction.

How could the mini wicker man be anything but a warning that I would be next? Dragged from my bed in the early hours and roasted.

But why? I still hadn't found what Jill unearthed, and the whole team discovered the coin. No longer a secret, it no longer held power. Everyone had heard about the coin by now, including the police and the National Trust. Why did I need to be silenced?

"That's it," Simon declared loudly, causing me to yelp.

I looked at him.

"Tea. Come along."

As we walked toward the Visitor Centre, he bumped my shoulder with his. Again, for Simon an unheard of display of public affection.

Quirking my eyebrows in his direction, he explained, "You were keening."

No way. "Keening?"

"High-pitched whining."

I rolled my eyes. "Duh. I refuse to believe I keened." Until I thought about how my mind spun on burning in a wicker man. "Maybe a little whine now and then, but not a keen."

With a strong cup of tea in me, my equilibrium returned. It didn't make any sense to threaten me and no one else. Lucky to be included in groundbreaking work, I pulled myself together.

So, no more ranting, no more whimpering, and instead, let the police do their job while I got back to work.

The problem with discovering one gold coin was that I wanted to find another. While the mapping process went well, the afternoon left me disillusioned.

As I entered the dining hall, I found the French back on dinner duty. Gabriel saw me from the kitchen and wiggled his eyebrows at me. It should have come across as goofy, but a hint of invitation caused me to throw a smile at him before I could stop myself.

Joining Sam and Simon at the picnic-style table, my mouth watered. "Smells fantastic!"

Dion emerged with a hefty pot of stew, followed by Gabriel with a trivet for the center of the table.

"Chicken bourguignon," they announced in unison. None of us were up for beef yet, so I thanked them for the thoughtful chicken substitution.

"I've missed your cooking," I said to Dion.

But Gabriel answered, "Anything for you, Miss Maddie."

In response to the first time he called me anything but Madeline, heat crawled up my cheeks at the intimacy of it. Hunching to hide my face, I dug into my stew.

Rich, velvety, and filled with herbs, the comforting dinner satisfied me down to my toes and provided an excellent distraction from Gabriel, who sat next to me.

Sleepily, Simon and I cleared and did dishes. Gabriel joined us, recounting tales of a childhood in Amiens, a cathedral city about two hours north of Paris. His hypnotic voice kept us entertained, but as soon as Simon showed signs of leaving, I quickly followed.

Without saying a word, Simon conveyed a vague amusement and slight disapproval.

"He's very charming," I said, defensive.

"Indeed."

"It's not like I'm into him or anything."

A noncommittal grunt from my companion.

"I'm going to call Edward," I decided as we split off to head to our rooms.

Without letting myself dwell on any of our teammates, I hit Edward's number.

"Lassie," he said, filling the word with longing, love, and comfort.

"Hi," I squeaked. The force of my reaction to his voice took me off guard, and my defenses crumbled. "My shirt was in a voodoo wicker man," I said, letting tears drip.

Activating his camera, his handsome face filled my little cell screen.

Torn between staring adoringly and the urgent need to blow my nose, I chose the latter. "Sec." Wishing I'd remembered to mute when I blew and snuffled, I quickly wiped my face and swiped on some lip gloss before pressing the video icon.

"Hi," I said again, this time more brightly.

"A what now?"

"A miniature wicker man. My favorite shirt went missing, and when I woke up, we found a piece of it burned in a doll-sized wicker man. Where do you even find something like that?"

"Prop store?" Edward must have noted my knitted eyebrows because he added, "Rhetorical question. Got it."

I nodded, and he continued, "As far as investigatory matters, it is valid though."

Thinking about it, I said, "I guess prop stores are mainly in London and not the countryside. I would focus on parasols and bonnets if I carried theater props in the Cotswolds. Maybe a quill pen."

"Aye, exactly." With a crooked smile, he asked, "How badly did Douglass treat you?"

"Completely!" I vented for a bit before turning the conversation to him. "How about you? Are you working on anything you can tell me about?"

"No details, but Parikh and I are closing in on drug activity. Cocaine mostly. The head seems to be in Bath, but we can't get a handle on him. But if we can close down enough distribution centers and gangs, it will gut the business."

"Wow! Look at you go, dealing with major crimes and all."

He attempted a haughty, important countenance with his nose in the air, then grinned. "I suspect my dodgy past played into the assignment, but I'll take it." He paused, then asked, "Anything else interesting?"

Annoyingly, Gabriel's dreamy eyes popped into my mind. Cursing my reaction, I said, "The coin we found in the fountain has significant value, both monetarily and as a commentary on the people who lived and stayed here."

"I bet Dr. Daniels will remember you now."

"Yeah, right after he orders lunch."

The mention of Dr. Daniels brought up my uncertain future again, and I began twisting a lock of hair around my finger.

"No one has told me what's going to happen," I said shakily.

"At the end of your internship at the Baths?"

I nodded.

"I know my mind, lassie, but the decision needs to be yours."

Sometimes, when someone is one hundred percent right, it is not helpful.

"A little cajoling wouldn't be bad," I said.

"Ah, ye say that, but I dinnae ken that it's true."

One long, drawn-out sigh later, I dropped the subject, and we chatted about nothing for a while. When I finally fell asleep, I dreamed of Scottish moors dotted with megalithic rocks. Each stone had three scratch marks on it.

* * *

Waking with a start, I recognized the significance of my dreamscape. Before the tourists arrived, I had found a place on the back of the nymphaeum wall where someone tried to pry up a stone. Tourists, then the mini wicker man, Douglass, and admittedly, Gabriel, drove the vital information from my brain.

Before I did anything else, I texted Sam and Simon with the information. Sam, who was awake early for breakfast duty, answered immediately. We would convene there after we ate.

The gray sky swirled with flurries of snow, and I shivered in spite of the warmth in my room. To combat the chill and gloom, I added lip gloss and a hint of eye shadow to my morning routine. Studying the effect in the mirror, I wondered if Gabriel would notice. With a shake, I pictured Simon's disapproving sneer and took off the extra makeup.

What was wrong with me? A little attention from the French and I turn into an idiot. Checking my face in the mirror, I intentionally messed up my hair. No extra effort to appear nice on my part. Not this girl. No way.

Secure in my relationship with Edward, I headed to breakfast.

The rest of the team was already digging into eggs and sausages. Unlike me, Gabriel had put extra effort into his appearance, wearing a white button-down shirt that emphasized his muscles.

Not that I paid attention.

The atmosphere seemed tense for a reason I couldn't identify. When Gabriel made eye contact with me, Dion sneered, muttering, "Idiot," quietly but clearly, but that diffused the tension rather than creating it.

Sam, however, paid no attention, focusing solely on her food. I wondered if something upset her.

The whole team headed to the spot in the nymphaeum where I found unauthorized digging. Sam gave a stern lecture about not going off-piste when it came to a national treasure like Chedworth. Her constant chatter didn't give me the chance to ask about her well-being.

"Ms. Niven," Dion said to Sam, bushy eyebrows knit together, "why would you say this to us? Clearly, it was this Jill person, rest in peace, causing the problem."

"Excitement can guide anyone's hand," she responded before dropping her following announcement. "I have something to tell everyone."

"Can we not go inside for this? It is not pleasant here," Dion interrupted.

I attempted to stop myself mid-eye roll, but Gabriel caught me and grinned.

"Do let her finish," Simon said.

"Simon will be heading the team for the rest of the week. All discoveries will be attributed to his leadership."

The news took everyone, including Simon, by surprise. I could tell because Simon's eyebrows quirked up.

Pelted with questions from every side, Sam hushed us with a hand gesture.

"I'm needed at the Baths. Dolly will join you here for sketching, and Simon deserves the recognition."

Much as I wanted to see Dolly, the idea of Sam leaving created a hollow pit in my stomach. A champion for us all, I counted on Sam to stand up for us—well, me, especially—with a constable who had it out for me.

Not that Simon wouldn't step in on my behalf, but his aristocratic background annoyed Douglass just as much as my existence did.

"No more poutin'," Sam insisted. "Maddie? Follow me inside for a mo'."

I did, reveling in the warmth while the rest of the team trudged through the snow.

Sam pulled a package about three inches long from her suitcase and handed it to me. Touched, I opened it to find the 3-D-printed padlock she asked her friend to create. A half-scale model of the piece from Chedworth Museum, I viewed it as an invaluable prize.

"OMG! This is the coolest thing ever."

"And it works," she said, taking it from me and snapping it shut. The gift also included a two-pronged printed key that I used to open the mini lock. "I had him do it half-size to save on the sturdy filament."

The lock measured longer than I expected, with a rectangle that encased the mechanism at one end with a metal loop sticking out.

"Thank you so much!" On impulse, I threw my arms around her and hugged, not only to thank her for the padlock but as a way to express how much I'd miss her.

"You are welcome." Disengaging, she patted my shoulder, then took her bag and returned outside.

Shaking myself, I squared my shoulders and marched out after her behind the curved stone wall of the nymphaeum. Snow accumulation masked the disturbance I had seen before, and I couldn't recall the exact location of the stone.

As a group, we carefully scooped away the drift, exposing the bricks at dirt level. In order not to disturb any fallen stones or mortar, we worked the snow as we would any excavation, except sifting turned into melting.

The work, tedious under the best of circumstances, proved cold and miserable in this weather. By the time the wall lay exposed, we all visibly shivered.

"Food," I said through chattering teeth.

"Agreed. And tea."

Hopefully, with sustenance, I could locate the marred stone. I debated whether to tell anyone I failed to see it, but of course, I had to.

"Hey, Simon," I began, "there didn't seem to be anything out of place."

"I agree, but that might have to do with moisture. While we eat, the wall should dry out, and the scratches reappear."

Two cups of tea, a tuna sandwich, and one pair of dry socks later, I returned to the nymphaeum's outer wall. Drier, its appearance changed. However, I still couldn't find the marred stone.

The rest of the team joined me. Tempted to shrug and find warmth, I couldn't let them down. We'd spent half a day on my word, and I needed to do something.

"I'll stay out here and keep looking," I volunteered. "You all go inside."

"Need I remind you of the miniature wicker man?" Simon asked. "You may be in danger."

True, but the thickly wooded hill behind the pool made it next to impossible to sneak up on me without creating noise.

Feeling relatively safe, I said, "Take turns checking on me every fifteen minutes."

Once alone, I stomped into the snow, which trickled freezing clumps into my shoes. I let my eyes relax, taking in the wall as a whole. The moss or lichen broke its pattern in one spot, subtle but there.

About to dig, I stopped when Gabriel appeared to check on me. Rather than leaving, he stayed and chatted so I didn't point out the discrepancy. When Dion came out fifteen minutes later, he cursed mildly under his breath, the sound muffled by the snow but distinguishable.

Dragging Gabriel back to the office with him, I caught a single phrase that chilled me more than my soaking feet.

"Bloody fool," Dion said in a distinct, non-French, very English accent.

Chapter Sixteen: A Visitor in the Night

A shudder of cold and confusion shook me. The sun dipped behind the trees, bringing darkness earlier than usual. As shadows grew, I wondered if I had heard Dion correctly. Had his French accent fallen off?

Leaves rustled behind me, and I bolted around, my eyes raking the gloomy forest.

A pheasant darted past me, its normally iridescent colors muted to gray in the weak sun.

"Jeez!" I complained at the bird. My hand patted my chest in an attempt to settle my heartbeat. "Right," I said, my voice approximating normal. "Get it together, McGuire."

Stamping my feet to restore some circulation, I rolled my shoulders and set to documenting the wall. I counted the bricks from both sides and made notations of the location of the stone with an odd moss pattern. After photographing it from several angles, I scampered to the office and announced I had finished for the night.

"Did you find it?" Dion asked, sounding fully French.

I hesitated for a split second before I said, "No, nothing. We will search again in the daylight." Not that I didn't trust Dion, but, well, okay. I totally didn't trust him.

"I'm heading back to my room." Picking up speed as I crossed the lawn to the Hunting Lodge, my head swiveled, looking for danger.

At a full sprint by the time I arrived at the door, I burst in, taking the stairs two at a time.

Inside my room, I closed the door and wished for a lock. Leaning against the wall, I texted Edward to call when he could. No hurry. No big deal.

When he didn't respond right away, I opened my computer and called Tori.

"It's not even the middle of the night," she said. "Did you pay attention to the time difference?"

"What do you think?" I said, grinning. Talking with Tori always brightened my mood.

"No, of course not. What's up?"

"We've got these two French exchange students, and I'm not sure if I trust them."

"Any particular reason?"

Gabriel's disarming charm caused suspicion, but Dion's changing accent took priority. When I explained it to Tori, she shrugged.

"Que sera. You never slip into an English accent?"

My eyeroll answered the question.

"No, you wouldn't. But for those of us who are bilingual, it's not unusual to change accents."

"But you never have an accent."

"I have a good ear. Maybe your French friend is developing his, especially if this is the first time he's been immersed in English." She studied my face. "Disappointed?"

"Partly," I admitted. "I wanted a solution to all the weird stuff that's been happening, but I'm also a little relieved."

"What about the other guy?"

"Gabriel," I said, trying to sound noncommittal.

"Enough said. Don't let Edward see that expression, by the way," Tori advised.

My phone buzzed before I could defend myself. Checking it, I said, "Speaking of which, there he is."

After disconnecting for Tori, I answered my cell.

"Lassie." Edward's voice made me tingle, but he sounded sad.

"How are you? Is everything okay?"

A slight chuckle. "You asked me to call. Isn't that my line?"

"Not when you've had a rough day. Come on. Tell me everything."

Without giving away secrets about police business, he filled me in on the drug ring. He and DI Parikh cut off fourteen sellers. Most of them refused to talk, but Parikh and Edward convinced a couple to give up their distributor.

"Classic good cop, bad cop, although, in my case, I used details about gangs that made them think I knew more than I actually did."

"You're amazing," I said, impressed. "But I bet you're exhausted."

"Aye, lassie, that I am. So far, the information points to a warehouse somewhere in Bath, but no one says who is in charge."

"Still, great progress!"

"Aye," he said again, the word infused with fatigue.

"You need sleep, Detective Constable," I said.

Instead of responding, he asked about my day.

"I'm not sure about Dion, one of the French students."

"Write everything down. Keep times, and if anything odd can be photographed, add that and make a note on your list that you have a picture."

"Why?" I asked as a jaw-cracking yawn echoed through the speaker.

"Go sleep," I told him, not paying attention to the relatively early hour.

"I will, lassie. You take care."

A distinctly odd conversation. At no point did Edward recommend telling Douglass about my suspicions. Instead, he wanted me to create a paper trail. Douglass must be building a case against me.

Opening a blank document on my phone, I made a list of everything, starting with the charred heart and including Jill wanting to speak to the constable without Dion present, her cryptic warnings, the voices I heard outside the window, and when I reported these things to Constable Grouchy-face. Adding his reaction to the information I shared built a solid foundation for me not to report anything else.

Wondering about Edward's intention to not share information with Douglass opened so many negative thoughts in my brain that I resembled a zombie at dinner. Frankly, so did Simon and Sam, and I wondered what ideas whirled in their heads.

Ignoring Gabriel's attempts to draw me into conversation after cleanup, I plodded upstairs and barricaded myself in my room.

After jotting a few more notes as proof against random Douglass accusations, I texted Edward goodnight, and slept like the dead.

* * *

The beeping of the alarm stabbed at my eardrums. Rubbing my head, I sat upright, and a pounding headache exploded behind my eyes.

"The hell?" I complained about the symptoms of a hangover but without the fun of getting tipsy.

Reaching for the phone to silence the assault, my hand found nothing but bedspread. The cell sat on the desk across the room.

Razor-sharp clarity cut through my foggy head. Someone had been in my room.

Sure that I texted Edward before bed, I knew my instinct wasn't paranoia. As I scanned every corner, minor discrepancies appeared, confirming my conclusion.

Leaping out of bed, I dressed in record time and ran downstairs as I pulled my hair into a ponytail.

Simon sat in the common room, his hands wrapped around a mug of coffee.

"Someone entered my room last night," I told him.

He quirked an eyebrow at me.

"Not like that. They searched. And I feel like someone drugged me."

That last statement got his attention, and he nodded slowly.

"Are you sure nothing in your room is missing or moved?"

"Not that I noticed."

"Well, come on. Let's look," I said. "And check on Sam, too."

Without any attempt to stand and follow me, Simon said, "Ms. Niven has already left."

"What?" Gutted that she hadn't said goodbye, I sank into a chair.

"We agreed that the fewer people who knew her location as she transported the coin, the better."

"And that included me? I thought she trusted me. I mean, we've—"

Before I could get too carried away, Simon held up a hand to stop me.

"While you have proven yourself reliable and discreet, the charms of the French cannot be underestimated."

Much as I wanted to argue that I could handle myself, I had caught myself divulging my first pet's name and the street I grew up on to Gabriel in one conversation. Both are used as passwords or security questions. I settled for a mild grunt of indignation before changing the subject.

"Have you heard from her? Do you know she's safe? Sam seemed as out of it as me last night. What if she never made it?"

That possibility had apparently not occurred to Simon as he finally got moving.

"Come."

Quietly, we crept upstairs, hoping the French wouldn't hear us.

After examining his room, Simon said, "Nothing out of place."

I pointed to the desk, which didn't sit right against the wall.

Approaching it, Simon set his hand on the surface, and the desk rocked from side to side.

"It never wobbled before," he said. "Good eye."

"Right," I said, vindicated. "Sam's room."

As expected, it sat empty. The armoire doors hung open, as did the desk drawer. We couldn't discern if Sam left it this way as she packed or if someone came in after she left, looking for something.

"Inconclusive," Simon said.

"Agreed. Text her, please. Make sure she got to her destination."

Better, Simon called her and left a message.

"Straight to voicemail, I'm afraid."

"Which makes sense as it's early after a late drive but is also upsetting because it's an unknown." Twisting my full ponytail around and around, I failed at keeping my mind from jumping to the worst scenario. I couldn't fathom a motivation to harm her, but my failure to understand didn't stop a bad guy.

Except, the gold coin. Priceless in terms of archaeology but also worth a ton of cash to a collector.

"The safe," I said to Simon, remembering Sam placing it in a lockbox and locking it in the Visitor Centre's safe.

Simon and I slipped across the grounds, the snow-turned-rain creating a sloppy mess. To keep upright, I focused all my attention on my feet and did not notice the police car until I stumbled into it.

"Oh no."

Inside, the woman whose name I still hadn't learned spoke to a constable, her voice shaky with tears.

"Here they are," she said, indicating us. "The archaeologists. I think they had something important in there."

Rushing around the counter, we found the safe open and empty, the lockbox with the gold coin nowhere in sight.

"No, no, no, no, no," I muttered continuously until Simon elbowed me in the ribs.

"Go get the French. The police will need to speak to them."

"Okay."

Outside, the weather greeted me with a slushy slap in the face. Cursing my lack of a jacket, I wrapped my arms around myself and ran as fast as I could.

Mistake.

Skating on a wet patch of grass, I started to fall backward, overcorrected, and landed hard on my hands and knees.

"Ouch."

Pelted by sleet, I stood and hobbled to the Hunting Lodge with chilling water dripping down my legs.

Gabriel and Dion still hadn't made it to breakfast.

The old lodge creaked in the wind, an unwelcome groan that sounded almost human.

Unless it was human.

"Gabriel? Dion? You guys up there?"

Nothing.

With my knees swelling, the staircase appeared four times steeper than reality. Gripping the handrail, I took one step at a time, listening for sounds of life.

"Guys?"

Step, together, step, together, I crept up.

If I hadn't needed to change out of my soaking clothes, I might have given up, but the chill kept me moving.

"Gabriel?" This time, it came out as a whisper. "Stupid," I said more loudly to bolster my confidence. "Guys, come on. You're late."

Still nothing.

For some reason, I tiptoed down the hallway, at odds with my goal of wanting them awake. I got to Dion's door first and knocked. More like pounded.

No response.

The handle turned easily, and when the door opened, it revealed nothing. Much like Sam's room, it stood empty.

Still, intruding on someone else's space was rude, so I crept quietly as I double-checked the drawers and under the bed.

Gabriel's room, also empty, evoked another emotion. Oddly betrayed that he hadn't said goodbye, I searched for a note.

"Twit," I said as I closed his door and went to my room to change.

I texted Simon my findings, and he sent a note back. 'Ms. Niven is safe and has ideas about the French. Come.'

Chapter Seventeen: Proper Villains

Relief that Sam made it safely to her destination lit me up. Beaming, I quickly changed and reread the message to confirm it.

How she had news about the missing French already intrigued me.

However, while I appreciated that Simon and I could now communicate with minimal words, his habit of commanding me like a faithful Labrador retriever needed to stop.

"Come," I muttered at his message. "Woof."

Propelled by good news, I threw fresh jeans on, careful not to rub my scraped knees, and returned to the Visitor Centre. Looking like an old man, I painfully headed to meet Simon.

"Did you tell her about the safe?" I asked, as I came in the door.

"You didn't think I'd keep our wee treasure there, did ye?" Sam's voice came through Simon's cell speaker.

"You're brilliant," I said, meaning it.

"Laying a bit of a trap," she continued. "The French were not what they seemed."

"I had that feeling as well. Dion's accent kept slipping. My bilingual friend said it's nothing to worry about, but I thought it odd."

"Odd indeed, Maddie me dearie," Sam said, her Irish accent in full force. "It's not unusual to slip in a stray word from your native tongue, but you usually keep your accent."

"That's true, isn't it?" When Tori used Spanish, her accent didn't modify English words. She just said a word in Spanish. "Also, he wasn't using French.

He used a British accent."

Simon raised an eyebrow at me.

"'Bloody fool.' That's what he called Gabriel. He sounded like that one reporter, Jeffery Dailey."

"An accent from East London?"

Casting an annoyed squint at Simon, I said, "I'm not Henry Higgins."

"Cockney?" he said without acknowledging *My Fair Lady* or his error that I could identify every accent in the country.

"Yeah, that."

"Well, well," Sam chimed in. "Let me do some digging at this end," and she disconnected.

The coin was safe, and my suspicion confirmed. Not a bad start to the day, except for the pounding headache from this morning.

"Do you think they drugged us?" I wondered.

Before he could answer, the local constable and cafe manager joined us, and I remembered we were not the only victims.

"Did they steal much?" I asked. Then, before I forgot again, I added, "I'm Maddie, by the way. It must have been scary to find the place broken into."

"Katherine," she said, her eyes too wide as she constantly wrung her hands. "Yes, violated, really. But no, not much cash. We only keep one hundred pounds overnight unless we hear a tour bus is coming."

"Are you okay? Do you need help with anything?"

In a masterful display of stiff upper lip, she pulled herself together. "No, no, of course not," she said and set to work.

"Call me anytime if you want," I offered before Simon caught my eye, and I went closer to him.

"Very likely," he said, continuing our previous conversation.

It took me a minute to remember what I asked. Had they slipped us something? "But what? I mean, people don't just walk around with chloroform." Having recently been the victim of a ketamine-level knockout drug, I knew it couldn't have been anything heavy-duty. But the thought of anyone giving me something turned my stomach.

"I would think they put chemist sleeping pills in our food. Ms. Niven didn't eat much, therefore not as affected."

Dion's belligerent glower came to mind, and as I planned a scathing diatribe against him, I stopped short. He and Gabriel must have planned everything together, otherwise they wouldn't both be gone.

Which meant gullibility clouded my judgment on way too many levels from professional to personal. I sighed.

"He fooled us all," Simon said, reading my mind.

Rather than confirming my train of thought, I worked on figuring it out. "Why now? What happened to make them leave last night?"

"Perhaps the fact that Ms. Niven removed the coin."

That idea made sense, but something didn't sit right. "Did they go into archaeology as treasure hunters?" A single coin hardly ever popped up. Caches of gold next to never. The Milton Keynes Hoard included gold coins, but it had been over two decades since its discovery. Again, a rarity, not the norm.

"That would be a silly mistake. But I am interested to hear what Sam uncovers about the two." And, as if summoning her, his phone rang.

"Ms. Niven, I have you on speaker."

"Did you find something else?" I asked. Only a few minutes had passed.

"An email from this morning with an apology from Dion and Gabriel for not joining us."

"What?" Simon and I said in unison.

"Turns out, their passports and other identification were stolen on the Chunnel train. And, to top matters off, someone reported them pickpocketing several tourists. The pickpocket victims insisted on pressing charges. The boys had quite a time sorting things out with the police and various French bureaucracies."

Nausea roiled in me at the memories of trusting two imposters. Totally taken in by a con artist, I recoiled at the thought of Gabriel as a friend. Dion's involvement was annoying, but Gabriel targeted me personally. He went out of his way to ingratiate himself with me, flirting and smiling his way into my psyche.

How many times would I read people wrong in this country? Far too often, I got myself into danger because of my trusting nature. One of these times, it would get me killed.

"Jill," I whispered. These two men I shared a house with, ate meals with, killed one of our team. Killed her in a horrific fashion.

That night we all went to the pub, Gabriel stayed behind to drink with the druids. He must have charmed them into telling him where the wicker man stood. Simply hire a truck, or steal one, and bring the wicker man here.

Had he stabbed Jill in the back or Dion? Which one of them started the fire? Did they watch as the flames engulfed her, snapping and popping?

The bile began to rise when Simon interrupted my thoughts.

"Spiraling out of control, are we?"

The skin on my face tightened, and my scalp itched. I searched his expression for any signs of panic. None. It took more than a betrayal, a con, and murder to affect Simon.

"As I said, they fooled us all."

"But they killed Jill," I squeaked.

"Chin up, old girl. We don't know that."

"That's worse," I said. Better to have only one set of proper villains than a mystery murderer still out there. "You should call Douglass and update him."

"And I am not delegating this responsibility to you because…"

"Because he hates me and will do anything to find an excuse to arrest me. The less I talk, the better."

With a superior stare down his nose at me, he said, "Dolly will be arriving soon. See she gets settled in."

"Thanks," I said, walking to the glass double doors that overlooked the parking lot. The clouds lifted, and sunshine broke through. On cue, a car appeared on the dirt track.

As I opened the doors and took the first step, my knees reminded me of this morning's fall. Opting for the ramp, I stiff-legged down to greet Dolly.

A delicate whir accompanied the car's progress. "Electric. Cool."

Dolly sprang from the small car with a wave to the driver. "Thank you, Gilbert," she said, and I ducked to see into the vehicle. One of the De Valence

Medispa servers waved enthusiastically and pointed to his chauffeur hat.

"Gilbert's moving up in the spa world, I see," I said to Dolly.

"I simply couldn't say no to that smile. Or the chauffeur hat." We hugged a bit awkwardly as she carried an artist's satchel.

"I love the car," I said as she eyed me critically. She read my distressed expression, but good breeding kept her from saying anything.

"It is all electric. I couldn't very well ride Merlin over. No facilities for him."

I grinned. Merlin, her spirited black thoroughbred, and his bay partner, Lancelot, helped establish Dolly and my friendship. A shared love of horses did a lot to make us, well, me mainly, more accepting of each other.

"Oh, but I would have loved to see him. How are the boys?"

"Absolutely perfect. You remember Rupert, yes?"

Nodding, I smiled at the thought of Simon's butler's nephew shoveling snow—an intelligent and industrious boy.

"Well, his mother and Uncle Hawthorn are allowing the boy to come over for a couple of hours once a week. He adores Old Nigel, and the other two are letting him brush them."

"Aww, I love that!" I really did. Old Nigel, an enormous draft horse, or Shire horse as he's called in the UK, provided a lot of comfort to me in some harrowing circumstances.

As we talked about horses, we moved, slowly on my account, back to the Visitor Centre.

Rushing to Simon's side, Dolly spread joy throughout the room. Her gorgeous long blonde hair swayed, and her bright smile took in everyone. Even Katherine, who had a rotten morning, smiled at the sight of Dolly.

"I have presents," she declared.

Starting with an utterly surprised Katherine in the cafe, Dolly handed her a sachet of lavender with the De Valence Medispa logo. "I can book a massage for you if needed. My staff are all local."

Next, she pulled a sketch pad out of her portfolio and displayed a series of drawings. The gold coin Sam and I pulled from the fountain was recreated in perfect detail.

"Oh," I sighed. "These are gorgeous. When did you see the coin?"

"Sam stayed at the spa last night, of course."

That made sense, and I should have thought of it myself. In my defense, I might have been given a sleeping pill.

"And for you," Dolly continued, turning to me.

I shook my head. "These drawings are enough. They're spectacular."

Ignoring my protest, she pulled what looked like lipstick out of a side pouch and handed it to me. The deep blue metal made me wonder what color she expected me to wear. Pulling off the top exposed not lip gloss but a spray bottle.

"Thieves' spray," she announced, and I almost dropped the thing on the floor. "But not the regular kind," she added quickly, steadying my hands. "Try it."

The original spray included five essential oils with antibacterial properties. For years, I always had some with me, and when I first got to England, the concoction contributed to saving me and Simon.

However, the mere idea of the scent brought back the terror of our entombment.

"I helped with the formula," Simon added, as the same terror would trigger in him.

Rather than sampling it on my hand, I spritzed a small puff into the air.

Cautiously, I sniffed. No blinding panic seized me, so I took in more of the scent.

The rosemary conjured memories, but most related to the spa. No clove or eucalyptus to remind me of the tomb.

Bravely, I sprayed it on my hands and rubbed. Citronella with hints of lavender floated up.

"You like it," Dolly said. "I absolutely knew you would."

"Thank you, Dolly. This is amazing," I said, but I made eye contact with Simon. Only he could have given her the idea and understood the significance of the scent.

Dolly explained how she got a small copper still designed to extract essential oils. Once she started with the lavender, she ordered a still for each of the herbs they grew at Simon's Comer Manor and the De Valence Medispa.

"You must visit the downstairs kitchen next time you come. It looks a bit like a mad scientist has set up shop."

"She was a simple whiskey maker, but he loved her still," I intoned one of my dad's many puns, getting a scowl from Simon and a delightful titter from Dolly.

Equilibrium began to settle over me. Still freaked out by Gabriel's evil plans, I knew I could handle it with Dolly and Simon there.

Wishing Edward could join us, I stepped aside and texted him all our news. He didn't answer right away, so I figured he and Parikh were busy rounding up drug dealers.

"What should I start on?" I asked shortly before the day turned unfriendly. Constable Douglass darkened our doorway.

"Good," he said with a peeved glare, "you're all here."

Supercilious. That's how my mother would describe him. No one used words as weapons better than my mom, and I missed her so much right then.

At least now, Douglass knew the bad guys were the French, which let me off the hook. Which probably annoyed him no end.

Recalling Tori's admonishment to be cooperative and not draw attention to myself, I inched behind Dolly. As a person to hide behind, Dolly didn't provide much cover since she barely hit five-two. I matched or towered over many of the men in England at five-nine. A comfort to have someone between me and Douglass, nonetheless.

"Who are you?" he demanded of Dolly.

"You must be Constable Douglass," Dolly said with the utmost grace. "I'm Gwendolyn De Valence, but please call me Dolly. I believe my uncle played croquet with your cousin?"

My mouth fell open. I snapped it shut before anyone saw, but how on earth did Dolly uncover a connection with Douglass? And who the heck plays croquet? Besides Alice and the Queen of Hearts.

Unbelievably, Douglass smiled.

I clamped my jaw tighter. Some people in this world always know how to charm others. My dad and Dolly possessed the gift. I did not.

Her charm, however, did not soften Douglass's attitude toward the rest of us. Douglass bossed us around like he owned the county, even though his job focused only on taking statements. A little power-hungry, in my opinion, which didn't make for a good detective. However, I played along and attempted meek as he separated us into different rooms.

By forcing me to wait until last, Douglass guaranteed that my conciliatory attitude had evaporated by the time he walked in.

"Howdy," I said with a smile, hoping it would bug him.

It did.

"This is no small matter, Ms. McGuire."

Technically, though, it was. The French being thieves, con artists, and possibly murderers, held importance, but Douglass taking interview statements didn't.

Puffing out air, I tried polite. "How can I help you?"

"You can start by telling me why you helped Gabriel and Dion escape."

Honestly?

Chapter Eighteen: The Douglass

"Dude," I said in response to Douglass's accusation that I helped the French escape before Tori's voice inserted itself in my mind and told me to be helpful.

With a shake of my head, I tried. "I'm sorry, but I honestly don't understand why you think I would be involved. I liked their cooking, but other than that, they tended to be belligerent, Especially Dion, who always glowered."

"You preferred Gabriel?"

"Yeah," popped out of my mouth before my brain caught up. "I mean, only in that he seemed friendly."

"So, you would describe your relationship as 'friendly,' then?"

Gnashing my teeth, I thought through my response. "No—"

"More than friendly?"

Note to self: no more "yes" or "no" answers.

"No relationship existed between me and the Frenchmen."

"So, just one?"

"Again, no relationships." I wanted to add, "except as teammates," but I didn't dare open the door to more questions.

Giving up on that tactic, Douglass started in on me about why I wanted to steal the coin.

I stuck to my guns, used clear, complete sentences, and didn't let him twist my words.

After a particularly heinous inquiry, I repeated, "Again, the coin only interested me as an archaeological find."

"That's not what I asked. Come now, Ms. McGuire, it's a simple yes or no question."

"It isn't. You're leading the witness."

Douglass set down his pen, folded his hands, and looked at me, questioning.

"Like, 'Do you deny that you stopped beating your wife?' However, you respond, you're admitting guilt, which is unfair."

He stared at me for a long moment, and I wondered how many petty criminals he trapped into a confession using that tactic. Quite a few, I imagined, but I'm not sure he understood the entrapment aspect.

With a snap, he closed his notebook, pushed back his chair, and stood. "Please keep yourself available for further questioning."

Surprised, I nodded, wisely kept my mouth shut, and bolted from the room.

Negative energy spun through me, and I had to work it off.

The sun and early morning rain washed the landscape clean of any snow. The chill in the air seemed more like a spring day than nearing the winter solstice. Following the road out of the parking lot, I headed to the open field below the villa. Tufts of green still poked out among the primarily brown vegetation, and as I aimed for those patches, the ground sprang back, spongy.

Thick forest offered a respite from any prying eyes, and by "any," I meant Douglass. Somehow sure he watched my movements, waiting for me to slip up and expose myself as an accomplice, I headed for the tree line.

Gray and waterlogged leaves carpeted the forest floor, muffling sound. An ancient evergreen tree protected the area underneath, and there, the leaves kept their color. I aimed for an oversized orange leaf, allowing the stress of my interview to slough off.

As I bent to pick it up, an alien image caught my eye. Poking through the mulch undergrowth, something grayish green and cylindrical. Tapered, pale at the tips. Almost like...

"Fingers," I screeched.

Dead, decaying, fingers, buried but reaching for escape.

Stumbling away from the horror, I turned and sprinted for the parking lot, knees protesting with every step.

Douglass's car headed down the dirt track, and I screamed his name, waving my arms.

"Aah! Help! Dead!" I shouted.

With a jerk, his car stopped, and he leaped out.

"What is wrong?" he asked with calm authority.

The tone of his voice helped to settle me enough to form sentences. "Over there. Under the pine tree," I gestured behind me.

"Yes?" he prompted, turning me around to return to the scene.

"Fingers. Dead, decayed…" Tears welled in my eyes, and I couldn't stop them. A sob escaped as I neared the spot.

"Wait here."

I nodded, crying.

Douglass put a calming hand on my shoulder. "It will be okay," he said, settling me.

As my opinion of him softened, I began to understand why Edward told me to give him a chance. This behavior presented potential as a detective.

And then he ruined it by barking, "Ms. McGuire. Come here."

I could live without another unforgettable, horrifying image seared into my brain.

"Uh." Eloquent, that's me.

"Now."

Cautiously, I inched forward, nerves causing tremors in my hands. Keeping my eyes on my feet to avoid seeing the hand again, I got within a few yards of the constable.

"Is this what you saw?"

No getting around it. He required me to face the horror.

Raising my gaze, I took in the sight of Constable Douglass with a decaying, severed finger pointing at me.

A scream tore from my throat, and I scrambled backward. Tripping on a tree root, I fell, turned onto my hands and knees, and crawled as fast as I could to get away from him, and the awful way he treated a dead body.

"Ms. McGuire!"

Rocks tore into my already scraped knees, so I staggered onto my feet and lunged back to the parking lot.

"Madeline!" he shouted, although it sounded mushy.

Finally catching up to me, Douglass grabbed my shoulder and halted my progress. Grabbed me with his putrid-covered hands.

I batted at him, dislodging his fingers as he shouted at me.

A single word penetrated my panic.

"...mushroom..."

Stillness settled over me. "What?"

"It's a mushroom," he said, all vestiges of politeness gone.

"A mushroom?" I asked, baffled.

Bugging his eyes at me, he said, "Yes, as in a fungus. Don't they have those in Arizona?"

"Well, no." Dry expanses of chaparral with cactus, palo verde trees, and mesquite, yes, but no mushrooms.

"Really," he said as a statement, disbelief dripping off him.

"No," I insisted, my earlier horror turning to anger. And embarrassment, which led to spewing facts from my high school science class. "We have twenty-two kinds of rattlesnakes that don't exist anywhere else on earth, Gila monsters, and the deadliest scorpions on the continent. But no, no mushrooms." To be fair, sometimes little white caps popped up by sprinkler heads, but accuracy only muddled things at this point.

With a supreme effort not to limp, I turned on my heel and stalked to the Hunting Lodge.

To change.

Again.

On the way, I looked up 'mushrooms that look like fingers' on my phone and found the offending fungus, called dead man's fingers mushroom. At least I wasn't the only one who thought so. Douglass could have given me this information to make me feel better, but no. Twit.

* * *

After a shower, applying Dolly's thieves' spray to my cut knees, and a couple of Band-Aids, or sticking plaster as the box said, I prepared myself mentally to join the team at the Visitor Centre.

Tactful as ever, neither Simon nor Dolly said anything about my absence or the scene they must have been able to hear if not see.

Katherine in the cafe, however, pounced. "Is everything quite alright? We heard screaming."

Heat rose to my cheeks as I said, "Fine. Fine. I'm fine. A misunderstanding is all."

Not allowing follow-up questions, I turned to Simon and asked, "What do you want me to do, boss?"

"Dolly will double-check the rather slipshod work the con artists attempted with the radar. If you wouldn't mind," he said in a way that made it clear my opinion did not matter, "could you go over the map of the nymphaeum again before starting on the new area."

"Excellent," I said and gathered the materials. When I noted the moss on the brick out of place, too much had happened for me to get back to it.

Rather than starting there like I wanted to, I followed Simon's directions and looked for inconsistencies in the entire area. One brick, the one used to whack Sam, had been moved again. Flipped over, most likely. I photographed and mapped the position.

Curious about why this stone fascinated the French so much, I examined underneath it thoroughly but found nothing. After fixing it and rephotographing, I let my vision soften as I took in the area.

Something clicked in my mind.

The brick in question on the floor inside the wall matched the scratch marks and misplaced moss on the wall facing the forest.

Counting, I confirmed the stone. Remembering the pictures earlier, I checked those too. Yes. Jill started something that the French saw and wanted a part of.

No one had caught her looking in the pond where Sam and I found the coin. Every time we saw her alone, she was working behind the nymphaeum.

After texting my theory to Simon and getting the go-ahead, I mapped out the back of the wall. With utmost care, I wiggled a bamboo skewer between the out-of-place bricks. The brick shifted, and I doubled my effort. Someone had already moved it at least twice, so I technically didn't have to be careful. But determination to do everything by the book ruled my movements.

After every inch or so, I documented my actions and photographed the progress. In addition, I bagged any mortar and dirt that came out as the stone became dislodged.

We needed to find out if the police got into Jill's laptop. She would have taken the same steps, especially if she wanted the glory of the find to be hers alone.

Not that I expected to find anything. The brick had been removed and replaced, so if there had been a buried treasure, it would have been found already.

Still, the brick needed to be restored to its original position in the wall, and the practice might impress Dr. Daniels back at the Baths Museum.

The Baths reminded me of my uncertain future, and I continued my work on automatic pilot, going through tedious motions carefully but distractedly.

What did I want? In Arizona, I never found dead bodies or freaky mushrooms that looked like them. But I also never got to do archaeology, especially anything two thousand years old.

If I stayed, so many logistics had to be figured out. Housing, Edward, food, Edward, school, boys in general, a job that paid. Why bother with the hassle?

As I dug, bagged, and took pictures, I answered every doubt with images of my work, my friends, my room.

Definitely.

Ninety percent sure.

Maybe.

If I remained, what would that mean to Edward? Staying sent a powerful message of commitment that I wasn't sure I meant. I mean, my mom and dad met when they were only nineteen, but that didn't work out so well for them.

But leaving would send an even stronger message, and I knew I didn't want that. After all, my grandparents married when they were seventeen and spent fifty-three wonderful years together.

Not that I necessarily expected such an outcome, but if I left, it wouldn't be on the table.

So, yeah, I'd stay in England for sure.

Except, would I still want to live here if Edward and I broke up? My initial alarmed reaction, "No way. Too many memories," was followed closely by an image of Gabriel perched on the kitchen counter.

"Get it together, McGuire," I chided myself. "No man defines you or your actions."

I stay. No matter what.

However, very little of the decision rested in my hands. Someone had to extend my student visa, and so far, no one had even broached the subject.

The last inch of brick came out as I wondered how to bring it up next semester to Simon.

After flipping the stone 180 degrees, I set it in front of the opening it created and examined the patterns. A perfect match.

Which begged the question, why had Jill, and then someone else, moved it in the first place?

After another photograph, I placed the brick to the side and chose a small, stiff brush to work at the mortar and dirt at ground level.

Not expecting to find anything, I continued to muse as I scratched at the soil.

Asking Simon would be easy. But he would then need to talk with his aunt and Dr. Daniels, which made me look weak and indecisive for not proposing the idea to them myself.

The brush on the hardened earth created a hypnotic rhythm. Scratch, scratch, swish. Scratch, scratch, swish. Whenever the debris pile became, well, a pile, I bagged and labeled it.

The next logical person to ask about keeping me on was Samantha Niven. After all, she approved my initial internship. The downside was that the museum might bind her to have a different student worker every term. And a negative from Sam, no matter what, would crush me.

Scratch, scratch, swish.

Lady Vivian's influence at the Roman Baths Museum carried a lot of weight, and a word from her could get me a position. But her endorsement didn't sit right with me. That Agatha Christie story about a boy ingratiating himself to the rich girl lingered with me.

Which left Dr. Daniels.

Scratch, swish, swish.

He could approve not only a student visa but also a work visa that would keep me in Britain indefinitely.

Swish, swish, swish.

"Wait," I told myself, interrupting my speculation.

The pattern changed. My incessant brushing hit softer dirt.

After bagging the most recent debris, I switched to a more delicate brush and paid more attention.

Cursing my lack of experience, I took extra care. The change in soil probably meant nothing, but logic told me that it should be more compact the further down I investigated. Soft meant someone digging there.

Ants, moles, or termites were my first guesses. The only time I ever saw loose soil in Tempe was when ants infested the area. Tiny, red, mean, biting ants.

Fortunately, any creepy crawlies should be sleeping this time of year, but I refocused my attention on excavation just in case I uncovered a nest.

Gently, I removed the soil. It came up quickly, but I took care not to go too fast. Every few minutes, I stopped to take pictures of my progress.

"Probably a waste of time," I said as I clicked. "But at least we don't have to develop film." Or worse, stop and draw every step like Howard Carter did when excavating in the Valley of the Kings in Egypt.

Swish, swish, swish, the dirt moved until a bristle of the brush caught on something.

Shining my phone's flashlight into the depression, I found exposed shapes that didn't look like rocks.

More carefully, I brushed, then blew the layers of debris away until what lay beneath became partially exposed.

Chapter Nineteen: All That Glitters

The sun dipped behind the hills, casting the area under the nymphaeum wall into deeper shadow, but I didn't let that stop me. Under the dirt, something caught my eye, just like the coin in the fountain had. But I didn't want to get excited yet.

After the fool I made of myself with the disturbing and totally realistic mushroom, I erred on the side of caution. The saying 'all that glitters is not gold' preached vigilance. In my case, 'all dead fingers in a forest don't belong to a corpse' taught the same lesson. Not as catchy, but a good phrase to internalize.

Leaning in more closely, I shone the light again and saw dirt. As I shifted, a beam of deep yellow flashed.

"Don't get carried away."

In Arizona, the phrase could be extended to 'all that glitters is not gold, it's pyrite.' Also called fool's gold, pyrite is a naturally occurring rock in the desert, a glittering golden color that, like gold, does not tarnish. More than one prospector staked a claim mistaking it for treasure.

Before I called for backup, I needed to be sure. If I made a mistake, becoming a fool was the least of my worries. No one extended a work visa to a girl who screamed at mushrooms and saw a trove where none existed.

"Slow and steady wins the…" I trailed off, the number of cliches running through my brain distracting me. The boy who cried wolf also came to mind.

"Huh, two from Aesop and only one from the Bard." Because of my mother,

I usually stuck to Shakespearean phrases.

Stalling, sure I would make another mistake.

"You can do it."

Two deep breaths later, I angled my phone to illuminate the area and snapped a series of pictures, including a closeup of what continued to look shiny.

Back to careful digging with an attempt to uncover the whole area and not focus on the foreign object.

However, as more became exposed, curves and glints multiplied. Rather than disproving the treasure concept, I uncovered what looked like a cache of gold coins.

Unlike the bronze money so often used, gold never tarnished, never dimmed. The precious metal shined even in the fading light, with dirt clinging to the uneven surfaces.

At this point, the discovery couldn't be ignored. Before taking more pictures, I texted Simon, 'Get out here now!'

A twig snapped, like a gunshot in the quiet evening. Something large must have been in the trees behind me. The forest floor lay damp and spongy, muffling all sound.

Whirling around, I shouted, "I've got mace!" while brandishing the small container of thieves' spray Dolly gave me. "Pepper spray!" I added, unsure of its name in the UK.

"Do be quiet," Simon said, his voice carrying from inside the nymphaeum.

"Aah!" I screeched. An unbecoming sound that emanated from me way too often.

He peeked around the wall. "Yes?" Disdain oozed from the word.

Ignoring his upper-class stuffiness and the fact that I yelled threats at trees, I said, "Drop down over there and tell me what you see." The flashlight glinted and danced off the gold.

"I say."

Slightly disappointed that he didn't make more of a fuss, I took a moment to collect myself before saying, "Right?" I could be cool when I wanted to.

Rather than barking orders to get the site active, he dragged me from the outside of wall to the relative protection by the pool.

"Why were you shouting about pepper spray?"

"Probably nothing," I said with a shrug.

"Illegal, you know."

Flabbergasted at the direction of our conversation, I dropped that little tidbit for the time being and instead admitted to hearing something lumbering in the woods.

"After everything that's happened, mushrooms aside, I feel we should err on the side of caution."

"Good point," I said before it registered that he knew about my dead man's fingers debacle. Either my screams were not only loud but coherent, or Douglass relayed the exchange to Simon, knowing it would embarrass me.

Which it did.

"We need protection," I continued. "How about the constable who came about the break-in?"

Eyeing me critically, Simon agreed to call the local constabulary rather than MCIT and Douglass.

"We work in pairs, no one alone at any point."

"Great idea, but if you recall, only three of us are left, Dolly included," I said.

This news surprised him momentarily. "Bloody Frenchmen."

After examining the hole and the quickly darkening sky, he started with new orders. "Call the local police and ask for a guard. We need lights on the area. You and I will work until the coins are mapped, cataloged, photographed, and secured. Dolly can draw as we work."

"Our cell phones will work for lighting if the Visitor Centre doesn't have floods," I pointed out as my call to the constabulary rang.

Although reduced in number, our team's excitement at the find kept us awake and focused. One at a time, we lifted a coin from the stash, noting its position. Simon took over official photography duty, but watching Dolly sketch at lightning speed was a sight to behold.

At one point, we switched positions, and he handed me the digital SLR, the official documentation camera.

"Why is it set to black and white?"

"The contrast is better. It allows for more detail."

"But it's digital," I pointed out. "We can just tell it to change the photos if we need to."

"A manipulated photo is hardly evidence, then, is it?"

Good point, but I wouldn't admit it out loud. I wanted to take more shots with my cell, but its position as a light source took priority.

Coin after coin came up from the stash.

Eighteen beautiful golden aurei, minted at the same time as the one from the fountain. Nothing as grand as the Milton Keynes Hoard, but the rarity of the Emperor Aurelian coin catapulted the discovery to exceptional.

Tomorrow, we would be descended on by the National Trust, which would report to the press.

Out of misguided fondness, I emailed Jeffery Dailey with details about the conference before shutting down my computer. A dodgy newspaper reporter on my side had more upsides than one who had it out for me. I didn't divulge any information about the coins, but I owed him a little for his help rebuilding the De Valence Medispa brand.

With the coins locked in the safe and guarded by the police, Dolly, Simon, and I shuffled to the Hunting Lodge to sleep. The stimulation of discovery that fueled us until the small hours of the morning deserted us now. Since I'd showered twice before, I ignored the dirt and tumbled into bed.

* * *

Grime and grit awoke me. Stiff and uncomfortable, I regretted my decision last night not to shower.

Pale light shone through the curtains, reminding me of what we had found the previous day.

Gold coins. Unbelievable. Worth being dirty.

However, instead of elation, my discomfort intensified. Disturbed not only by my current state of filth but also by a creepiness invading the room.

A quiet, measured sound repeated.

Almost like breathing.

Chancing a look, I lifted my head to find a lump in the second bed.

Frozen, heart pounding, I scanned the room, looking for a weapon. My computer proved to be the heaviest, sharpest thing in the room. Better than nothing. Creeping from under the covers, I willed the floorboards not to creak. Stealthily, I gripped the laptop with both hands, sure my silence didn't wake the intruder.

Ready to swing, I turned to discover a man sitting in bed, fully awake.

"Aah!" I screamed, swung, and promptly let go of my weapon.

With cat-like reflexes, Edward snatched my computer before it crashed to the floor.

With too much adrenaline coursing through my system, I said somewhat aggressively, "What are you doing?"

"I'm sorry I scared you," Edward said, jumping to the heart of the matter.

Not that I wanted to admit it. "I'm not scared. I'm mad," I said, ignoring the fear. "You can't just come into a girl's room in the middle of the night. It's not proper." Great, I sounded like my mom. Just what I wanted.

He smiled and held out a hand, and I went to him, letting him wrap his arms around me.

"I'm covered in dirt," I said.

Instead of agreeing, he kissed my forehead.

"You don't think I'm daft enough to let a constable with two months on the job protect my lassie, do ye?"

"When did you get here?"

"Right after I saw your lights go out. I patrolled the grounds first. Frightened a stag, I think. Then came in here, and the pillow looked too inviting to pass up."

Torn between the invasion of privacy and the gushy warmth bubbling in me, I avoided further comment on the situation.

"Why didn't you call or text me?"

"I did. Your cell's dead."

True. Using it as a lighting instrument for the dig drained it to nothing. Swiveling my head, I checked to see if I plugged it in before passing out. I had. Good for me, past self.

"I heard something in the woods earlier, too." A deer watching over me and not an evil human would be a much nicer scenario. "How did you recognize it as a stag and not a doe?"

"Massive, by the sound of it. And my torch caught a flash of antlers when I turned toward it."

Taking a deep breath to release tension, I caught my scent.

"I'm going to shower. Be right back."

Something about falling water spurs clarity and creativity, no matter how little sleep I ran on. However, rather than forming a brilliant speech that I could deliver to the press if anyone asked, something negative niggled at me.

The stag Edward encountered didn't sit right. Yes, deer roam at night, but it struck me as too convenient. None of us had spotted that level of wildlife since we arrived.

Disquiet continued to poke me. The image that popped into my head showed a tall man in a robe with ceremonial antlers standing in the woods—a druid priest, but I couldn't remember if I saw it in a movie, a drawing, or a history book.

With no time to research, I dressed in the best clothes I brought, jeans and a plaid shirt, since my pretty blouse was burned up in a voodoo wicker man doll. Then we met Simon and Dolly downstairs.

"Edward! How absolutely lovely to see you."

In spite of the fact that she stayed up as late as me, Dolly looked refreshed and stunning.

"How do you look so lovely?" I complained. "I already want a nap."

"Rubbish," she responded. "Every camera will be focused on the beautiful American girl who found a cache of golden coins."

We hugged and I sent a silent prayer of thanks to Sam for getting Dolly here.

"Shall we go?" Simon asked formally.

No one from the Trust or press had arrived yet except for one reporter.

At the sight of Jeffery, the cockney reporter who lived in a village near

Bath, Simon groaned, and I waved.

"Mr. Dailey, what a pleasant surprise."

"Lady Gwendolyn," Jeffery said with a slight bow.

He didn't show that much deference to Simon's aunt. I wondered if Dolly offered lessons in English charm.

"What's the Jackanory?" he asked.

Using cockney rhyming slang to confuse me delighted Jeffery no end. Someday, I needed to pit my mother against him.

Silently, I went over words that rhymed with "nory." Glory held me up until I finally landed on something that fit the situation.

"Story?"

He grinned.

"But Jackanory isn't even a word."

"Cor, you ain't never 'eard of Jackanory? Best part of me childhood, it was."

"A children's show," Simon clarified in a rare attempt at helpfulness. My guess is that he provided the info to annoy the reporter.

Shaking my head to clear out useless information, I said, "No, not an exclusive. I told you about the press conference because I doubted anyone else would. And it's prestigious."

"Sandshoe," he replied, tipping an imaginary hat.

He could be making it up as he went, for all I knew. After a beat or two, I said, "Wait out here. They'll be arriving soon."

In an extraordinary display of incredulity, Simon raised both eyebrows at me.

"Better the devil you know," I said, explaining Jeffery's presence.

With a shrug, he gestured Dolly and me into the building, but not before Edward pulled me aside in a bear hug. "I'm so proud of you, lassie."

Before I could get all gushy, he straightened and put on his neutral cop face. The next time he spoke, his accent would be gone. Official business from here on out.

The constable on duty chatted up Katherine, who fed him a steady stream of cookies. When he saw Edward, he straightened and attempted to look official as crumbs tumbled off his chin.

Technically, he and Edward were the same rank in different divisions, but something lurked beneath the surface in my Scottish lad that people responded to. Often, the response included not entirely unfounded fear.

Simon got a report from the constable who insisted he hadn't moved from the spot until Katherine came to open the cafe and gift store, at which point he used the facilities.

Since Katherine knew the safe's combination, it seemed logical to trust her with it. Although, I worried about her safety.

Before we got any further, the National Trust's Cultural Heritage Curator appeared with two associates. After introducing herself as Julie and her staff, whose names I didn't catch, assistants pulled up, adding to the confusion. The Visitor Centre, not sizable, flooded with way too many people. Excited chaos swirled around the find. Chatter came from every corner. Strangers patted us on the back, congratulations all around.

Edward directed the constable to handle incoming traffic in the car park. The lot, small to begin with, provided even fewer spaces after the rain and snow created mud bogs.

Meanwhile, Edward drifted to the back door, standing guard without drawing attention to himself. Grateful for his organizational skills and watchful eye, I relaxed, getting swept up in the electricity of the moment.

"Were you the one who found them? The coins?" a middle-aged woman asked me, light shining in her eyes.

Much as I wanted to take all the credit, my childhood theater director drilled into our heads that most things in life were a team effort.

"I couldn't have done it without Simon Pacock and Samantha Niven, the dig's directors. And you should see Gwendolyn De Valence's drawings. They make the discovery come to life."

From my peripheral vision, I caught a glimpse of someone who looked familiar. As I turned to follow him, the woman I spoke to leaned in.

"Of course, of course. But really?"

With a smile, I said, "I'm sure any find is thrilling, but there is something about gold. Even buried for two millennia, it still shines like the sun when uncovered. It's almost like it wants to be found."

"You're so lucky," she said with a sigh.

Nodding, I agreed, "So lucky."

Not long after Simon showed the pieces to Julie, her associates, and the assistants, the press appeared and jammed themselves into any remaining open spaces.

The room's energy doubled if possible, and Julie started the conference, announcing the find, giving full credit to Simon and me by name.

Tears of joy welled up, and I fought for composure. Simon would banish me if I made a scene, but the stimulation threatened to overcome me.

Simon spoke a few words I didn't listen to as I beamed at the assembled crowd. Cameras flashed, and questions flew in a polite and orderly way.

Finally, Julie ended the gathering by saying they needed to get the sixteen aurei back to London with the other one I'd found earlier that week, again naming me specifically.

My heart pounded so loud I thought the press mics would pick up the sound.

Sixteen?

"Once the lab finished, they would be returned to the Chedworth Museum for display," she concluded, thanking everyone.

There were eighteen coins last night. Weren't there?

Chapter Twenty: Two Coins

The crowd dissipated as quickly as it formed, leaving us with the curator and her two assistants, who radiated energy.

"Oh, that went well, didn't it? I do so hope it gets international attention."

"I'm sure it will!"

"It's the find of the decade."

Voices melded into static as I concentrated. Julie said sixteen coins, but I remembered counting eighteen the night before. Maybe.

When we finished in the wee hours of the morning, we were all dead tired. I could have counted wrong.

Except, I paid close attention to my find of a lifetime.

"Simon," I called him closer to me, interrupting the inventory conducted by the National Trust team under his watchful eye. "Did she say sixteen? I thought it was eighteen aureus."

"Eighteen," Julie said, overhearing my question, "yes. The gold aureus and then the two bronze ones."

Bronze? All the coins we found were gold. Again, fatigue robbed me of my confidence.

Still, we had photographic evidence that would tell the story —and Dolly's sketches, too. Pulling out my phone, I checked a couple of pictures, but they were from early in the process. The official camera, already packed away with the National Trust team, would confirm my memory. The black-and-white photos would detail the lack of decay and rust, indicating gold over bronze.

"Simon, about the sixteen coins," I began, but he stopped me with a minute shake of his head, which then tilted toward the corner of the gift shop.

Rather than turning around, I said, "How long do you think it will take to build a secure display for them?"

He and Julie exchanged opinions while I stealthily moved to where Simon indicated.

A sole reporter remained, and one I recognized. Allowing Simon to uphold my end of the conversation with Julie, I faced off with Jeffery.

"Jeffery, first in, last out, I see."

"Nowhere else to be today. Thought I'd look around, see what else I could find."

"Ah, well," I said in a fit of brilliance. *Come on, brain.* I had used up my cleverness to cover my question to Simon.

With Jeffery still in the room, we couldn't bring up the possible substitution of two missing coins. And the blasted reporter showed no signs of leaving.

"Simon, I'm exhausted. Do you mind if I take a break until noon?"

Nodding, he said, "We all will," before turning to Julie. "Let me help you out with these."

Certain that Simon wanted to use the opportunity to bring up the discrepancy, I puffed out air, relaxing.

But Jeffery piped up with, "I'll stay for that transportation phase. Make the story complete."

"Sorry," I mouthed at Simon, who shrugged as only a young lord could.

Once the coins were off to London, I found Edward and asked him to meet me back at the lodge. Drained, I lumbered to my room. Every ache and pain forgotten in this morning's excitement came back tenfold. Even my scraped knees complained, the skin too tight over the swelling.

In my room, I intended to scour every photo I took. As I settled onto my bed, I understood why Edward thought the pillow looked so inviting and figured I would give it a try for a moment.

* * *

Waking up in the dark, no matter the time, made me spacey. The shorter days thing was weird. The sun came up about the same time as in Arizona in the winter, but it set two hours earlier.

Turning on the only lights in my room, I found notes from Edward and Dolly, plus texts from those two and Simon. My phone assured me the time was only 4:00 p.m., and I had ignored my messages.

Saving Edward's for last, I read texts first. Simon followed Julie and the National Trust to London. Dolly left for the Medispa but sent Gilbert to drive me to the train station.

Edward had tried to wake me, unsuccessfully and regrettably had to join DI Parikh at an interrogation.

Alone.

In a Victorian lodge where a recent vandalism, murder, and theft occurred. "Not good."

As quickly as possible, I threw my things into my suitcase and backpack. Within fifteen minutes, I stood in the Visitor Centre chatting with Katherine.

"It looks like you were abandoned," she said.

"A little bit, yeah. I'm super happy you're still here. When do you close?" Information I should have noticed but didn't.

"4:30, but I will stay if you need me to. I would really rather not stay alone in that lodge."

"How about in the center?"

"It's all good here. Besides, that lovely constable gave me his number."

For a horrible moment, I thought she meant Douglass, but then I realized it must have been the local officer who spent most of his time chatting with her.

The conversation shifted to him and the fact that he planned on joining her for Christmas dinner.

"Christmas?" I said, horrified to realize that other than the basket of delicacies I'd picked up at the Markets in Bath for Edward, I didn't have anything to give anyone.

Inspiration hit when I saw the Chedworth Roman Villa playing cards in the gift shop. "Is it okay to get a last sale in for the day?"

A book collaboration of poetry and art for the Priestlys, a guide to Chedworth for my dad, National Trust note cards for Mom, a deck of cards for Lily, matching teacups for Dolly and Simon, and thick mugs for Edward and James.

"You're a lifesaver," I told Katherine.

"My pleasure," she said as she gestured toward the glass doors. "Your ride is here, I think."

"Merry Christmas!" I called as I scampered out to meet Gilbert.

"And a very happy Christmas to you."

A lovely basket filled to the brim with medispa items perched on the front seat of De Valence Medispa's electric car.

"Whack that in the back. You can sit up front. Lady Dolly wanted you and the family you're staying with to open it and report back."

"Thank you so much for the ride, Gilbert. I thought you'd be driving Simon and Dolly to London."

Shaking his head, he said, "Ain't never been as far as that. This is plenty of adventure for me, ta very much."

The first road sign we passed reported Gloucester twenty-four kilometers away, roughly fifteen miles. My mom drove me further than that to get to high school every morning.

"You've never been outside the Cotswolds?"

"Oh no. Stroud is as far as I go. Except today!" He straightened. "The big city. Gloucester."

Gloucester, smaller than Tempe and not part of a massive metropolitan area, hardly counted as intimidating. "Big city," I said, marveling at how overwhelming a country of small square footage was for locals from a country village.

After bidding a vaguely terrified Gilbert happy holidays at the train station, I rode to Bath with a carload of jolly travelers.

"Home," I sighed, disembarking. Only a few months in the elegant city, but it stole my heart. When I stepped out the side doors to catch a bus, my heart just about pounded out of my chest at the sight of Edward.

"You're home!" I cried, expecting his detective duties would keep him away.

"Aye, lassie. Parikh dismissed the team to spend time with family."

Picking up my bags, we went to the SmartCar, which he sometimes borrowed from a friend's mum. I still hadn't met this friend, but I didn't need the information right then.

"Will you come inside with me?" I asked as we pulled up, suddenly shy. The time away from each other with intermittent contact had me second-guessing our relationship.

Yesterday at the villa, we were both working with built-in conversation, but now our only reason to be together was each other.

"Aye," he agreed, but he looked nervous, and I wondered if he sensed my discomfort or if my intuition picked up on something in him.

Since he carried my suitcase and backpack, we couldn't hug properly or hold hands as we approached the house.

The boot room, stacked with overshoes and puffy jackets for the season, didn't hold the invitation I expected. Dim and cold, the sight drove away the sense of home that welcomed me to the Bath Spa station.

Panicked, I regretted all my decisions about everything. Why stay? Freezing weather, surrounded by strangers, away from my mom for the holidays. For what? A boy who didn't let me meet his friends and an internship full of people who didn't make any attempt to keep me on even when I found a cache of Roman gold. With that discovery on my resume, I could be anywhere.

Breath coming in jagged gasps, and dizziness swept over me. I should leave. I should leave now. My dad would get me home, take care of me, make sure I had everything I needed.

"Maddie, my love," Edward said, his arms encircling me.

My love?

My internal rant stopped, my breathing stilled, and I quietly wept, all the stress, excitement, doubt, and unease seeping out of me.

A minute of indulgence, then I sniffed, rubbed my wet cheeks on Edward's shirt, and braved looking at him.

The crooked smile didn't mask the concern in his eyes but filled me with happiness.

"Ready?" he asked, hand on the doorknob.

"Yeah."

It wouldn't be home, not the same, not familiar, but I was ready.

Chapter Twenty-One: Christmas in England

When Edward and I opened the front door, a pine scent welcomed us, followed quickly by baking bread and cinnamon. "Hello?" I called.

"Maddie, dear! Thank goodness. I could use your help if you don't mind."

The last time Meryl needed my help in the kitchen, she had clogged the sink with noodles and created an unholy mess.

Rushing along the entry hall, I pushed open the kitchen door to find her elbow-deep in flour, constructing dozens of cinnamon rolls.

Spices wafted from the oven. Edward collided into my back, worried at my sudden sprint.

"You're cooking magic in here," Edward said.

"It smells like heaven," I agreed.

"Edward, you too. Wash up. The first batch is almost ready to come out."

Dough in various stages covered every surface. A folding table acted as the proofing area, with four bowls of yeasty goodness rising. On the center island, Meryl rolled out a ten-by-fifteen-inch rectangle. The counters held filled rolls not yet sliced, plus several pans of rising buns waiting to bake.

A timer beeped.

After drying my hands, I grabbed potholders and removed two pans with six buns each from the oven. Then I stared, having no landing pad for the delightful treats.

Heat worked its way through the hot pads.

"Ouch, ouch," I said, setting them on the stovetop. Dangerous. I once destroyed a batch of cookies by setting the pan on a hot burner. But it was better than dropping Meryl's creations on the floor.

"Dining room table," she said, pointing a buttery flour-covered finger in that direction. "All set up with table protection and cooling racks."

I carried the rolls to the dining room one pan at a time. Many more pans awaited the table, which expanded to its full length for eight.

"Do I need to turn them out so you can reuse the pans?" I asked when I reentered the kitchen to find Edward in an apron, having taken over rolling duties. All fears and paranoia about our relationship dissolved at that moment. Grinning, I said, "Good look for you."

"I love foods he said, returning my smile.

If possible, my estimation of him increased.

Patiently, Meryl waited for us to finish making googly eyes at each other and answered my question.

"No, I have a stack in the pantry borrowed from the ladies in the church. Most are returning for our Christmas Eve community outreach tonight, but there will be plenty here for Christmas. Will you be joining us, Edward?"

"Yes, ma'am, if it's not an imposition."

Laughing, she said, "The more the merrier. Bring James, of course." Turning to me, she asked, "Anyone else away from home for the holidays?"

"Lily might be."

"Ask her too, then."

An afternoon spent kneading, rolling, filling, and baking cinnamon-infused—deliciousness soothed my soul. Indecision and a lack of knowledge about my future left my mind as I reveled in baking.

Once the final batch came out of the oven, Meryl said, "I'll get these to the church. Why don't you two head to the local?"

Confused, I asked what she meant.

"Surely, you'll want to go to a pub or two. It's Christmas Eve!"

Never did anyone permit me to go to a bar, as I was still two years under the drinking age in Arizona, let alone have it encouraged. And by a minister's wife. I didn't need to be asked twice.

As we drove, I texted Lily to meet us at the Crystal Palace in the Abbey Green.

The pub vibrated with good cheer. Somehow, we found a table, and Edward ordered drinks, including a pot of tea for Lily.

When he set everything down, Lily appeared with Donny, the bartender.

"What can I get you?" Edward asked Donny.

"That's my line."

"You deserve a break, mate."

After our first round, we headed to The Huntsman, the pub closest to us.

"Unless you want Scottish whisky, in which case we should detour to The Hideout," Donny suggested.

Shaking my head, I said, "Too strong for me. I think I'm expected at midnight service later."

The Huntsman proved jollier than The Crystal Palace. Greeted by cheers from the crowd the moment we entered, we were roped into singing Christmas carols with either different words or a strange tune.

Rather than dwelling on the differences, I embraced the experience with joy.

"Do you want to try The Boater, or would you rather avoid it on your night off?" I asked Donny.

"Avoid, avoid, avoid!" he responded.

As we laughed, he explained, "Mac has been a bear lately. You might almost say—"

"Unbearable!" Edward and I finished the sentence in unison while Lily clapped.

"No Boater, then. Slug and Lettuce or The Raven?"

We wound up sticking our heads in both for a song, if not a drink, and then caroled our way to the Priestlys' church for a candlelight service and more singing.

* * *

"Merry Christmas," I said when my alarm went off. No stockings hung by the fire, bursting with my favorite things.

Homesick, I turned on my computer to check for messages.

Tori, Scott, Naomi, and friends from Chicago and Tempe filled my inbox.

The one that caught my attention said Special Delivery from Mom. Opening it, I discovered an animated desert Christmas scene, ending in stockings by an outdoor fire pit. Attached were gift certificates to restaurants and shops around the Cotswolds. Mom's thoughtfulness acted like a warm hug.

The note from my dad said, 'Hey Pumpkin! I deposited cash into your account. Tell me if you need more. Yasmin says I should shop for something more personal, but I've never known you to say no to cash. Merry Merry, Firecracker!'

My parents' abilities to cheer me up bordered on psychic, even from thousands of miles away.

Unsure of the expected attire for breakfast, I dressed in attractive sweats, comfy but not too formal. I headed downstairs to find Edward, in full plaid flannel jammies and robe, sipping tea with the similarly dressed Priestlys.

"Happy Christmas!" all three chimed.

Curling beside Edward, I whispered, "I like your outfit."

With a grin, he jumped up and modeled. "My gran sent it. She's quite chuffed that James is with me and not in a gang in Scotland."

"Is that a family tartan?" I asked, indicating the green plaid pattern as he sat.

"It is, actually, although we don't hold ties with the ancient clan. Perfect color, though. It'd look good on you with your dancing green eyes."

For some reason, his statement brought a flush of heat to my cheeks. More than a compliment, his words invited me into his circle.

To hide my embarrassment, I said, "Dolly sent a basket. Be right back." Since the gift didn't have wrapping paper, I hid it in my room. A perfect excuse to run off and get blushing under control.

Adding a bathrobe to my ensemble, I returned to the celebration with the De Valence Medispa gift basket.

"Dolly is going to open a gift shop, and she wants us to sample everything and report back."

Roger went straight for a brown bottle with a locking stopper. "Mead. Oh, she's a good one, she is."

When scamming alcohol as an underaged teen, one rarely aims for the mead aisle. "What's mead?"

"Fermented honey. She must have beekeepers."

"She does! They keep hives at Comer Manor as well as the De Valence property."

Roger's normally pristine silver hair stood up at odd angles, and his robe, had a bear on the pocket. Still, I leaned forward to listen to his wisdom when he nodded sagely.

"The honey takes on characteristics of the flowers they use. Comer Manor honey will have a different flavor from hives at Dolly's."

"I've heard that," I said, remembering something my best friend back home had told me. "Tori's mom used local honey to get her immune to pollen she's allergic to. They have to be careful about oleander, though, because bees feeding on the flower make honey poisonous."

The basket delighted us for quite some time, mainly providing wins with only a couple of losses. Roddy the Rabbit warranted a gift of fresh parsley.

Happy that my furry friend had run of the house, I held my hand out and called him. "Roddy! Do you want some yummy greens?"

Nose twitching, he bounded across the room and into my lap. While stroking his soft black and white ears, I poised a piece of the herb in front of his face. Carefully, he took it in his mouth and munched. When he finished, he placed his paws on my arm, then my shoulder, stretching until his face leveled with mine.

Vying for the cutest creature on earth at that moment, his message became clear. "More, please," Roddy indicated.

"Quite the treasure, isn't it?" I said, then wished I hadn't. I managed to forget the two missing coins for a while, but the mention of treasure brought it back.

After a few pieces of parsley, I cut him off, not versed in rabbit nutrition. "I'll put this in the kitchen for you tomorrow," I told the rabbit, who hopped off to sleep in front of the fire.

The rest of us indulged in cinnamon or sausage rolls, which paired beautifully with the coffee, tea, and drinking chocolate Meryl warmed on the stove.

"I must say," Meryl declared with a dramatic flair, "if it were my daughter, that stocking would be in pieces by now."

I avoided looking at the mantle because I didn't want to see a row of stockings without my name. When I did, I saw a beautiful velvet stocking hung in the center with "Maddie" embroidered on it.

"Oh," I squeaked, tears forming. Swiping at them, I chastised myself. I never used to be emotional, and now, all of a sudden, a kind gesture melts me into a puddle of goo. "It's lovely."

Overflowing with useful trinkets and Bath souvenirs, I enjoyed each piece.

Lily stopped by for breakfast and to exchange gifts, then headed to Donny's for dinner with his family.

"Wow! Meeting his parents," I teased.

Blushing, she whispered, "Exciting, don't you think?"

A little pang of jealousy at how confident Lily was in what she wanted lasted only a moment before I wished her luck.

Edward gave me two Scottish wool scarves: my original one, which he retrieved from the hospital after I used it to bandage Sam's head wound, and another in the Bailey tartan. I draped the green one over my neck and hugged him fiercely. "Now you have one for work," he said, indicating the cream one, still a bit stained, "and one for going out."

He pulled a small, rectangular package from his pocket. Too short for a necklace or bracelet and not ring-shaped. "Not really a gift, as much as a safety precaution," he warned.

The package contained a tiny, deep green Swiss Army knife. "I thought pocketknives were illegal here."

"Anything more than three inches with a locking blade, yes. That is a Jetsetter knife. No blade."

Intrigued, I pulled out a pair of tweezers, scissors, a toothpick, and a bottle opener with a screwdriver head. "Cool," I said, playing with the little tools.

"Keep it with you. Always," he warned as I slipped it into my sweatshirt pocket.

*****

Christmas dinner continued the festivities.

James arrived, looking incredibly sharp, and I suspected he had borrowed Edward's new work clothes for the occasion. The Bailey brothers ate enough food for five, pleasing Meryl no end.

A basket of silver and gold tubes appeared after we cleared the dishes.

"What are these?" I asked.

"Christmas crackers!" everyone declared.

"Come on," Roger said, handing me one, then promptly yanking it out of my hand.

Eyebrows knit together, my gaze shifted from him to the cracker.

"You're supposed to pull, dear," Meryl told me.

"Ah. Okay."

Prepared, I accepted the end Roger placed in my hand and gave it a mighty tug. It popped like a gunshot.

I screamed, dropping the paper on the floor, much to the amusement of everyone else.

"We don't have Christmas crackers in Arizona," I said.

"You must have something with prizes for the children."

After thinking for a moment, I came up with the closest tradition. "Piñatas. Papier mâché in bright colors filled with candy. You hit it with a baseball bat. Blindfolded." Explaining it sounded a lot more dangerous than I remembered as a kid.

A couple of blank stares later, Roger indicated the half tube on the floor. "You got the bigger half. Put on the crown and show us your prize!"

To my surprise and delight, a little whistle, a paper crown, and a piece of paper with a bad joke spilled out. My dad would love this tradition.

"Why can't penguins fly?" I read from the paper. "Because they're not tall enough to be pilots."

After much popping without screaming on my part, trivia, trinkets, and jokes later, Meryl brought out the Christmas cake, and we adjourned to sit in front of the fire.

A nutty, boozy fruitcake made weeks in advance, its spices warmed me. Nothing like the candied fruit doorstops packaged in the US. This cake made a believer out of me.

As my head drooped onto Edward's shoulder, his cell rang.

"Work," he said, shifting me onto a comfy pillow and taking the call in the boot room. When he returned, he kissed me on the forehead and told the room, "Fire at the co-op on Mount. I have to leave."

The only reason Edward would go to a local fire meant something extra awful happened.

Chapter Twenty-Two: Boxing Day at Chedworth

A note from Simon cut short my time off. Without the chance to say goodbye to Edward, I re-packed my clothes and caught the train to Gloucester, where Simon met me.

"What is Boxing Day, and why are we the only ones working?"

Skipping the definition, he broke the news. "Dolly and I successfully convinced the National Trust that the two bronze coins were substituted for gold ones that were stolen. Now, we need to do everything we can to recover them."

"Are you flippin' kidding me? After everything we found, we're the ones in trouble?"

He threw me a bemused expression.

I groaned.

"You mean, I'm the one in trouble. I swear Douglass has poisoned the world against me." Crossing my arms across my chest, I glared out the window. Right up until I caught my reflection and realized I looked like a petulant toddler.

"Why aren't the imposters- slash- thieves their main suspects? I mean, come on, they have records."

"Well," Simon began, always a signal of impending unwanted information, "they left."

Point, but I didn't want to admit it.

Rounding the corner to the dirt road that led to Chedworth, Simon's

Citroen slid in the mud.

"Please don't crash," I advised.

"Working on it."

A few sloshy, slippy minutes later, he pulled onto high ground. Wet, but at least covered in gravel, the only safe spot.

"Dolly's not here?" I asked, as we had the only car, and the area oozed abandon and unease.

"I'm afraid her Boxing Day is a bit more involved than mine with the spa and all."

Scurrying across the grounds to the Hunting Lodge, I put the conversation on hold until we got inside and turned on the heat.

Once the kettle whistled and hot tea was in hand, I repeated, "What is Boxing Day?"

With a sneer, he said, "If you hadn't run off to the colonies, you'd know such things."

Sneering back, we tried to out-scowl each other until we broke into a laughing fit.

"Traditionally," he began with an attempt at serious, "servants work on Christmas, serving meals, cooking, cleaning, and preparing food for the following day."

"We wouldn't have run off to the colonies if you treated people better."

"You did ask."

"Okay, fine. Continue." As an afterthought, I added, "Please."

"On the day after Christmas, servants were free to celebrate with their families."

"How kind."

"Indeed. As a thank you, the lord and/or lady of the house would send them home with boxes of gifts, as a thank you for their loyalty and work the previous day."

That part sounded more positive. "So, it's Boxing Day because you, the aristocracy, gave people boxes of stuff."

"Yes."

"It has nothing to do with the actual sport of boxing?"

"No." Simon's sneer returned. "Why would it?"

A multitude of responses surfaced, but I chose to discard them in favor of, "You made the Hawthorns work on Christmas Day?" The idea of the sweet elderly couple having to wait hand and foot on the lord of the manor appalled me.

"I agree," he said, surprising me. "Aunt Viv tried to give them the day off, but they wouldn't hear of it. Mrs. H muttered about being put out to pasture while Hawthorn harrumphed and bashed the silver about."

That surreal, out-of-body feeling I experienced way too often in England occurred. I plain didn't get it. Why would anyone be offended at an offer to relax?

"The aristocracy is part of the landscape in some villages. It's expected," Simon explained, accurately reading my mood. "And besides, I slipped a bonus into his paycheck. Dolly's duties are quite a bit more extensive today, with her household and spa staff."

Blowing air out of my mouth, I changed the subject.

"Anyway, what are we doing here? When did the coins disappear? Did anyone from the National Trust count all gold coins, or did everyone note the two bronze ones? In other words, what time did the swap happen?"

"Answering those questions," Simon said, which made me stop and recall what I asked.

"We're here to establish a timeline?"

"Exactly."

Mapping graph paper worked for timelines, so I grabbed a roll, pencils, and copies of our notes from the excavation.

Our pictures had exact time codes until we used them to light the site. After that, we had to refer to the computer with copies from the digital SLR camera.

Starting shortly before sundown, when I started brushing under the wall, I created a timeline of each level of discovery. At 3:03 a.m., I recorded Simon, Dolly, and me storing eighteen gold aurei in the safe in a lockbox. A local constable stood guard.

"What does that tell us?" Simon asked.

"That the theft happened between 3:03 and 11:00 a.m. when the doors opened for the press conference, unless the cop stole them."

Unfortunately, the next part of the timeline wasn't as straightforward as no one had documented it with pictures.

Except the one journalist who arrived first.

"Jeffery Dailey," I said.

"A scoundrel, certainly, but not a thief."

"No, not as a suspect, but he might have pictures of everyone who arrived and at what time."

In response, Simon lifted one shoulder in artful nonchalance.

"I'll text him to see if I can get the pictures."

I did and regretted it the second I got a response.

'And what do I get in return?'

Muttering a string of derogatory phrases about the man and his profession, I considered typing them verbatim but stopped.

"If he helps, I'll offer him an exclusive on the theft," I told Simon.

"Is that wise?"

"As long as I don't give him any hints about what is happening now, I think it's okay."

He twitched his head, which I took as consent. I sent an offer to Jeffery, only mentioning an exclusive on something juicy if he helped me now.

'What about?' Jeffery's text asked.

'I'll tell you once I have all the facts. Email the pictures. I'll contact you in a couple of days.'

Surprisingly, he let it go and sent a link to an account with his pictures from the event.

Groaning, I scrolled through the file. "It's massive," I complained to Simon. "He must have walked around with his finger on the camera's button the whole time."

"Won't that help?"

"It's like trying to find a needle in a haystack—or, more accurately, a piece of hay in a haystack since I have no idea what I'm looking for."

"Arrival times. Start with every picture with a new person in it."

"What are you going to do?"

"Supervise," he said with a smirk.

Instead, Simon sat next to me and stopped at each significant photo, dictating the time and person, which sped up the process a ton.

"Okay," I said when the Visitor Centre doors opened in the photos. If possible, let's focus on the area by the safe. For now, our only suspects are the local constable and Katherine, who works in the gift shop and cafe and has the combination to the safe."

"Suspects?" Simon asked.

"Turning amateur sleuth, are you?" I asked, giggling.

Somehow fabricating a critical exhale, Simon sighed and said, "What, exactly, have you been doing since your arrival in town? And what are we doing now?"

After a very long pause that I used to come up with an argument, I gave up. "Sleuthing. But not on purpose. We wouldn't be doing this now if Douglass didn't keep accusing me of stuff."

"Stuff," he muttered, followed by, "Americans."

Grinning, I indicated that he should restart scrolling through photos.

As we scanned, I said, "Anyway, I don't think Katherine, or the constable had time to plan a heist. They were too busy flirting."

Simon regarded me skeptically.

"Seriously. He went to her house for Christmas dinner."

"How do you find out these things?"

Shrugging, I said, "People talk to me."

Even though I didn't suspect Katherine or the local officer, I started a Suspects list with a column for Opportunity.

"Shouldn't there be one for motive?" Simon asked.

I rolled my eyes, forgetting that I promised myself to stop the habit as it made me look like a middle-schooler. "Money. The motive is priceless gold coins. Duh."

"An excellent observation," he conceded, something he never did. He must be worried about my position.

Photos slide by in rapid succession.

"Okay, wait. Go slower," I said, tamping down the anxiety by focusing on the hundreds of pictures Jeffery took of the event.

One shot showed Katherine and the constable behind the counter with the safe. After a billion more photos, another shot showed them at the opposite end of the center.

"Stop," I said. "The safe is unguarded at…" Simon read the time code, and I recorded it on our timeline. "Go back and locate the National Trust folks."

It didn't take long to find several pictures of Julie and her team surrounded by the press. No way one of them could sneak off.

"You look for the constable while I check for people near the safe."

Several more shots of the couple looking happy passed before Jeffery captured another shot of the area where the coins were locked away.

No one looked suspicious, and my enthusiasm flagged. "Bored," I declared.

"Your attention span is appallingly short."

"And you sound like an old man."

Again, his sigh conveyed a ton of information that I interpreted as, 'Don't let our lack of progress get you down.' At least, that's what I chose to believe instead of something about me being annoying.

Pushing my chair back, I stood, did a few jumping jacks, remembered why I hated them in PE class, and sat back down.

"Carry on."

More and more people appeared in the photos as more of the press filtered in.

As they scrolled by, intuition nagged at me. "Wait. Go back. Something's not right."

Simon did so without question, an implied trust in my instincts.

"Stop!"

Leaning in close, I pinpointed the man who had caused my unease. The body language of a blond young man caught my attention. Without being overly tall, he seemed to loom, his shoulders hunched.

"Look at that guy."

"Hmm," Simon said noncommittally but flicked through the following few photos slowly until the man's profile came into view. "Yes, that's something, isn't it."

"His hair is dyed," I pointed out.

Compelling me to explain with a look, I said, "His eyebrows are dark and brooding. And not natural with that hair color."

"Brooding," Simon repeated.

"Like a glower," I said, recognizing the man through his disguise. "It's Dion!"

Reversing, we found the first sighting of the faux Frenchman and added him to our timeline.

"Now, let's see if Jeffery caught him on camera by the coins."

No picture of Dion with his hand in the safe laughing maniacally existed. However, we found one that showed a blond head just above the counter which could count as Dion ducking to get into the safe. To be fair, Simon had blond hair, too, but since we knew it wasn't him, we added 'Dion behind the counter by safe' on the timeline.

All for calling it a job well done and moving on, I couldn't wait to stop looking at photos. Simon had different ideas.

"You will never be a top-rate archaeologist without patience and persistence."

"Patience? Me? Who sifts dirt for hours? And in a stairwell, no less? I can do patience. And persistence. Even when plunged into darkness and covered in dirt, I stuck to that stairwell and sifted like nobody's business. Don't you lecture me about persistence. Just because I find looking at pictures tedious doesn't mean I won't be top-rate. I mean, honestly, look at what I've discovered, and I don't have a degree yet."

"You sometimes tell people you do."

As I took a breath to launch another rant, he said, "No more stalling."

"Fine."

As expected, Simon's thorough nature paid dividends. Dion disappeared from every photo after the blond head below the counter shot. Jeffery's camera aimed every which way in the room during Julie's speech.

"He's as unfocused as you," Simon commented.

I might have growled in response before proving that I, too, could formulate a plan. "We need to find out where Dion got the two bronze coins that replaced the gold ones. Can the National Trust people test it to see if it's been professionally cleaned? Also, can you buy them anywhere around here?"

"I've never seen them at an antiques gallery, but I believe there is an ancient coin dealer in Cheltenham."

"Antiques gallery," I chuckled.

"What are you on about?"

"In Arizona, ninety-year-old potato mashers and Depression Era glass counted as antiques. A gallery that carries ancient Roman coins? No way."

Ignoring my distraction, he insisted, "Coin dealers. Now."

"Also," I said, annoyed at his bossy tone, "did you mark the coin's materials on the artifact bags? Like, writing 'gold coin.'"

Since my digging and sifting jobs required me to hand over all the finds to another team member, Simon completed the cataloging.

"No, of course not. It would be presumptuous to identify metal in the field."

It made sense, but he could have said it nicer.

"Then, Dion could have just swapped the coins and not the whole bag."

"Correct."

"Why would he have gotten artifact bags?" A good thief would have identical backup packing materials, but how would the thief know what they would find?

"A better question," Simon said, "is why did he bother?"

About to answer, I stopped myself, acknowledging the point. "Yeah, true. He could have just taken a handful of coins and not bothered to replace them."

"The Trust was satisfied that the number remained the same, eighteen coins. If I hadn't gone to London and insisted two were missing, no one but us would have known."

Chapter Twenty-Three: The Timeline

Replacing two gold coins with bronze, rather than stealing one or all of them, didn't make sense. Why take the risk of tracing the bronze coins back somehow? And what kind of thief shows restraint in the face of priceless treasure?

From his expression, Simon seemed to be contemplating the same questions.

I left him musing and called the coin dealers on the search engine's list.

"Hi," I began, eliciting a glare from Simon, probably for sounding too American. "I'm looking for a bronze aureus. Do you have any in stock?"

The second store had a recorded message that they would be closed for two weeks for Christmas. Dion wouldn't have known which coin to buy prior to that, so I eliminated them from the list.

A mug of steaming tea appeared by my elbow, and I saw Simon disappearing into the kitchen. While I didn't understand not marrying for love, I got why Dolly wanted to spend her life with Simon.

Adding a dollop of milk, I sipped the fortifying brew and made another call.

The fifth try landed info. "Such a popular coin these days," the clerk said.

"Really?" I prompted.

"Oh yes. Well, you must have seen the discovery at Chedworth. Gold aureus, right on my doorstep. Who would have thought?"

Waiting for a beat, I willed him to go on. He did. "Although you are the second person this holiday to ask about them. A young man bought the only ones I had in stock just before Christmas."

"So you're out?" I asked, employing my acting skills to sound crushed.

"Yes, he bought the last two."

"Okay, thank you."

After disconnecting, I shouted my findings to Simon.

Emerging from the kitchen with a plate of grilled cheese sandwiches, or cheese toasties, as he called them, Simon set them within arm's reach. The caramelized butter created a crunch, followed by a deep, rich, gooey Red Leicester cheese, creating a perfect bite.

"Thanks. I didn't realize how hungry I was."

"I do admit to missing the Frenchmen's cooking."

"Yeah, me too. They were magic in the kitchen. Which makes me wonder if they were actually French."

"We will turn the timeline and coin dealer information over to the police and let them worry about it," Simon said.

We ate in silence until he broached the subject I'd been thinking about earlier. "Since only two coins were available, that solves the mystery of why only two were taken."

"True," I agreed, "but I don't understand why they cared enough to replace any. Why not steal them all?"

"Two thoughts come to mind. One, the treasured coins would be too difficult to fence. It might take years before they could sell any without triggering the police. If I had not convinced the National Trust that the coins were substituted with bronze versions, the gold coins would have immense interest after your discovery, without any red flags attached to a sale."

"Wow, smart." The genius of a plan eluded me until Simon's deductive powers laid it out. "That has to be it, right? It benefits Dion in two ways."

Rather than agreeing, Simon explained his other thoughts. "The only other scenario that makes sense is from Gabriel's perspective."

"But Gabriel wasn't in any of the pictures," I pointed out too quickly.

"Why send two recognizable people to steal the coins instead of one? Plus, a driver is required for a quick retreat." With a sidelong glance, he added, "A 'getaway car,' as you Americans would say."

"I got it," I said, annoyed that Simon was right. Of course, it wasn't just Dion stealing the coins. He and Gabriel were a team, and they abandoned Chedworth together. If Dion committed a crime, Gabriel backed him up. *Damn.*

"I still can't believe they murdered Jill." As I said it, the truth of the statement surfaced. I couldn't believe it. They may have fooled me as to their identities, but unless they both tested as high-functioning sociopaths, they weren't killers.

"Nor I, but again, we leave that to the police."

After clearing the dishes, I ignored Simon's logic and cleaned the kitchen. It didn't take nearly long enough.

"My second theory," Simon resumed.

Relentless, that man.

"Gabriel seemed to find you, shall we say, interesting."

Shaking my head, I said, "He didn't. No more so than anyone—"

"Don't interrupt. A less delicate description might be that he drooled after you like a Saint Bernard."

"Eww, gross."

"This will go faster if you remain quiet."

While I wanted this conversation to be over, I didn't want to hear it in the first place.

"And," Simon continued, "I will be brief."

"Brief, brief, or brief like Polonius?" The king's advisor from Hamlet famously rambled on after claiming "…brevity is the soul of wit."

"Do be—"

"Quiet. Yeah, yeah."

He blinked at me slowly.

Instead of letting him go on, I took over. "Gabriel liked me, I get it. You think he's willing to give up gold for a girl he just met who's dating a cop? I don't think so."

"Never underestimate the power of attraction," Simon advised.

"Anyway, your first theory makes a lot more sense. Let's operate using that as a guideline. This means our next steps—"

"Are to go through all the pictures more thoroughly. Like, girl dating a cop thorough," he added with a solid American accent.

"Yawn," I responded.

"You'll be happy for the effort when you aren't in jail."

"And after I finish?"

"If you are thorough—"

"Stop saying thorough. It doesn't sound like a word anymore."

"If you are conscientious, it will take you most of the evening."

With an exaggerated sigh, I pulled his laptop with the pictures on it toward me. I flipped the pictures back to the beginning like a Wheel of Fortune spin. After the first two, I noticed Simon did not join me.

"And what will you be doing, Mr. Too Good for Tedious Work?"

In another surprise, he laughed at that.

"I will be with Lady Gwendolyn."

"What?"

"Dolly wants me there for the spa employees' Boxing Day, setting a precedence for joining her in the future."

"I'll come too," I said, appalled that he hadn't extended the invitation already.

"You will be fine here. Every news outlet reported that the coins are in London, and the villa is closed to visitors. You're perfectly safe."

"But why can't I come to the spa?"

A long-suffering expression forced his eyes closed. "Because if you are there, the staff will wait on you. Most balked at the idea of taking the evening off."

"I thought traditions were strongly held in small villages."

"At Comer, yes," he said, shuffling me to an easy chair and inviting me to sit. "Hawthorn is the nephew of my grandfather's butler. The tradition goes back years. Dolly's uncle wasn't technically in charge, as he is the younger brother, and the estate passes to Dolly. The customs were lost in the transition."

Simon usually didn't take the time to explain things in detail, even when he should. This kind of speech established the importance of these relationships to him.

"When will you be back?" I asked, hoping the slight, sad whine in my voice might change his mind.

It didn't.

"First thing in the morning. We'll bring breakfast. Don't break my computer." He waived farewell. "Toodle-pip!"

"You know this is how people die in horror movies, right?"

Silence.

"Well," I said to no one, "I wish I hadn't put that thought in my mind." I changed to singing. "Raindrops on roses and whiskers on kittens." The song helped to calm my nerves, so I belted out the whole thing, chasing the Hunting Lodge's shadows away.

"To work!" I called, drumming enthusiastically on the table.

Organization made tedious work go faster, so I took the total number of pictures and divided that by four per hour, which gave me manageable fifteen-minute chunks to work in. For fun, I did the calculation again in my mind for ten minutes, which created a less daunting number of pictures.

"Right then," I said loudly, dissipating any lingering spookiness, "photos!"

As I scanned Jeffery's documentation of the press conference, the wind picked up. Sodden leaves battered the windows, sticking momentarily before sliding off.

The first few pictures told me nothing new.

A powerful gust rattled the door, so I got up and re-locked every lock, wishing I'd done it when Simon first left.

The lodge continued to creak and moan as the storm intensified. Ignoring the sounds, I continued my search of the pictures. Rewarded with an additional sighting of Dion, I deserved a treat.

After noting Dion on the timeline, I headed to the kitchen, for drinking chocolate and toast.

Bang, the door to the lodge blew open with a howl.

"Eek!" I screeched as I ran out of the kitchen to the front door and slammed it shut. When I checked the locks, I must have opened the deadbolt instead of securing it.

Heart pounding, I leaned against the door for a moment before re-stacking my timeline and notes, spread across the floor in the wind.

A movement caught my attention, and I swear a flash of something sizable flew by the window.

"Probably an owl," I rationalized, glaring at the blinds that blocked views in, but allowed me to see out because of the floodlights on the grounds.

I cupped my hands around my eyes to block light from inside, pressed against the window, and searched outside for animals. The floodlights exposed only trees rocking violently in the wind.

Returning to the search, I took solace from the chocolate and found another picture of the constable buying something from the gift shop instead of standing guard.

The lights flickered momentarily.

"Do I know where the breakers are?" I asked, again hoping to fill the house with sounds from me and not scary weather. The words sounded hollow and small.

Partly because, no, I never noticed a breaker box.

In the kitchen, I grabbed a flashlight, just in case, and checked inside the pantry.

Nothing.

It hid in the laundry room at home, so I checked there next. No luck.

That's when I remembered we had a second box in the backyard in Tempe. As the wind howled, I vowed to call Simon to come and get me if I had to go outside.

Before that last resort, I called Edward and left a message, asking where the breakers were hidden in England.

A text came in a few moments later. 'Sorry I can't answer lassie. Work. Going dark.'

Whenever I worked in the Undercroft at the Roman Baths, where no cell signal could penetrate, I texted Edward that I turned my phone off so he wouldn't worry about me. My happiness that he returned the favor dampened when I couldn't help but think if he had to turn off his phone, he might be in a sticky situation. Which, naturally, made me worry more.

Lights dimmed briefly, spurring my quest to find something electrical-looking.

I hit pay dirt in the kitchen's cleaning supply closet. Behind a broom and two mops lay a box with a lightning bolt.

"Gotcha," I said, and the lights went out with a pop.

I screamed, my first thought sabotage, that a bad guy had thrown the breakers. But as I stared at the electrical box when it happened, I ruled out that unpleasant possibility. Natural forces must have overloaded a circuit.

Flashlight on, I opened the box and found a series of round glass knobs.

There were enough electrical storms in Tempe that I knew a thing or two about popped breakers. Open the box, and anything that got flipped off, you flip to on. Easy.

This box contained no breakers, nothing to flip—just weird circular things.

Examining them, I saw most were filled with light-colored fibers, except for one brown one.

"Like a burned-out lightbulb," I said, pleased with myself for figuring it out.

The problem now became finding replacements.

If it were me, I'd put the fresh lightbulb-thingies near the box, so I played my light around the room. The beam glinted off something on the top of the box. Carefully, I felt around and pulled down a fresh…

A fresh what?

Then it hit me. *Blowing a fuse.* I'd heard the expression enough times but had never seen an actual fuse before.

Excited by my success, I poked at the bad fuse until I discovered that, like a lightbulb, it screwed out. When I screwed the fresh one in its place, light flooded the closet.

"Look at me go," I said, grinning, and pushed on the door. It didn't budge.

The closet door had swung shut during my search and didn't have a knob on the inside.

Mood deflating, I muttered, "You have got to be kidding me." Rather than a full handle, a plate with a slot confronted me.

Casting around the little room, I found a small tool chest complete with a large flathead screwdriver. "Perfect."

After only two slips, I managed to turn the contraption and set myself free.

Pleased with my accomplishment, I refilled my mug of chocolate and resumed my station at the computer to scan photos.

Only the computer shut off. Not just asleep. Off.

The power button didn't bring it back to life—dead battery. Okay, that made sense. I had the resolution on high to view the pictures.

I fetched my charger from my bag, which still sat by the front door, but it had a different connector.

Well, at least I had an excuse for not finishing my dull task.

When I picked up my cell to text Simon about the setback, I discovered that it, too, was turned off.

Flies fluttered in my stomach. Not pleasant like butterflies, the buzzing echoed the skittery panic in my mind.

I charged my phone earlier.

Hitting power, I waited for it to boot up and confirm the battery level at sixty-seven percent.

Neither device was plugged into the grid during the storm, so they were not subject to surges or faulty fuses. No way they overloaded or shorted out.

I texted Simon, "I think I'm in trouble. Come and get me, please." The message only loaded halfway, stuck in limbo.

The storm could have knocked out a cell tower. Maybe.

Hands trembling, I tried to call, but it didn't connect.

A floorboard upstairs groaned.

Stock still, I held my breath and listened. Clenching my hands into fists, I counted to ten, then twenty. My childhood ritual calmed me, and with the decrease in my heartbeat, I questioned if I heard correctly.

But if there was one lesson I learned during my time in England, it's that I should never second-guess my fear.

Someone prowled upstairs.

Chapter Twenty-Four: The Visitor

The tell-tale floorboard didn't make another sound, but the atmosphere in the lodge changed. No longer empty and abandoned, the air closed around me, suffocating. A weird, high-pitched keening sound filled my ears.

Keening.

Like Simon accused me of the other day.

"Get it together, McGuire."

With considerable effort, I took a deep, slow inhale, counting to five, followed by exhaling all the air out of my lungs by counting to ten. The strange sound stopped as my breath returned to normal.

The lodge's air hung close and suffocating.

My choices included to run, hide, or fight.

Running away sounded great, but I vetoed the idea because I had nowhere to go and no hope of finding help in a raging storm.

The person upstairs knew about my presence in the house, or they wouldn't have bothered to turn off my electronics. If I hid, they would hunt me down.

Which left me, with fighting.

Back in the supply closet, I grabbed the screwdriver and a spray cleaner bottle. Both could be used to defend or attack and didn't weigh me down.

The element of surprise offered my only advantage. Rather than waiting to be chased down like a scared rabbit, I would go on the attack. Roddy's long claws and strong legs came to mind, and I amended my resolve to not be a frightened mouse. Rabbits could hold their own.

Armed, I crept up the stairs, alert for any sound. A board creaked, and not under my foot. Shouting like a banshee, I rounded the corner at the top of the stairs, laying down a stream of cleaning spray.

"Bloody 'ell! Oi, stop it, Maddie."

Hands reached through the spray and snatched the bottle away.

I cocked my arm and aimed the screwdriver at the assailant's neck.

Barely scratching his skin, he grabbed my arm using my forward motion against me and tossed me behind him.

Tori's brother used this move on me. In answer, I did what always worked on him—launched myself at the legs.

Disturbingly, my attacker possessed more skills than an obnoxious teenage boy and gracefully leaped over me as I careened into the wall.

"Miss Madeline," the stranger called with a familiar accent.

Rolling onto my back, I gazed up. "Gabriel?"

His accent left and was replaced by a cockney one when he said, "Harold, if I'm being honest."

All my preservation instincts fled, replaced by the absurdity of the situation. "Harold?"

While holding out a hand to help me stand, he said, "It's a perfectly good name."

An engaging smile sparked mischief in his eyes, and I momentarily forgot about our intertwined fingers.

Alarm bells sounded in my mind, a little late, but they got there. Yanking my arm away from him, I broke contact and backed away.

"You're a liar and a thief," I said, as much to remind myself as to accuse him.

In response, he bowed low, flourishing an imaginary hat that painted a picture of a rogue pirate. "At your service."

Drawing on my fear from earlier, I slapped my fist into the wall to break his spell. "And you killed Jill!"

Consternation knit his eyebrows together. "I did no such thing."

"Dion, or whatever his name is, then. And you let him. Encouraged him."

"No, he did not. Tame as a pussycat, that one."

The fact that I wanted to believe him probably contributed to the sincerity I sensed in his answer, but I wasn't ready to give up yet.

"Of course, you would say that. You're impressively good at lying. You set up the real French students."

In a decidedly Gallic gesture, he shrugged.

"You couldn't possibly think you'd find anything worth money. The value of archaeology is in the people and how much we're still the same after thousands of years."

Skepticism painted his expression, similar to the faces that my parents and friends had when I told them what I wanted to major in. This caused me to launch into a lecture.

"In the Roman Baths, there are curses that citizens wrote and tossed into the water for the gods to carry out vengeance. The glorious thing about them is that sometimes it's just about someone stealing a chicken or wanting revenge for a neighbor, making them sick. It's exactly the same petty stuff we complain about today."

Gabriel nodded, but I continued. Spying the 3-D printed mini-padlock that Sam had made for me.

"Take that lock," I said with a head gesture toward it, then thought better of my phrasing. "Not literally. It's mine, but the point is that we're still using padlocks after two millennia to keep things away from thieves. We think we've evolved because we have space travel, but we act and think like our ancestors."

Appreciative of my mom like never before, I said, "It's why my mother studies Shakespeare. That understanding of human nature transcends centuries." I'd need to remember to tell her if she bugged me about my choice of fields again.

"The little weasels bragged about buried treasure. How could we resist?"

My mouth opened and closed a few times before the correct response surfaced. "Because it was wrong."

Another shoulder twitch.

"As is murder!"

"Maddie, me beautiful girl, we're thieves, to be sure, but not murderers.

We're as upset by Jill as you were."

Logically, a straight-out murderous sociopath would lie about everything, including being a con artist. Gabriel, or Harold, I supposed, pretty much bragged about being a thief, which made his denial of the murder more plausible.

Not that I wanted him to see that I came to that conclusion. I kept my skeptical expression firmly in place.

"Good," he said, grinning, "you believe me."

Someday, I vowed to myself, I would get a poker face. But not today. "Maybe," I told him.

On the bright side, Gabriel/ Harold wasn't a murderer, which means I hadn't been flirting with a monster. Good.

However, that meant said monster ran around the countryside still, and I didn't have any other suspects. Except Katherine in the Visitor Centre or the local constable, neither of which seemed likely, but I'd been wrong about people before.

"Why are you here? I already have proof that Dion stole the coins, so why risk coming back?"

"Is that really the question you want to ask me?" His voice dripped with innuendo, which, frankly, pissed me off.

"No. What I really want to know is if you killed all those birds."

Looking skyward, his lip jutted out, and his head wavered from side to side. "That we did. Dion—"

"That's not his real name."

"No, it's not. It's also not my secret to give away."

He winked, indicating that by telling me his name, we shared a confidence that I wished didn't create warmth in my chest.

"Dion convinced me we could find the treasure ourselves if the rest of you were gone. Jill was mouthy about what she was doing. She thought we were too thick to understand English, so she let loose around Dion."

"Why did you pick Celtic warnings?" Curiosity got the better of me.

He laughed, a joyful sound that lowered my guard further. "We were too thick to know better, weren't we?" he admitted. "Felt a right fool when I heard you carrying on about how the Celts had been gone for centuries. Also, the heart set the tone. Not us."

His expression softened. "I am sorry about the little wicker man. Dion thought it would do the trick, but I didn't like to see you that upset."

It is incredibly difficult to stay angry at someone who sounds so sweet. Fighting to hold onto my justified ire, I stamped my foot. "I can't trust anything you say since you've been lying since I've met you."

The convincing chagrin looked rehearsed.

"Oh, please," I complained as he turned on the smile.

"You can see right through me. An open book, am I."

"No, not completely. Why did you come back?" I repeated.

With a quick step toward me, his hand caressed my cheek and pulled a gold coin out of my ear. Like a magician manipulating the aureus, it floated across his fingers until it disappeared into nothing.

"Why doesn't Dion have it?"

"You 'ave 'eard about zee cat, non?" he asked in an exaggerated French accent.

"Curiosity, yes. Answer the question."

Rather than acknowledging my bossy tone, Gabriel answered, "He left it here in case we were stopped driving off. It was supposed to be empty today. Boxing Day, you know."

"Well, no, not until today. But I do now and will never forget as this has been a doozy."

Tension bloomed awkwardly, and I sensed we were crossing into new territory. I knew he had the coins and that he wasn't French.

I was a loose end.

He must have read the conclusion in my face because he said, "Cor, you're a smart one. I can't let ya go. Not just yet."

All the fluttering of warmth in my chest left a cold trickle of panic taking its place. "Sure you can," I tried.

For a moment, he tilted his head and studied me. Finally, he said, "Nah, I don't think you're suited for a life of crime. Come on."

Indicating that I go downstairs, I did with a tight grip on the handrail.

"Don't be daft," he said, taking hold of my free arm. "I wouldn't push you down the stairs."

As I didn't have a way to confirm that, I kept hold until we were in the communal area.

"Pick a chair."

Choosing the one closest to my phone, I sat as he produced zip ties.

No, no, no, no, no.

I stood, scuttling away from him.

A charming smile stopped me. "I can't have ya followin' me or callin' your copper friend. You'll be okay for a bit. Come on," he said again with a gentlemanly gesture to the chair.

"How am I supposed to defend myself if the murderer comes? Not that I made much of a dent on you," I commented, a tad bitter. I hadn't fared better during our fight.

"The spray worked," he conceded as he cinched a zip tie around one leg. "Can you wiggle your ankle?"

After ensuring my circulation wouldn't be cut off, I nodded and said, "Not nearly well enough. And don't patronize me."

"Nah, that wouldn't do. No other opponents ever got that close to me."

Unable to help feeling pleased, I replied modestly, "It's nice of you to say, but I didn't stand a chance."

"Well, me girl, I do have a black belt in karate. There's not many who can take me down."

Stupidly, given that my wrists were being attached to chair arms, I preened at how well I did against him.

Wondering if he might let me go, I attempted guilt. "You're going to feel awful if you hear about an American intern who died of thirst while strapped to a chair over the holiday break."

"That I would, but don't you worry. Lord So- and- So will be back in only a few hours. Take a kip. You'll be a bit stiff, but other than that, right as rain."

Once he secured me to the chair, both coins appeared out of nowhere. One in each hand, they danced across his knuckles. Mesmerized by them, Gabriel asked, "How much do you think they're worth?"

At that moment, I saw the real Harold. The carefree rake disappeared, and a man, probably poor, saw his future in his hands.

I shrugged. "Priceless as archaeological pieces go. On the black market to unscrupulous dealers," I pondered, calculated exchange rates, and shrugged as best as I could considering my restrictions, "thousands of pounds each. Maybe as much as ten grand." Never having considered selling or buying a Roman treasure, I never looked it up, but my estimation seemed reasonable.

"You're not going to leave me here like this, are you?"

The coins disappeared into a black velvet bag, and his cocky expression resumed.

"But what if I have to go to the bathroom?" I asked, hoping for a reprieve.

"Do you?"

I sighed. "No."

"Then don't drink anything in the next couple of hours, and you'll be fine."

"And how do you know that?" I asked, stalling. "How many times have you been zip-tied?"

His eyes traveled up and to the right as he considered it. "Four. Only once to a chair, though, and I didn't mind that one. Only the best for you," he said with a chuckle.

"Gee, thanks," I said, attempting not to smile. Damn that charm.

"I'd like to stay and chat all night and into the early morn, but I must be gettin' on. Otherwise, you might just set me on the straight and narrow."

"I hardly believe that," I said, laughing.

"You never know." He touched my cheek and said, "If you ever need me, contact the Captain Kidd pub in London."

"I will never need you," I assured him.

"You never know, lovely," he repeated, then kissed me full on the mouth. Soft, sensual, and somehow polite.

I may have enjoyed it more than I liked to admit.

Chapter Twenty-Five: Tied Up

Depressingly, Gabriel, aka Harold, left me zip-tied to a chair in the Victorian Hunting Lodge at Chedworth. Running the sentence through my mind a few times, I concluded that my situation was as hopeless as I thought.

Also, what kind of guy kisses a girl like that and then abandons her? A rogue, that's who. A scoundrel, as Simon would say.

One whom I made a fool of myself over. "Arg, I'm such an idiot!" How could I let him trick me like that, take advantage of me, and compromise everything I'd worked so hard for, both personally and professionally?

When I got out of here, I would have DI Parikh and Edward hunt him down like a dog. Did he think he would get away with it? Hell hath no fury, like a woman scorned and tying me up and leaving counted. I wouldn't rest until he paid for everything he did.

Just as soon as I could escape. Or when Simon showed up.

Revenge plan on hold, I contemplated what to do next.

A nap sounded appealing. It would pass the time, but I didn't think much of the idea as the chair wasn't tall enough to support my head.

"Okay, McGuire, you've been trapped before and survived," I said as a pep talk.

The thing is, when you've suffered a disturbing entrapment, you want to forget it, not make a game plan for the next time it happens. Dredging up unpleasant memories, I discarded anything not pertinent to my current situation. Taking inventory helped before.

Confined to the chair meant a catalog of things on my person. A ponytail holder in my hair, tee shirt, flannel shirt, jeans, underthings. Trying not to get discouraged by the pathetic list, I clung to the memory that clothes had helped save me before.

"What else?"

Pockets! Gabriel hadn't emptied them. The unfortunately named thieves spray, a hair scrunchie, loose change, and something else. I could feel the lump through my jeans.

A smile crept over my face. I had the Swiss army tool Edward told me to carry with me always. It didn't have a blade, but a bottle opener would work on my plastic restraints.

Without thinking it through clearly, I reached for the gadget too forcefully, and the zip tie cut into my flesh.

"Ow."

Until I could escape, the things that I needed to escape were inaccessible. Awesome.

After a few calisthenic moves where I tried to get my pocket closer to my hand, I realized I needed a better plan.

Whenever I saw a movie with someone tied to a chair, I thought they could tip themselves over onto the floor and be able to get around or to a pocket. Looking at the polished solid wood, I decided that plan involved a lot of pain with the possibility of knocking myself senseless if my head made contact.

Maybe I should nap.

I closed my eyes, slowed my breathing, and forced my fury at how Gabriel used me from my brain. When my head dropped to my chest, I jerked awake, not sure from discomfort or if I heard something.

The floodlights exposed movement that I caught out of the corner of my eye. Antlers.

"Edward's stag," I said, trying to convince myself. The animal's gait didn't seem natural, as if it had a lame leg. Maybe it came close to the buildings for food.

Not that I had any idea what deer ate, but grass seemed likely.

"Sigh." Contemplating the deer diet woke me up, and I had no idea what time it was. Still dark meant anytime between 2:00 and 8:00 a.m.

My phone sat on the table behind me, alluringly close. If nothing else, I could check how much longer I might be alone.

Planting my feet as best I could, I stood on my toes and heaved an inch toward the table. It worked, so I tried it again, inelegantly hopping several inches. Once my back bumped into the table's edge, I needed to rotate to face the surface.

On my toes, I gave the chair a mighty twist. Rather than achieving a turn, my seated prison tipped, rocking back and forth alarmingly. The floor appeared far away, and my stomach swooped in protest.

"New technique," I recommended to myself.

The chair stopped moving, and I waited for my heart rate to return to normal. Again, I considered waiting for Simon to show up, but truth be told, boredom kept me moving.

Shifting my toes, sort of like a sideways moonwalk, I heel-toe lift-turned and managed to move the legs in the correct direction. Way too many times later, I faced the table, but I had also pushed myself so far away that I couldn't wake up the phone with my nose.

Resettling my feet, I lift-hopped forward. The back two legs tilted off the ground, and I bashed face-first into the table. Fortunately, I turned my face to the side so that my ear took most of the blow.

"Ow."

Not willing to give up my progress, I planted my forehead on the table for leverage and scooted-dragged the front legs closer until I could tip back and be seated at the table.

Except for a throbbing cheek and ringing ear, I relished my accomplishment.

The movement woke my phone up, and the time read 7:32 a.m., meaning Simon would return soon. Although, why hadn't he shown up when he got my text? The message must have been sent once the storm wound down.

However, I needed to call the police sooner rather than later, so I tilted forward again and put my chin near the phone. Much like the trust game we played in acting class, where I clenched an orange between my chin and chest and then transferred to another person, I used my chin to pull the cell toward me.

Once square in front of me, I used my nose to press the unlock code. At least, I attempted that. The tip of my nose didn't carry enough mass to make a difference. Bending over the screen, I plonked the area closer to the bridge of my nose. Satisfying clicking noises occurred, but my first two attacks did not unlock the phone.

Worried the security system might engage and shut down the cell for fifteen minutes, I gently rested my undamaged cheek on the table and listened to the ringing in my ear. My vision focused on the wood grain in a pathetic attempt to occupy my brain.

Or to show me something helpful! A pencil sat next to the laptop, and if I stood and scraped my body over the tabletop, I could pick it up with my teeth.

After bruising my wrists and collarbone, I acquired my prize.

Firmly clutched in my teeth, the pencil eraser descended toward my Lock Screen.

Success! Relief quickly gave way to dismay when Simon's text from the previous evening still tried to load. It was never sent.

"Uh-oh."

Studying the tabletop, I saw a small addition that hadn't been there the night before: a tiny, flat electronic square—the cell's SIM card.

When I arrived in England, my dad got me a local phone, so I didn't need to bother swapping the SIM. One thing I knew I couldn't do with a pencil and no hands was replace an ultra-thin piece of plastic in a narrow slot. Without the card or WiFi, my phone became a fancy clock I could play games on.

Excellent.

A knock on the door startled me so much that I jumped.

"Ack!" I might have screamed as well.

"Y'alright, are you?"

Tilting my non-ringing ear toward the door, I concentrated, trying to place the voice. It wasn't Simon's, Edward's, or even Gabriel's.

"Hello?" I called.

"Will the Visitor Centre be open today?" a familiar, hopeful voice asked.

"I need help!"

The knob rattled, and I groaned, remembering that I checked the locks. He couldn't get in. I'd be stuck here, zip-tied to a chair, until someone with a key showed up.

A cold breeze swirled around me, and I realized the stranger had entered. With an eye roll, I thought, *Gabriel. He just left it unlocked.*

To be fair, leaving it open helped with my rescue.

"What have we here?" George the Druid asked.

"George, thank goodness. Can you find some scissors and get me out of these things?"

"You poor love," he said, sympathy clear as he gently probed the zip ties. "Cruel this."

"Honestly, if I hadn't moved around so much, I wouldn't be in such bad shape."

Opening a pocket on his cargo slacks, he extracted a folding buck knife with a bone handle, just like one of my high school boyfriends had for hunting. The blade locked in place, and George carefully cut the bands. Pressing a button, it collapsed, and he stowed it.

"Let me get you some ice for those cuts," he volunteered, pointing to the kitchen.

I nodded, grateful.

As George rattled around in the kitchen, I rotated my ankles in every direction, then flexed and pointed. Sure of adequate blood flow, I stood on wobbly legs.

"Hey there, Miss Maddie, don't try too much," George said when he returned. Placing a baggie of ice on my bruised and torn wrists, he said, "You must have quite a tale, you must." His polite grin wasn't pushy but invited my story.

"Unfortunately, yes," I chuckled.

"Let's take a spin around the room to check your balance," he offered.

"Thank you," I said, appreciating the kindness he and all the druids displayed.

Giving me space but remaining close by to catch me if I stumbled, George followed me around the common room until I felt steady on my feet.

"I think I'm okay, thanks."

Holding the ice bags to my wrists made me shiver, which George seemed to notice.

"Better put the kettle on," he said, and we went into the kitchen together.

Leery of the pain in my wrists, I boosted myself onto the counter to wait for the water to boil. The action reminded me of Gabriel sitting here, entertaining me with life in France. Briefly, I forgot my anger and had to examine my bloody forearms to rekindle the proper level of indignation.

Watching George fuss with the tea settled me. The ritual had its desired effect, and once the hot brew hit my mouth, I relaxed.

Except, I couldn't figure out his presence. Odd that he showed up in time to rescue me. Not that I objected to freedom from my torture chair, but the Knight in Shining Armor meme didn't fit George.

"Now, tell me that tale," he said as he settled on the kitchen bench.

"Thank you so much for rescuing and caring for me. But why are you here? Everything is closed down for the season."

"My pleasure. How often do you get a chance to rescue a damsel in distress? I'm not the type. I'm not," he said with a chuckle.

The innocuous words sent a shiver through me. Somehow, echoing my thoughts boosted my awareness. I sensed something wrong. Taking a sip of tea, I kept the mug in front of my face. Contemplating the steam hid any giveaway expression I displayed.

Rather than repeating my question, I waited, hoping silence would spur his side of the conversation.

It did, but only after it became awkward.

Artfully, he covered the unease with a jolly slap of the knee. "You asked why I'm here, you did. Of course, of course. My brethren have packed up their robes and moved out of Far Peak. Headed back to our normal lives, if you can call them that." Another chuckle, this time with more warmth.

Much as I wanted to engage in the conversation and ask what he did for a living, I held my tongue. George still hadn't answered my question.

I smiled at his joke, encouraging him to continue.

"Well, lo and behold," he said, apparently warming to the idea of story-telling, "you'll never guess the first thing I encountered when back in polite society. A newspaper with my friends at Chedworth Roman Villa and with ancient Roman coins, yet! Unbelievable, I thought to myself, and decided to nip up here and give you a visit."

Frowning, he admitted, "I thought the site would be open to visitors after such a discovery. Imagine my surprise at finding everything all dark and gloomy."

Plausible. A good idea, actually. I grinned at him. "You should do marketing for the place. Staying open is a great idea to excite more interest in the site."

His shoulders relaxed, falling away from his ears, and he settled deeper into his seat. It was almost like a relief that I had bought his story.

Yesterday may not have been the day I managed a poker face, but an uncomfortable coldness in my gut told me today needed to be. Rather than neutral, which I knew I couldn't manage, I created the character of Polite Tour Guide for myself. Her back story included a fear of being yelled at, with a motivation to please and be accepted.

"Well," I said, gingerly scooting off the counter and testing my feet before putting my full weight on them, "since you came all this way, let me show you the area of interest, as they say. Thank you so much for being here," I said, oozing earnestness. "Both for rescuing me, which I still need to tell you about my perils, by the way, and so that I can talk about the discovery."

"The credit goes to," a warning stayed my tongue as I almost mentioned Jill, "uh, Simon Pacock and Ms. Niven. Their guidance and mentorship elevated our whole experience."

Grabbing my jacket and lovely new Bailey tartan scarf Edward gave me, I considered going for my phone. But, not only would it make me appear suspicious, the thing didn't work without the SIM card that I hadn't had time to install.

In a spectacular display of it's always darkest before the dawn, the timers shut off the outside floods as soon as I opened the door. No moonlight shone, and the sun stubbornly refused to rise.

"Chilly, isn't it?" I asked, jumping up and down in a show of warming up. In reality, the action helped make me more alert. After being strapped in a seated position for hours, I couldn't run. And even with George's kindly manner, I didn't trust him.

I often failed at spotting bad guys, so erring on the side of caution topped my to-do list. Bad enough that Gabriel tricked me. *Just because you're paranoid*, as the saying goes.

"Right over here at the nymphaeum," I said, arm extended to show the way.

But George had already started toward the spot. The newspaper article he read could have mentioned the pool, and he knew its location from my previous tour. It was perfectly reasonable for him to head in that direction.

However, the image of a man snapping a twig in the woods as he hid, ready to bash Sam or me over the head with a brick, played in my mind. But my Tour Guide persona wouldn't let that bother her.

A genuine bright smile graced my features, dredged up from the time I ended my first successful talk at the Roman Baths Museum. "Right this way," I said officially as I trailed behind.

"As you may be aware, the nymphaeum had several masters. Nymphs to start, then Christ, and at some point, nymphs made a comeback."

"Right," he said, assuming the role of expert.

The Tour Guide character needed to up her game.

"The chi rho stone moved—"

"And was used over at the bathhouse. I read the book."

George's sudden impatience confirmed my misgivings about him. He was searching for something, but I couldn't fathom what.

"What about the second stone?" he asked.

This question pulled my Tour Guide character up short. Me, as well. "What second stone?" I asked, curious.

Gabriel's warning about the cat surfaced in my thoughts, and I snapped back to my role.

"The one in the wall," he said.

Voice too gruff, my character said, "Sir, I'm sure I don't know what you're talking about." Quite proper for someone with her back story.

A delightfully mischievous smile appeared on George's face, and he said, "Is that so? Well, you never can tell about the things you hear. My mistake, my mistake." He flapped a hand toward the pool, inviting me to enter the enclosure before him.

The warning bells crescendoed. *Do not go near the little pool.* Not in the dark, not in the cold, not in a box, nor with a fox. Dr. Seuss's rhyming scheme brought a hysterical little giggle to my mouth, but I didn't let it out. A toothless grin that didn't reach my eyes didn't suit my character, and I gave a polite bow with my head.

"I've seen the area up close and personal. Please, you enjoy."

The little play we acted out began to fray around the edges, but I kept at it as I didn't have a backup plan. The show must go on, after all.

Marching straight to the tape we strapped up to keep tourists away from the dig, George dropped and stuck his hand toward the wall, shining a small flashlight around.

His composure slipped, and I heard him mutter, "Jill described it right here. The cow."

Thinking back to my first week at the site, I pictured the scene at the pub when we met the druids. George must have met her then.

Only Jill and Dion stayed behind to talk to the police about the charred heart on the lodge door.

How did George know the murder victim?

Chapter Twenty-Six: A Tomb-like Entrance

The sky finally brightened, cloudless and still. The storm's ferocity blew out, leaving a cold, sparkling winter day in its place.

Simon said he would be here bright and early, which left me with a decision. Should I wait for him or run away from George?

Waiting meant I'd need to stay in my Tour Guide character longer, and I suspected George didn't believe it. It also required Simon to walk unprepared into a life-threatening situation, endangering him as well.

Escaping, however, required agility I didn't currently possess.

While George continued to hunt for something Jill told him about, I took cautious steps away from the confines of the nymphaeum walls. With sunlight, the contours of the villa came into view, and in my mind, I built the ancient home in 3-D. Nothing as convenient as a hidden passage existed. The villa's builders wanted to show off their wealth and status, not hide it.

Turning to the dining room and west bathhouse, where the first mosaics were revealed, I contemplated the structure that preserved the site. There was no place to hide, and I didn't have a key to enter.

I longed for the Roman Baths Museum. Its twists and turns provided hiding places around every corner.

Curses emitted from George as he continued to search.

Spurred by the crack in his personality, I backed further away, casting about for safety.

In no shape to navigate the woods, I considered crawling on the roof of the National Trust building. But if I could get up there, so could he, and I didn't have anything to defend myself with.

Scritch, scratch, snick came the sound of a knife on stone.

Indignation roiled in me, crawling up my throat, begging to be released in a furious roar. *You're defacing ancient ruins, you heathen!* I screamed in my head, clamping my hand over my mouth.

Turning away so George didn't hear my labored breath through my fingers, I counted to ten, which helped a little. *Three point one four one five nine two six five three five eight...* Reciting the digits in pi in my head took more concentration, and I settled, able to think again.

The knife.

When I first saw it, my relief at being set free prevented me from making the proper connections.

When Edward gave me my Swiss Army tool, he emphasized it didn't have a blade. Blades, especially locking ones, were illegal in the UK.

George, not Jill, made the scratches I saw on the nymphaeum wall.

Poor Jill. She was obnoxious, noisy, and pushy, but she didn't deserve that death or my unkind thoughts.

Tremors shook my body as realization slammed into my gut.

Although turned to ashes in the wicker man, Jill was already dead when the fire started.

She had been stabbed in the back.

Stabbed by a hunting knife very like the one George used.

Playing a role to placate a possible suspect contrasted greatly with what I needed to do now.

I had to escape from a murderer.

Eyes bulging, I turned to the grounds.

There. Built into the end of the west bath house covering, a tomb-like entrance to a tunnel under the building gaped.

Scrambling to it, I crammed into the opening and smashed my body against a grate. The metal groaned, and I willed it to silence as it opened a crack.

The space hid me from view but provided no security. If I went into the tunnel, I could block the grate from him. However, if I moved it, the rusted creaks would draw George straight to me.

"Miss Maddie, you'll be interested in this." George's voice, pleasant, floated in my direction. Apparently, he still wanted to play our game. "A second chi…" He trailed off.

The genial personality convinced me, and my legs uncurled unconsciously, ready to head in his direction.

Stopping myself, I instead drew a circle with six petals inside, like the apotropaic in the Bath Abbey. Something to keep the demon away.

The differences between a con artist and a true sociopath became apparent. Gabriel enjoyed putting on a show, while George didn't seem to realize the changes in his personality.

"Maddie?" he called, curious. "You'll enjoy this. I promise you will."

Footsteps squelched through mud, back and forth as he looked for me.

I wouldn't stay hidden for long. Readying for the noise, I grasped the cold iron of the grate covering the tunnel and pushed. As I did, George let out an inhuman bellow, masking at least some of the sound I created.

Not knowing if he heard me, I needed to hide. I stuck my head into the dark, smelly opening.

And stopped.

Paralyzed, I couldn't do it. Couldn't go into the dark, not after what happened to me before. I couldn't willingly subject myself to entombment.

Heart pounding loud enough to block anything else, I stared into the abyss, breath coming in ragged gasps. Defying the frozen ground, sweat formed on my hands and forehead.

"Squeak. Squeak. Squeak," came a sound suspiciously like rats from inside the hole.

Still frozen in claustrophobic panic, I couldn't move backward to escape from the rodents I visualized as a swirling mass of scaly tails, claws, and jagged teeth.

Curling into a fetal position as the will to save myself seeped out of me, I chanted, "Not again, not again, not again." An unwelcome refrain, blocking helpful thoughts.

Ominous footsteps pounded, breaking my mind from its stone prison. Extending my head from the ball I'd formed into, I peeked around the corner.

A seven-foot-tall human stag towered over the grounds. A black robe swirled around its heavily booted feet, and a massive spread of antlers crowned the head.

Lifting his arms, George bellowed again.

Time stopped as the nerves in my fingers tingled painfully.

Dressed as an ancient Celtic priest, the druid mocked his connection with nature rather than embracing it. This stag wouldn't protect the forest creatures but kill them without mercy.

"Maddie!" His shout cut through my terror, spurring action.

Nowhere to run.

Only one place to hide.

"You can do it, McGuire," I whispered.

Shifting onto my hands and knees, I stuck my head in the rat-infested death trap.

A flutter and another squeak of protest. I convulsed, causing the grate to emit a rusted howl.

"Shh, shh," I begged it to be quiet.

The distraction dislodged a thought. Rats didn't flutter.

As my eyes adjusted, I focused on a tiny creature hanging from a crevice in the bricks. Less than two inches long, a bat complained about my disruption.

"Bats," I said in relief.

I cocked an ear and listened for more footsteps, my voice too loud.

Nothing.

Pulling my arms tight and smashing my eyes closed, I inched forward.

Rather than experiencing my current position, I focused on Arizona, with its dry air, and warm sand. And bats. Bats were good.

In Tempe, we had a bat house mounted under the eaves of our home. Every evening, bats, far larger than these little guys, swooped and squeaked, eating mosquitoes, white flies, and other nasty bugs.

I liked bats, but that didn't mean I wanted an angry one in my hair. Dropping to my belly, I army crawled further in the foul-smelling ooze until I could close the grate with my feet. It screeched in protest, but I had a barrier between me and Stag-George.

The tunnel opened higher further along, but I couldn't venture further into the unknown. Regretting not bringing my phone for its flashlight, I rolled over, effectively covering myself with a layer of icy slime, front and back. From my new vantage point, though, I could experience the outdoors, feel fresh air, and experience sunshine. The view kept the walls of my prison from closing in on me.

Relatively safe, I could do this. Focus on the light; wait for Simon.

A shadow fell across the opening, blocking my freedom, my hope, my sanity. Tears formed as my jaw clenched, and I fought to keep the sob from erupting.

George's face, flushed and crazed, came into view. "Ello, ducks," his kind, solicitous voice said as he showed me my printed mini-padlock. "Had a feeling this would come in handy. Very handy."

The lock slipped between a slat and the iron post cemented into the foundation, snapping shut. My metaphorical prison became a literal one.

The sobs, no longer held at bay, tore from my throat, but I stopped short of begging.

Since I seemed destined to share the cat's fate, I let curiosity drive me. "Why? What did Jill ever do to you?"

"The cow wanted this position so badly she turned to me to forge a letter for her." Flipping his robe up to expose jeans, he plopped onto the ground, apparently happy with the idea of storytelling. "I work in her tutor's office two days a week. Mostly filing and jobs too demeaning for educated blokes. They never caught on that I listened to every word, looking for my opportunity."

Incredulity broke into thoughts. What possessed these people to think that archaeology led to riches? "What possible opportunities could you find?"

"Falsify a few papers overstating the archaeological significance of an area, slip them to a nervous buyer so they pull out, and Bob's your uncle. Land for cheap, land for cheap."

"That's…" I almost said, "appalling," but didn't think it would help my situation. "Pretty smart. So, what was Jill supposed to do here? You couldn't think we'd discover anything."

"Not really. But she owed me one, you see, she owed me. My plan, making the druids cause such a fuss that the meadow would be deeded to us, had nothing to do with treasure. I could get my hands on the land from within the group and build on it. Worth a bundle, innit? It'd make right fine summer cottages it would."

Stupidly, I pointed out, "But there were no druids when Chedworth—"

Sudden fury sparked in his eyes, stilling my voice. He yelled, "Jill didn't tell me that, the worthless b—"

"Maybe she hadn't researched that," I shouted over his profane insults. Somehow, I thought Jill would object more to being called worthless than anything else.

Then, curiosity got the better of me. Again. "But why did you return today?" His story from earlier made sense then, but not now.

"An archaeological discovery can be worth a lot to the right people," he said, smiling affably while wiping spit off his chin. The antlers settled askew over one ear.

The sudden change reminded me of another person I'd encountered on my travels, and it turned my insides to ice.

George was crazy.

Heartfelt charm made it impossible not to like him. Friendly, sweet, the life of the party, all described this man who stabbed Jill in the back and burned her body in an ancient sacrifice.

One may smile, and smile and be a villain, I quoted Hamlet in my mind, hoping I survived long enough to tell my mom. She loved it when I referred to the Bard.

"Must be getting on, I'm afraid," George said as though we were sharing cocktails at a party. His face disappeared as he stood, and light trickled in as he walked away.

Waiting for the other shoe to drop, I listened for any sign of his return. The longer nothing happened, the more my teeth chattered. Cold settled into my bones as I considered his words. He must have believed in a second chi rho stone, and if he removed it, he could sell it.

As I propped up on my elbows, mossy moisture dripping off the back of my shirt, I wondered if he had defaced the wall by taking a brick. One marked with a chi for Christ. The discovery would be almost as thrilling as the coins.

My movement caused a chorus of little chirrups to erupt above me, but I kept still, and the bats stopped complaining.

"Bats are awesome," I told them for something to do while I waited for rescue. "I'm sorry to bother you, but I won't be here too much longer."

A single squeak answered me. I took it to mean, "Fine."

Distant grunting, followed by a crash, then a thud filtered into the tunnel, muted but menacing.

"He's still here," I warned the bats.

Concentrating, I concluded that the groans were George hauling something he dumped unceremoniously on the grounds. The clattering sounded metallic, almost like something electronic breaking.

As in breaking and entering. The image of him stomping and kicking the delicate 2000-year-old mosaics into dust chilled me more than the muck I wallowed in. Continuing to visualize my worst fear, I pulled myself up short.

Honestly, my worst fears included dark places, confined spaces, stabbing, and burning. The list went on. But as far as the Chedworth Roman Villa went, anyone defacing the place made my blood boil.

Another crash echoed into my chamber. A long pause, then another.

I pictured George with a tree branch taking swings at random, defiling the site and what had once been someone's home.

My teeth stopped chattering, and I wondered if a good, angry rant would warm me further. First, though, I checked for numbness associated with frostbite. Fingers and toes moved fine, and there was a hint of warmth in the soothing air.

Finally, I had a bit of luck. The sun's rays irradiated the earth, providing me with a small bit of comfort.

A sudden flurry of activity overhead caused me to drop onto my back, giving the bats room.

With cheeps and the beating of tiny leathery wings, they exited the tunnel in a dark mass.

I knew about Arizona bats, which only came out at dusk and night. Did English bats hunt during the day in winter? Unlikely.

More likely, they sensed danger.

Chapter Twenty-Seven: The Hypocaust

When a vaguely freaky thing gets freaked out, it clearly indicates that the situation has worsened. Always.

Pursued by a crazy guy dressed as a stag, locked into a wet, stinky, slimy tunnel inhabited by bats was terrible enough. Something even more horrific happened when the bats got agitated enough to flee.

But what? Maybe George's crashing about, disturbed the bats. Not so bad.

A drip of sweat fell from my forehead, which I pushed away with my sleeve.

My eyes rapidly adjusted to the dark, allowing me to see around. A foot further toward the Bath House, the floor rose, dry and goo-free. Careful to pick my way around discarded stones, some of which looked like the same material as the pilae, I appreciated the reprieve from the wetness.

Snap, swoosh.

The sounds stopped my heart for too long, recalling a terror I wanted to forget: spraying retardant on the flaming wicker man that encased Jill, the wood snapping, shifting, and collapsing into red-hot coals.

Fire, here.

Another snap.

Very close.

Laying out the floor plan of the building in my mind, I pictured the access points of the West Bath House. Half the floor was intact, showing off the intricate mosaic. The other half was missing, exposing the hypocaust that funneled warm air under the room to heat it.

A fire would be built at one end, and a passage to open air would draw the flames throughout the room's length.

A passage very like my current prison. Architecturally, the exact one, I confirmed, recalling the layout.

No wonder the bats left.

Wiggling away from the heat toward the open air, my clothes absorbed more gunk.

Hotter than I imagined, my shirt had already dried, leaving it stiff. Now, the cloth acted like a sponge, holding the chill against my skin. The sensation had already faded to coolness.

"It's getting hotter." Saying it out loud did nothing for my frayed composure.

Pulling both knees to my chest, I exploded straight, kicking the grate with all my might. Metal shrieked, but the 3-D filament of the padlock held strong.

My knees and ankles screamed in pain from the effort. I couldn't attempt it again.

If I had more time, I could wiggle the iron brackets loose from the stone. As I reached for it, a flicker of light danced on the wall.

No time.

As the hypocaust did its magic of directing heat, I gritted my teeth and coated my hair in the mossy sludge, protecting it from bursting into flames.

A temporary solution.

I had to block the fire. Even if it were to burn itself out soon, it sent flames dangerously close now.

"The pilae stones," I said, gasping as smoke crept toward me.

I counted to ten to avoid panicking, then counted in squares, which made me smile. Edward's collar number on his constable uniform was perfect squares backward, sixteen, nine, four, one. Absurd.

"Focus."

Gathering the loose stones and clay, I recalled Sam's lecture about flue stones. They were a barrier, with an opening for the heat to be directed upward to warm the floor above.

One by one, I stacked the debris between me and the hypocaust, creating as much of a curve as possible. The concave form acted like a funnel, guiding heat up.

Two full rows were completed, and the temperature had already diminished. My shoes no longer felt warm to the touch.

Encouraged, I slapped bricks and tiles on top of each other, not bothering to measure my movements.

A mistake.

One I wouldn't have made had I not been worried about burning to death. Unrelenting fear puts a damper on common sense.

All the pieces except my first two rows collapsed in a heap, and heat rushed toward my face.

After a justifiable sob or two, I worked more carefully. The structure grew as heat from the blaze reached it.

Fingers burning, I placed the last of my brick stash on the makeshift fire break. Unstable, but already directing flames away from me.

"Maddie?" an incredibly well-bred and cultured voice called.

"Simon," I croaked. Heat had dried my voice, vocal chords, and mouth. Impossible to shout. "Simon." Hoarsely whispering his name, I inspected the barrier a final time, then turned toward my prison's gate.

At least, I tried to turn. Moving took more time than expected as I blocked off the tall portion of the tunnel with the flue. Careful not to knock down my work, I pulled my knees in tight, and lift-spun in short bursts, much like when I moved the chair. A technique I had never used before today, but I could teach classes in it with my newfound expertise.

As I crawled toward the grate, I wracked my brain for something to make noise with. If I couldn't shout, I probably couldn't whistle either. Fortunately, noisy, rusted metal stood between me and my rescuers.

Blisters materialized on my fingers as I thrust them into the winter sunshine. Now that I could see them, they throbbed, pulsating pain with every heartbeat.

"Ow."

Attempting to ignore the pain, I grabbed the grate and rattled it. It didn't produce the echoing shrieks it made when I wanted to hide.

"Honestly?" I complained at it in a whisper.

Wriggling backward, I aimed a kick, reminding me that my ankles and knees had taken a lot of abuse.

My hands cupped, I tried clapping, but the muffled sound refused to carry.

With my nails, I untied one gloopy shoelace and pulled the shoe off my foot.

Yep, swollen. A problem I hoped to survive long enough to deal with.

The shoe, however, formed an excellent stick.

Whack, screech, whack, groan, whack, shriek. I used an unsteady rhythm, hitting my shoe on the grate.

"This way, Simon," Dolly's calm, cool, collected voice came my way.

"What's this?" Simon said. Instead of coming into life-saving view, I heard Simon on the phone. "Fire, yes. The Chedworth Roman Villa. Hurry."

Frustration boiled over, and I smacked my shoe into the grate like a two-year-old throwing a tantrum.

"Fire," I muttered, voice cracking. A good policeman and an ambulance sounded better to me. Smack, smack, smack.

The effort wore me out, and I rested my forehead against the bricks. With silence, I could hear Dolly's voice, more directive but as pleasant as ever. "Simon, please come at once. And call nine-nine-nine again. This time, ask for the police and an ambulance."

Finally, she bent over and looked for me in the tunnel. Her beautiful face transformed with a look of horror when she saw me. "Oh, my giddy aunt."

"Hi," I responded.

For once, at a loss for the perfect thing to say, she stammered, "Is that? Why are? Who did—"

"Help," I interrupted hoarsely.

With a subtle shake, she said, "Absolutely." Taking stock of the printed padlock, she asked, "Can this be cut with scissors?"

I shook my head. "Bolt cutters."

As she asked Simon to find something useful, I contemplated how far 3-D printed materials had come. The technology started as brittle novelties, but now printers existed that could build a house. Not useful, but better than thoughts of fiery doom.

"He's looking," Dolly said. "Can we pick it, do you think?"

Not comfortable sitting around waiting, Dolly built contingencies. Brilliant.

"Two thin prongs," I said, nodding and wanting to explain how the key looked like a hair pick missing teeth and that I had studied the contraption's inner workings. But I couldn't speak.

"Simon, hunt for skewers and bring Maddie water."

If I hadn't been a shriveled prune, I would have cried at her thoughtfulness.

A brick in my wall shifted, allowing a tendril of smoke to curl around me.

"We need to hurry," I attempted, but my voice cracked, and it came out "urry."

Rather than asking me to repeat myself, she mused, "What else can we use? Toothpicks would be too soft. Safety pins too small. Pens too big."

Her Goldilocks musing inspired a memory. Edward's gift of the Swiss Army tool bulged in my pocket.

Straightening my leg, I lifted my pocket as far as the encrusted, wet denim would allow, and jammed my blistered fingers into the pocket. Skin ripping, I ignored the shillings and pence, exploring by touch, until I landed on the lozenge of the tool.

Face scrunched in pain, I yanked. The abrasive action broke open pustules, jarring the utensil from my grasp with a plop.

It landed in one of the remaining pools on the tunnel floor. Gritting my teeth, I plunged my hand into the muck. Visualizing the plethora of viruses and bacteria that flowed into my open wounds, I relocated the Jetsetter tool.

Uselessly, I wiped in on my equally gunky shirt before handing it to Dolly.

Without a word, she turned it in every direction, pulling out the screwdriver, tiny scissors, and tweezers.

"These should work," she concluded.

I gave her a thumbs up, then flapped my hand toward the tool. "Other side" came out as "Hnn i."

Understanding my caveman style of communication, she located the toothpick.

Thus armed, she turned the 3-D printed padlock, located the keyhole, and looked at me.

Since I couldn't talk her through the lock-picking process, I chose to mime.

First, I used both hands to show imaginary picks in each. Then, I moved them forward and indicated an upward thrust. Next, one hand became the lock, the other a pick, and I indicated that a lever had to be depressed to open.

As she worked, another tile fell out of the wall that protected me from the fire.

How much wood had George piled? Impossible to find out, but I heard him make several crashing noises. If each was a pile of wood, he could make quite a bonfire.

Not wanting to stress Dolly as she worked the lock, I pulled into a tighter ball, closed my eyes, and whimpered.

Another brick, tile, stone, or whatever fell, causing a chain reaction. The barrier's structural integrity gave way, and flames searching for oxygen shot toward me.

Chapter Twenty-Eight: A New and Interesting Smell

"Why does this always happen to you?" Simon complained after having dragged me from a fiery tomb.

Staring up at the sky from my prone position, I considered thanking him for unceremoniously plucking me from the jaws of certain death.

As the collapsing wall consumed my attention, I hadn't heard Dolly's cry of triumph as the padlock clicked open nor Simon's arrival on the scene.

Now, I lay on my back in the muddy, dead grass and stared at puffy white clouds floating by as Simon wiped gunk off his hands.

Dolly handed me a lovely flask of tea. Grateful didn't cover it, but I couldn't gush at Simon without embarrassing him.

"It happened to you once," I retorted. "And her," I said, gesturing at Dolly.

"But always to you."

"I told you not to leave me here by myself. I might have even begged a little."

Ever the hostess, Dolly said, "We'll need to find a way to keep you safer, won't we, Simon?"

After a long gulp of tea, I said, "Thank you, Dolly. You were brilliant."

"I rather was, wasn't I?"

"Absolutely," I said, usurping her favorite word. She answered with delightful laughter.

"And what is that smell you're steeped in?"

While his voice sounded gruff, Simon's relief and affection were evident in every worried gaze he directed my way.

"Right? I'm disgusting." I wondered where I could change. And into what? "The lodge is a crime scene so no one should go in there. And check the nymphaeum. I think George stole a brick. Does anyone have a key to the Visitor Centre bathrooms? I can at least rinse off my hair."

With every movement, my formerly strawberry-blonde locks crackled with green slime. Every time I heard a snap, I worried that more of my hair had broken off.

No one responded about the key.

Propping up on my elbows, I looked at my saviors. "What?"

"I'm afraid," Dolly began.

"The Douglass wants to see you immediately."

Finally, I turned my attention from throbbing pain in every part of my body to the Chedworth Roman Villa grounds. Firemen put the conflagration out, local police cars blocked the parking lot, and the distant weeoo weeoo of an ambulance echoed.

"How long have I been here?" I asked, wondering how everyone had arrived so quickly.

"Well, you sort of passed out for a while. Not long," Dolly assured me quickly, to what must have been my panicked expression. "Forty minutes, maybe. But the lorry got stuck sideways on a lane trying to avoid traffic, and the ambulance had to go around the long way."

"Is the villa—?"

"Safe," Simon assured me. "The hypocaust actually did what it was designed to do. No fire touched the building."

"Such great news," I said before scowling at Simon. "Why did you call Douglass?"

Shaking his head and sneering to indicate my general level of idiocy, he said, "I didn't. The emergency services operator did."

"The wall?" I asked.

"A brick is missing, as you said. Do you know why?"

"Jill had discovered a second chi mark. It's what made her look for the treasure. George thought he could sell the brick."

Simon offered me a hand and then a silk handkerchief. It still cracked me up that he carried them.

"You sure?" I said, indicating the fine square of material.

"I'll burn it after."

Wiping my face, I trudged toward the room where Constable Meany-face Douglass awaited.

"Ugh!" he greeted me, waving a hand in front of his nose. "What is that stench?"

"Bat guano and primordial ooze. I'm probably infested with an appalling number of diseases. And you're the one who wanted to see me right away instead of giving me a chance to clean up. You can't possibly still think I have anything to do with this. A seven-foot-tall stag man tried to kill me, which, saying it like that, does sound a little unbelievable. George. The stag, George, with antlers. Remember him? Dressed as a Druid with antlers and a robe. He killed Jill. He told me. But Dion and Gabriel stole the coins and tied me to a chair, but they weren't the violent ones; George is because he tried to kill me, too. And burning—"

"Go," Douglass interrupted loudly as he ushered me out of the building, "talk to the ambulance technician." If he'd had a broom, he would have poked me with it.

"I need clothes and a shower, and the Hunting Lodge is a crime scene," I said as he hurried me toward the ambulance.

"What happened there?"

Two EMTs, or whatever he called them, ran up and efficiently fussed. "It's where Dion hid the coins; Gabriel retrieved them and tied me to a chair to keep me from getting help."

Douglass took one technician aside and said, "Get a SOCO over here. The clothes need to be bagged for evidence."

Shrugging at the thought, I supposed it made sense. The victim of two crimes in one evening, I'm sure my clothes picked up something important along the way.

"What am I supposed to wear?" I interrupted Douglass as he directed a local constable to cordon off the lodge.

The so-called SOCO, a man in white overalls, shower cap, and booties, came over. "We'll get you taken care of, pet," he told me in a round accent I didn't recognize.

As he scraped goo and muck from my hair, skin, and clothing, I asked, "Where are you from?"

"Newcastle. North of here."

"My dad likes your beer."

"Most do, pet," he said with a grin as he guided me toward the Visitor Centre bathrooms. Handing me oversized plastic bags for my clothes and a smaller packet with a set of overalls, he pointed to the door of the lady's room.

"Is it okay to wash?" I asked.

"Yes, I got what I needed from your skin and nails. Be careful of your burns, though. The water will sting."

Not heeding his advice, I turn the water on and thrust my hands underneath. "Aaaaaaaaagh!"

"Sting, did it? Y'alright?" I heard the SOCO ask through the door.

"Yes, and yes, and I promise never to ignore you again."

After setting my clothes in the provided bag, I turned to the sink again. This time, I stuck my head under the faucet until the green slime turned to mostly clear water. Thrusting my head under the loud and awkward air-blade style hand dryer knocked a lot of water out. At least my hair didn't drip after a minute of tornado-force winds.

"What's SOCO mean?" I yelled through the door as I pulled on the coveralls he gave me.

"Scene of Crime Officer," he called back. "We collect the forensic evidence before the detectives get here."

"Is this a Gloucester case or MCIT?" I asked, opening the door.

"It started local but is moving up in the world, I hear," he said, wrapping a wool blanket around me and escorting me to the medic team.

MCIT meant that my information about George killing Jill sunk into Douglass's brain and that he wasn't on site simply to annoy me. Hopefully,

DI Parikh would appear, and I could deal with a logical and kind person instead of Constable Grouchy-Face.

Speak of the devil, Douglass appeared at my side, trying to assert authority he didn't possess and get me back to interrogation.

Fortunately, the ambulance team intercepted me.

"Sorry, luv, these burns need looking after," a medic said, taking my wrists.

"Ow," I said.

Letting go she gently rested my wrist on hers and lifted the coverall's elastic band. "Where did these abrasions come from?"

"Zip ties," I said. "It's been a rough day."

She raised her eyebrows but refrained from commenting.

Another round of cleaning involved medieval torture in the form of antiseptic. As the technician gently dabbed, I considered confessing to any number of crimes.

She redeemed herself with the burn salve, turning my pulsating blisters into cool lumps I could almost forget. Until the bandages went on. Covering my wrists, fingers, and ankles, the white gauze quickly turned me into a skinny marshmallow.

"Y'alright?" a familiar Scottish burr inquired.

"Edward!" With the intention of flying into his arms, I bounced onto my feet, shooting needles of pain into my swollen ankles and knees.

In the nick of time, the ambulance tech caught me gently around the waist and sat me back on the bumper of her truck.

"Sorry," I muttered.

"We will need covers for those bandages," she said, adding medical tape to protect the fabric. "There. Now when you fall over, your wounds will stay clean."

Embarrassed, I said, "You're strong."

"Helps to keep bolters in place," she said with a smile, then helped me stand. After an injection of something for pain, she dismissed me.

Edward took over, supporting me, and kissed me on the forehead.

"I thought you were undercover and wouldn't be able to be here," I said, grateful at his miraculous appearance.

"I'm beginning to develop a sixth sense when it comes to you being in danger. It goes off a lot."

"Not my fault," I told him.

"Never is."

"Is DI Parikh coming? I know who murdered Jill."

"The manhunt has started. Douglass went to Far Peak, APW went out, and—"

"All points what?"

"What?

"What's an APW? I expected you to say APB or All Points Bulletin."

"Similar. All Ports Warning, so the fellow doesn't leave the isle."

With a sigh, I confessed, "I'm never going to get what's going on in this country."

"You're alright," Edward said with another kiss. "Fancy a cup of coffee?"

Shaking my head, I said, "I'd rather have coffee. Wait. What?" Everyone always offered tea, but sometimes a dark roast brimming with caffeine hit the spot.

"Come on."

He gently and slowly took my blanket and bandage-wrapped form to the Visitor Centre, and installed me at a table. He then produced an American-sized coffee flask and poured me a cup.

Subtle hints of hazelnut complimented a dark coffee with chocolate undertones.

"This is an excellent cup of coffee," I told him.

"Only the best for my lassie."

Safe, warm, and pleasantly numb from whatever the technician gave me, exhaustion asserted itself. My eyes fought to stay open, and my head lolled. The moment sleep took over, I dreamed of being engulfed in flames. My leg jerked uncontrollably, and I kicked a table leg, waking me up.

Dolly and Simon joined our company and rushed to my side while Edward spoke into his cell.

"When can she go home? The poor girl is absolutely knackered," Dolly asked. A guardian angel, that one.

We looked to Edward, who held up a finger to indicate one moment. After several, he hung up. "I can take you home now, lassie, but you'll need to talk to Parikh and Douglass tomorrow. They need the information on the coin."

Barely able to hold my head up, I nodded in what could have been construed as agreement.

What coin? I wanted to ask as sleep overtook me.

Chapter Twenty-Nine: One Coin

Disoriented, I rubbed at sleepy eyes with a baseball mitt.

"Wha?" I said, unable to complete the word over a thick tongue.

Scrunching my eyes tight and opening them a few times allowed me to take in my surroundings: lace curtains, a bed nestled into bookshelves, and a desk in the corner.

Home, safe in my very own princess tower at the Priestlys'. Good.

An attempt to run my fingers through my hair failed, and my attention shifted. My hands bulged with gauze and tape.

"Oh, yeah."

Before going downstairs, I put the electric kettle on in my room and made a cup of cocoa for a little sweetness to chase away the effects of the pain medicine. Using both hands, I cradled the mug and sipped.

The sugar hit my system like electricity, waking up every sense. Two prevailed: pain in my fingers and hunger. Turning back to my desk, I smiled at a glass of water with two ibuprofen tablets beside it. Meryl must have put them there when I got home.

After taking them, I pulled on a robe, finished my drinking chocolate, and headed downstairs.

Another storm moved into Bath. Thick, gray clouds laden with moisture spit slushy snow at the house.

As I pushed open the kitchen door, I shuddered at the cold. Empty, with no evidence of Meryl's freshly baked bread or Roger's famous scrambled eggs.

Probably at work, I thought, having completely forgotten the date.

The breadbox still had a partial loaf from earlier in the week. I picked up the serrated bread knife, dropped it, and glared at it. The bandages didn't allow my fingers to bend enough for a proper grip.

My stomach was in no mood for problem-solving. Gracelessly, I grabbed the bread with both mitts and took a bite like a barbarian. Rude if I planned to leave the bread behind, but I didn't. Stomach rumbling like a freight train, I couldn't remember the last time I ate.

The front door jiggled and then slammed open.

"That wind!" Meryl said.

"It'll be worth it," Roger promised, pushing into the kitchen, arms laden with food.

His eyes grew wide when he saw me.

"Uh," I said, pawing crumbs from my chin as I placed the bread on the counter, thought better of it, put it in the bread box, realized my germs covered it, yanked it out, and hugged the loaf to my chest. Like a crazy person. "Hungry."

"We thought you might be, lassie," Edward said, entering the kitchen with more bags brimming with goodies.

That's when I remembered my hair had not only not been brushed but had, in fact, been mauled by my clumsy hands.

"Uh." Eloquence personified.

Meryl must have seen my look of embarrassed horror as she took over the situation. Sweeping me upstairs, she brushed my hair and picked out clothes with no buttons.

We returned downstairs once I approximated the appearance of a sane, twenty-first-century woman and not something akin to a werewolf.

The men had covered the dining room table with small plates of finger foods.

"A feast for the day," Roger said, extending an arm to invite us to eat. "No cooking required, and food is waiting whenever anyone is a bit peckish."

"Silly, really," Meryl said. "I could have made most of this."

"Of course you could," Roger agreed, "and it would taste better. But after all those cinnamon rolls and Christmas dinner, you deserved a break."

They embraced, and I longed to hug Edward, but not enough to keep from stuffing an oatcake with marmalade into my face. Luckily, Edward knew better than to come between me and food, and he waited until I finished the cake, then a handful of almonds and dried apricots, before he approached.

"I cannae tell ya how sorry I am that my phone was off."

Squeezing him, I said, "It wouldn't have mattered. Gabriel took the SIM card out of my cell specifically so I couldn't warn you."

The Priestlys joined us, and we nibbled and chatted about inconsequential things. Eventually, Roger addressed Edward. "I never get to say this in a non-metaphorical way, but where was the fire you rushed off to?"

So much had happened since Christmas Day, I hadn't heard anything about what Edward and DI Parikh found either. I looked at him expectantly.

Laughing at my expression, he said, "I cannae believe you're curious. Dangerous that."

Gabriel had said something similar. Rather than mentioning that, I said, "It makes me a good researcher." But didn't add that Tori directed most of my research for me.

"An empty warehouse, so no one got hurt," Edward began. "Looked like arson."

"Was it insured for quite a bit?" Roger asked.

"Something like that," Edward answered vaguely.

Edward hadn't confided in Roger that he and the DI had systematically dismantled a drug operation, effectively stopping distribution. My guess, the fire destroyed evidenced linked to the kingpin, if that's what they were called in Britain, and probably a fair amount of product.

When we finished our meal, Edward gave me a look.

I knew that look.

I wished I didn't.

"I have to talk to Parikh now, don't I?"

"Aye."

Refraining from saying "Fine," I harrumphed.

"Get the gauze changed and have your burns looked at," Meryl said as we left, handing me a note with the address of a medical clinic near the church.

"Do we have to go to Keynsham?" Most police stations in the UK were centralized for efficiency. A small town a few miles away housed Bath's station house.

"Nae. Parikh is here," Edward answered, opening the door of the SmartCar he borrowed from a mate's mum.

"And who is the mystery friend with the car? When do I meet him?" Considering why I hadn't met them yet, I added, "Or her?"

"How do you know you haven't?"

"Because," I paused, wondering about the various people I'd seen Edward around. "Have I?"

A twinkle in his eye matched his mischievous smile.

"That's not an answer."

"Let's get those bandages changed first," he said, pulling into the public car park by Roger's church, another church, the medical office, and, conveniently, the police. The One Stop housed not only on-duty police constables but also tourist information and city offices.

As we stepped into the doctor's office, Edward pulled rank, something I never saw him do. "This woman needs bandages changed, and I need to move her quickly." A flash of his MCIT badge and I walked straight ahead of the line.

The doctor smirked at my marshmallow-looking hands.

"The ambulance technician wanted to make sure I didn't get anything dirty. It had been a rough morning."

She and Edward exchanged a nod, but she didn't say anything until my fingers were cleaned and redressed.

"Use this ointment," she said, handing me a paper bag with extra gauze and a yellow tube, "and change the dressings every morning. They're healing fine."

After thanking her, we entered the One Stop building. Edward guided me to the back corner by the constables. An electric lock buzzed, and he ushered me to a back room with a kettle and snacks.

DI Parikh sat at a table, cleaning his wireframe glasses.

"What a relief to see you," I said.

His mouth twitched in the briefest of smiles, and he covered it by replacing his glasses on his narrow nose.

"As expected, you have had quite an adventure," he said as Edward pulled out a chair for me to sit on.

"Adventure isn't my word for it."

"How did you come to be alone at Chedworth?"

"Wait," I said, then pulled out my phone and emailed him the notes Edward asked me to take, plus a picture of the timeline Simon and I created. "I kept track of everything suspicious. It might help."

He nodded his thanks, then asked me to start with being alone at Chedworth

Launching into an unnecessarily long and vaguely bitter account of Simon abandoning me, I noted the detective inspector stopped taking notes. He actually checked his phone a couple of times.

Meanwhile, Edward prowled behind me. To see him, I craned my head around and raised both eyebrows. He checked his phone, too.

Since nobody seemed to pay much attention anyway, I covered Gabriel's appearance with no fanfare.

Before I could mention the coin, Edward answered a vibrating phone and exited the room.

Parikh said, "Continue," but he stared fixedly at the door Edward left through.

It opened, and Edward said, "We may have him, sir."

They departed without another word.

The two men looked intense. Since I'd be stuck waiting for them to return for a long time, I needed entertainment. Despite my sleeker bandages, it took my total concentration to pull my phone out of my jacket pocket.

When the door opened a few minutes later, I said, "That was fast," before looking up.

Constable Meany-Face-Douglass entered carrying an evidence bag.

"How long have you been in league with the Frenchmen?" he asked, skipping niceties that normal humans would use.

Twit.

"Still? You still think I'm guilty?"

"Evidence points that you are clear of Jill's murder."

"Of course I am," I barked. The statement was so ridiculous that it held no relief. "Listen to me. I am clear of everything. All of it. One hundred percent."

"We shall see," he said, sounding more pompous than ominous.

"What makes you think I have anything to do with any of this?"

Douglass placed an evidence bag on the table and pushed it toward me. Gold gleamed through the plastic.

An aureus.

"OMG, you found the missing coins! Did you catch Dion?" After too long of a pause, I added, "Or Gabriel? Where were they? How did you do it?"

Overlooking Douglass's sour expression, I pushed the coin back to him to expose the emperor as I explained its value. "Emperor Aurelius only served for about five years, so not many coins would have been made, and most of those were out of bronze. These gold ones—"

"Ms. McGuire," he interrupted, a nasty habit he needed to curb. "Where did you get this coin?"

I blinked several times. "You handed it to me."

He responded with an epic, long-suffering sigh worthy of a thirteen-year-old girl.

"What?"

"We found the coin in the pocket of your jeans."

More blinking as I processed his words.

No good. It still didn't make sense.

"Wait, what?"

"The jeans encrusted with," he paused, flipped through some notes, and continued, "primordial ooze, as you put it. In said pocket of said jeans—"

"Stop saying said," popped out of my mouth before I could stop it.

"In said pocket of said jeans," he repeated, rather peevishly, I thought, "were a Swiss Army knife, a hair tie, two shillings, and a priceless gold coin."

"Not a knife. No blade. Edward gave it to me. It saved me."

Eyebrows knit together as he said, "Explain."

"Well, the half-scale 3-D printed padlock had two levers inside that must be depressed to bypass the key. This little tool had a toothpick and tweezers that were just the right size."

"Not," he growled, "the lock. The coin."

"Ooooooh," I said, exaggerating the word. If he treated me like a criminal, there was no reason not to act like one. "No idea."

"I find that hard to believe."

"True, though." Which, actually, it was. I had no idea how the coin got there. Last I saw, Gabriel slipped both into a velvet bag. Douglass needed to be civil before I cooperated by revealing that information.

"You mean to tell me that the coin magically appeared in your pocket?"

Magic.

No matter how much I didn't want to help Douglass, I wanted to solve the puzzle.

"Gabriel," I said, "did magic, pulling the coin out of my ear."

"You didn't mention Gabriel before. Why did you choose to keep this information from me."

Unable to stop glaring, I said, "I told Detective Inspector Parikh before he left."

"But not me."

"When, exactly, did I have time for that? Pinpoint it for me. Go on. Spell it out. Did I have time during your delightful greeting? Or your open-ended questions about my experience? Hmm?"

Yes, okay, not the best response to a cop, but the guy pushed my buttons.

Uncharacteristically, he ignored my outburst and said, "What about Gabriel?"

Petulance kept me from revealing Gabriel's real name, Harold. "As I told the detective inspector," I said, employing Parikh's full title again to put Douglass in his place, "Simon Pacock left me at the Hunting Lodge to attend a function in a nearby village." Not too much detail, because I didn't want Douglass to use the aristocracy connection against me. At least I listened to that much of Tori's admonishment to lay low.

"Why were you at the lodge on Boxing Day?"

"We went through press photos of the day to find when the coins were taken."

"Photos?"

"Yes, press photos. We saw Dion, one of the fake Frenchmen. He dyed his hair, but we recognized him. Anyway, he hid the coins in the lodge in case he got stopped on the way out. Gabriel picked them up on Boxing Day since the lodge should have been empty. Only Simon left me there alone."

"And Gabriel performed magic tricks?"

Skepticism dripped from his words, and I didn't blame him this time.

"Well, yeah. Showing off, I think." Sam had found out that Dion and Gabriel were both pickpockets. Gabriel could have slipped the coin into my pocket during that goodbye kiss, and I wouldn't have known. I was understandably distracted.

"Finds you fit, does he?"

Temper flaring, mostly out of guilt about the kiss, I reigned in my first admittedly inappropriate response and answered coolly, "I do not presume to know the minds of others."

"Well, that's one thing you don't presume to know, then."

Any hint of cool fled. "How dare you," I said, slamming my palm into the table, forgetting my wounds. "Ow." Tears stung my eyes in response to thrumming pain.

"Let's try this from a different angle, shall we?"

Like I had a choice.

Cradling my hand to my chest, I ignored his next few words.

"Ms. McGuire." His nasal tone cut through the pain.

"What?"

"Answer the question."

"What question?" Again, not the best approach to take with an officer of the law, but my fingers hurt. And he was mean.

"Why would the French imposter leave the coin with you?"

To be fair, it was a good question. One I'd like the answer to. Not that I wanted Douglass to feel justified in asking. "How would I know?"

"Speculate," he suggested.

"Oh no. You hold that against me."

His attempted smile looked like a grimace. "Believe it or not, we are on the same side here. We both want the coins back."

Well, I got one. You get the other, came to mind but I did not say it out loud. I can be trained.

"The only thing I can think is that Gabriel felt guilty and left the coin with me because he knew I would return it." Guilty, or he didn't want me to get into trouble. Everyone noticed that Douglass had it out for me. If Gabriel thought I might get thrown in jail for helping him, giving me the coin would guarantee my safety.

The enormity of his sacrifice hit me. Gabriel's eyes had locked onto the gold like a lifeline. He asked what it was worth, and I told him thousands of pounds, possibly tens of thousands. And he left it with me.

A waving hand appeared in front of my face. Douglass, getting my attention.

"Huh?"

"Why wouldn't guilt make him leave both coins?"

Shrugging, I said, "Only one was his to give away. The other one belonged to Dion."

"'Belonged' is a stretch."

"Agreed. But Gabriel had a strong sense of honor among thieves, I guess. He didn't give anything away about his partner."

Douglass steepled his fingers, turning him into an evil overlord. "And why didn't you turn the coin over when you found it?"

"Wha, why, how dare you?" Never in my life have I used that phrase so often. "Have you not paid any attention to anything that happened to me? A crazy man dressed as a Druidic priest tried to kill me. I obviously didn't feel the coin in my pocket."

"Really?" The skepticism returned.

"First off, didn't you say you found it in the same pocket as my Jetsetter tool?"

He nodded.

"No way I would do that. Gold is soft, and putting it next to anything metal could have damaged it. I'm here to preserve Roman antiquities."

"Perhaps."

"And secondly, why would I hand you my jeans if I wanted to keep it a secret?"

"You are wily."

Unable to stop, I burst out laughing, which became a coughing fit. Leftover smoke haunted my lungs. "Wily?" I choked. "Who says that?"

Instead of joining in my mirth, Douglass stood, shut his notebook, and left me alone.

Alone with my very conflicted thoughts.

Chapter Thirty: Dr. Daniels

A short time later, one of the officers who manned the desk came in. "Sorry to keep you waiting, miss. You're free to go."

"Thank you," I said and smiled in an attempt to appear innocent. Not that I had anything to look guilty about, I reminded myself. It's not like I bullied Gabriel into leaving the coin with me. Or used my wily ways.

And it's also not like I purposefully kept information from the police. Except his name is Harold, but that won't be much help. I didn't have a last name.

You have the name of a pub, my inner voice, which sounded like my mother, reminded me.

Still, there must be dozens of pubs with that name. Besides, no one asked if I knew his location.

"Y'alright?" Edward's voice sounded in my ear, and I screamed.

"Sorry! Sorry. Deep in thought." I shook my head to clear it before asking, "Did you catch him? I'm guessing not, or you wouldn't be here."

Squeezing my shoulders, he said, "Brilliant, you are. Either false information, or he did a runner before we arrived. Disappointing, but I'm proud of how much of his empire we destroyed. He'll think twice about setting up shop in Bath again."

I wrapped my arms around him. "Fantastic result for your first MCIT case."

"That it was." Proudly surveying the city, he helped make safe, he said, "I take it Douglass didn't arrest you."

"The coin surprised me as much as it did all of you," I said. "I'm still baffled."

"You underestimate your charms," he commented with a kiss on my cheek. Before I could protest, he added, "If you and Simon weren't so honest, no one would have deduced the substitution. At least now, reputable dealers will avoid them or notify us."

"I wonder how mad Dion will be when he finds out what Gabriel did."

"That's a conversation I'd like to hear."

At the steps of the Roman Baths, Edward and I maneuvered around the line of tourists and ducked inside. "I'll leave you to it," he said, slipping back outside.

What exactly "it" was, I couldn't guess. Maybe my future.

Now that I had completed the work to protect Chedworth Roman Villa for the winter, discovered gold coins, reported two missing, and recovered one, I didn't know how much longer I'd be welcome in the country.

In the Oversight Office, I discovered Lady Vivian perched at Sam's desk.

"I'm glad to see you," I said by way of greeting, preferring not to have to figure out her proper form of address. Unable to stop myself from an awkward partial curtsy, I quickly sat.

And waited.

One does not pounce on a lady with undue questions.

Placing the cap on her Mont Blanc pen, she carefully laid it next to her notepad. The subtle scent of roses wafted toward me.

"Would you prefer to be put on tours or go back to sifting for the next two weeks?"

My heart sank. Two weeks, when my internship ended. In three weeks, I'd be in the US. A myriad of questions swirled in my brain, every other one relating to Edward.

"Don't pout, girl. It's a simple enough question," Lady Vivian interrupted my downward spiral.

"I—"

The door opened, interrupting my answer. And my questions. Like, should I ask to be extended? Maybe staying required an official request on my part.

"What, what?" Dr. Daniels said, catching sight of me.

Back straight, I tried not to resemble a beleaguered kitten in front of the eminent archaeologist.

"I heard you had a spot of trouble at Chedworth."

"Nothing I couldn't handle, sir," I said, hiding my bandaged hands that stuck out like, well, a sore thumb. "I'm ready to get to work for you."

"Perhaps," he said in an infuriatingly vague response.

"We could help with the tours, actually," Lady Vivian responded. "That Drake person left," she said, conveying a level of disdain akin to running away with the circus.

"Shakespeare," I provided.

"Yes, well, be that as it may, we're down a Roman guard."

"I could do that," I said in direct contradiction to history. "Well, not a guard, but I could take on a role if you needed me to."

"Have you any acting ability?"

"You should have seen me with…" I couldn't finish the sentence. The persona I adopted with George the Murderer kept me alive but not out of danger.

Black dots danced before my eyes as my brain played a soundtrack of burning wood.

Roses and kindness enveloped me as Lady Vivian hugged. One penetrating stare later, she must have decided I wouldn't faint and stepped back behind the desk.

"I'll add you to the schedule for tours tomorrow, and then we shall see what happens next."

"Thank you," I responded to the dismissal and left.

My ankles and knees still throbbed, but the clear sky and calm wind convinced me to walk up the hill to Ash Tree Cottage.

Replaying every bit of the conversation with Lady Vivian and Dr. Daniels on an endless loop, I searched for nuances that indicated they wanted me to stay.

Whenever I thought I hit on something, the nagging voice reminded me that I hadn't told anyone I wanted to stay. Obvious to me, but maybe I needed to say something.

Had it been obvious? There were moments when I wanted to be home so badly that I didn't care. Did anyone at the museum pick up my misgivings? Edward had, and took me to the Thermae Spa, the perfect remedy for my doubt.

And where was Sam? She didn't make me nearly as nervous as Lady Vivian. I could have asked her.

"Ask her," I said out loud as I crossed through Bear Flats and smiled at the polar bear on a bar roof.

Yes, ask her. And cc Lady Vivian. When I got back to my room, I would shoot off an email to both, formally requesting an extension of my internship or approval of a student work visa so that I could stay on at the Baths.

Somehow, I needed to include Dr. Daniels in my request, too.

Stumbling on the curb to Greenway Lane, I used my hand to steady myself on the stone wall that lined the street.

Wrapped up in my plan's excitement, I stopped paying attention to my surroundings. Since I made it to Greenway Lane, I didn't feel the need to change that.

In my formal request, I could also ask that if the Baths didn't have a position, I would be honored to be added to Dr. Daniel's team.

The gate to the cottage lay open, and I pushed it, still deep in thought.

"As a volunteer, even. Could I get a visa for that?" I asked aloud.

"That a mystery it is, it is," a male voice said, freezing me to my spot on the second step.

George the Druid, dressed in a proper tweed jacket, blond curls bobbing cheerfully, smiled at me. Friendly, sweet, psychotic, sociopathic George. With Roddy.

The impulse to turn, go up one step, and bolt shuddered through me, but I stayed still.

I couldn't leave George with the rabbit.

Holding the struggling bunny by his ears, George's hunting knife aimed at Roderick's midsection.

Chapter Thirty-One: Roderick

"Roddy," I said, voice trembling. "Don't hurt him. Please."

The mad druid held the rabbit, like an expert who could gut the creature in one swipe.

"You left before I could show you Jill's discovery; you did." His serene, inviting smile contained the slightest hint of hurt at my rude betrayal.

"I didn't…" I began, but my vocal cords couldn't produce sound. Paralyzed by fear for the rabbit, I had to shut my eyes to regain my voice.

A couple of deep breaths took me back to the conversation we had while I looked for escape at Chedworth.

"Another chi rho stone," I said, relieved I could remember. Glancing toward the house, I saw no indication that George had been inside. Praying he hadn't, I squinted, hoping for some indication that the Priestlys were safe. That they hadn't suffered the same fate as Roddy.

George's gaze shifted to the house, and I took the third stair down toward him to keep his attention focused on me. I didn't want him to find Meryl and Roger if he hadn't.

"How did Jill find it?" I asked, my voice loud to draw his attention.

"Dumb luck, much like everything about the girl."

Jill had been many things, but not dumb. Obviously, her manners needed work. But I wondered how often she'd been overlooked or stepped on to form that abrasive personality. If she had had a mentor like Sam from the beginning of her career, her fate would have changed for the better.

"The mark, chi as you say, the one that looks like an X."

He waited, and I nodded my agreement.

Roddy's legs kicked twice, but George merely moved the tiring animal further from his body. The bunny went limp.

"The Romans etched the chi at an angle, more like a lowercase 't.' Jill convinced me it pointed to something important."

"Boy, was she right," I said, trying to sound interested and non-threatening. My concern for Roddy's safety overrode everything else in my brain.

Roddy offered me comfort when I arrived in England. The Priestlys were on a cruise, but Roderick the Rabbit welcomed me to their home.

Granted, his rampant nibbling uncovered a gruesome threat on my doorstep, but I didn't hold it against him.

"What did it look like?" I asked, hoping George would set the rabbit down to demonstrate.

"It looked," his jovial voice broke as he growled, "like a 't!' Just said that, didn't I?"

The buck knife brushed against Roddy's soft black and white fur.

"I meant," I practically screeched in panic, "where in the wall? I checked the other bricks along the bottom."

The smile returned, relaxed.

"Two bricks up, innit? Pointing the way to the treasure below."

He folded his legs with agile grace and sat crisscrossed on the frozen ground. Placing Roddy across his knees, George repositioned the knife at the base of the bunny's skull.

Roddy, who knew a thing or two about danger, lay perfectly still, eyes wide. Silently, I vowed to rescue him.

Continuing his story, George said, "It seems she cleaned some moss with particular vigor. That girl was nothing if not tenacious, was Jill. A, what did she call it now, a veneer of plaster broke off, revealing the symbol."

It was a discovery of a lifetime, and she didn't feel she could share it with the rest of us. A pang of guilt that I didn't do more to make her a friend shook me.

"Poor Jill," I muttered, sad for my former roommate.

"What's that?"

"Why did she tell you? I mean," I added quickly, not wanting to set him off again, "You were her patron, sort of, but she could have kept it to herself."

Pointing the knife at me, he said, "Astute. She instituted a change of plans, convincing me of untold riches, that I'd make far more than on a real estate deal."

"That makes sense," I said, lowering to a seated position on the steps by the gate. Conversational, non-threatening, friendly. "She was right about that, too."

Like my conversation with Douglass, I couldn't help antagonistic phrases from leaping out of my face.

Guilt, the little voice in my mind said.

"I don't think Jill meant to double-cross you," I said, hoping to conjure a hint of guilt in George. Cold seeped into my jeans, but I stayed still, hoping to appear relaxed and conversational.

"Is that right?"

"Well, she didn't tell the team what she had found, and if she had, she would have gotten all the credit. It would have made her career forever." An exaggeration on my part as I discovered the gold, and no one leaped to offer me jobs. Or internships. Or visas.

"But she told you," I continued, stamping down my disappointment so I could rescue Roddy. And me. "Jill must have considered you a partner."

"Good try, me ducks, but she didn't act like it."

"You weren't there, though!" I said, excited to have some proof to provide. "The night we met you, she wanted everyone out of the lodge so she could talk to the police alone. Dion made her furious by staying. She wanted you there for the big announcement." Not only did this idea ring true, it painted Jill in a pleasant light.

It struck me that I often spun stories for others, usually negative. Tori's boyfriend, Scott, got the brunt of it through high school. Then Simon and Edward when I first arrived in England. And poor Dolly. The things I attributed to her, bordered on evil.

"Once she found the gold, I'm sure she would have shared it with you."

A movement flickered near the base of the garden wall that bordered the ravine. Concentrating on George, I floundered for something to say to keep him talking. He seemed to be contemplating my assessment of Jill, but if I was right, he killed her for no reason, and that tidbit might spark another fit.

"Rabbits make a fine meal, fine meal," he said, brushing Roddy with the hand that held the hunting knife. "Nice and juicy, this one. Perfect for lapin a la cocotte."

My almost non-existent understanding of French didn't dampen the threat to put Roddy in a stew.

A whimper escaped my throat, causing George to smile.

"It's why you never name animals. Makes it harder to skin them."

Refusing to take my eyes off George, I watched motion from my peripheral vision. Roger approached Roddy's enclosure, trying to get close enough to George to do something. Silent for such a tall man.

He was also a kind man. If he were faced with a knife, I doubted his ability to leap in and save the bunny. This meant he required the element of surprise, so I had to keep George focused on me.

Without much of a plan, I stood and said, "It's cold sitting on the cement."

At least, I intended to say that. What came out was, "It's cold, sitting—whoa, crap, help, stuck," as I crumpled on numb and swollen feet.

From my prone position on the garden path's stepping stones, I added, "Ow."

What started as an obvious ploy to distract George succeeded through no invention of my own. However, the act put me in considerable danger.

Standing over me, knife in one hand and Roddy in the other, George let loose with an inhuman howl.

Chapter Thirty-Two: Not Quite Cricket

The bellowing, knife-wielding man immobilized me with terror. Unable to roll out of his path, I stared into his manic face.

Roger's sneaking didn't make it in time, plus I didn't want him in danger anyway.

George stood close enough for me to land a good kick, but the hunting knife would take out the bunny. I couldn't risk it.

Unfamiliar hopelessness settled over me. Nothing I did mattered. I failed at protecting the sweet, fluffy bunny, my wonderful landlords, and me. Shutting my eyes, I gave up, expecting the point of the knife at my neck any moment.

You can do it, Pumpkin, my dad's voice played in my mind. *You can do anything. Always could.*

Two things struck simultaneously. One, usually my mom's voice haunted my subconscious, and two, yeah, Dad was right.

My eyes flew open. I rolled, tucked my knees, and shot both feet toward George's privates. I missed the mark, but my blow caused the knife to clatter to the cement.

Furious, George roared again, lifting Roddy over his head, readying a mighty throw. I cocked my knees. If he tossed that rabbit, I would do anything to catch it. But first, I needed to take down George.

This time, I aimed my aching feet at his shins, and he doubled over, dropping Roddy in the process.

Aiming at George's face, I struck again, but he snatched my ankle in his hand, lightning-fast.

With a mighty jerk, he snapped my leg, and I heard a pop in my knee as my head clunked into the cement.

Dizzy, I clutched at the ground, coming away with a handful of dead twigs as George's anger-fueled strength dragged me.

A high-pitched scream split the air, and it took me a moment to realize it came from me. The pain from my knee caught up to my nervous system. Flailing, no inspiration came to me as George reached for the knife with his free hand.

Bonk.

George collapsed beside me.

I thought at first that agony played tricks with my vision. "What?"

Free of threat, Roderick hopped over my prone form and shakily went to Roger.

Dropping the spade he used to clunk George on the head; Roger scooped the rabbit into his arms.

He knelt beside me and said, "No one threatens my rabbit." He stroked Roddy's long ears, once, twice, then set the bunny down and checked me.

"I heard the pop. You've either got a bad knee sprain or a torn ACL. I've heard it before at a rugby match."

"It hurts," I said pointlessly as the crying and screaming indicated it.

Unbelievably, Meryl arrived with zip ties. "Will these do?"

Blinking back tears, I realized Meryl arrived ready to bind the man who threatened her pet and tenant.

"Very well," I said from experience, marveling at the calmness with which the couple handled the situation.

Stringing two plastic ties together, she made a loop and worked it over his feet. "I'm afraid I only brought two," she said apologetically. Like it was her fault that a crazy man attacked me and her rabbit, and she wasn't prepared to subdue and detain him.

"That's okay, but we need to do something about his arms," I said, lifting my hands in a shrug. My thick, gauze-covered hands.

After unwinding the bandages, I tied each piece together and crawled toward George. Roger stopped me, handed the bunny to Meryl, and then bound George's hands himself—tightly, from the sound of the man's grunt.

I managed a smile even with the persistent pulsating in my knee. "Did you call nine-nine-nine?" I asked.

"Well," Meryl said, nuzzling the rabbit's fur, "I wasn't entirely sure what I would say. A man holding a knife on my bunny sounded a bit like a crank call."

True, but my habit of shielding the Priestlys from the things I encountered landed them with a murderer in their front garden. They could have been seriously hurt. Or worse.

"What have you got yourself there?" a Scottish burr asked.

"So we called dear Edward," Meryl added.

With a hop and a step, he knelt by my side, and I wrapped my arms around him. "George," I told him. "A druid, but not really because he only joined to steal land. He killed Jill."

"So sorry, but did you say he killed someone?" Roger asked, his composure finally breaking.

"I need to be more forthcoming about my adventures. You could have been hurt." When saying it, I pictured one more door closing, against my staying in England. They wouldn't want a tenant who brought killers to their doorstep.

"How did you knock him out?" Edward asked.

Color returned to Roger's face, and he took on a hint of swagger. "I was quite the batsman in my day."

To my look of confusion, he answered, "Cricket," and made a swinging motion.

"Ah." When faced with a nonsense answer, I liked to clarify things with equally vague sounds.

Taking charge, Edward corralled the Priestlys and Roddy to the house, carried me to the couch in the living room, and then made phone calls and took pictures.

Uniformed officers arrived first and carted George away. The rest of the MCIT team from Chedworth arrived shortly after.

Resurrecting the buffet from earlier, Meryl and Roger hosted the team like they were old friends.

Notebook in hand, Douglass set up an interview schedule. "Right then. You first, Ms. McGuire, then Reverend Priestly, and whenever you have a moment, Mrs. Priestly."

Apparently, food and tea created a chink in Douglass's armor, and he positively beamed at Meryl.

However, DI Parikh stepped in. "Thank you for the itinerary, Constable Douglass. But as Bailey here arrived first on the scene and made the arrest, he will interview the witnesses."

Throwing a glare at me, like I engineered the whole ordeal, he accepted a cup of hot tea from Meryl and left the house.

Edward and DI Parikh stood stony-faced, but I smirked a little. Douglass worked hard, but his constant mistrust of me crossed the boundary into harassment.

"Miss McGuire," Parikh said, shaking his head. "If you could answer a question before the ambulance arrives?"

I nodded.

"Do you have any idea how George found you in Bath?"

Shaking my head, I said, "No, none. I gave him a tour of the Villa, but that was after the pub..." I trailed off. The Wheatsheaf, where I first met George and the druids.

"Yes?"

"I may have mentioned Ash Tree Cottage when I first met him."

Parikh raised his eyebrows over the wire frames of his glasses.

"I know. It's just that it's so charming to have a house with a name."

We sat in the glow of Christmas lights. "Charming, indeed," he commented, taking in the festive decor.

Nodding, a lump formed in my throat. The house oozed charm, and I considered it home. And I might need to leave it in just a couple of weeks.

"It'll be alright, Maddie," DI Parikh said gently.

This brought a flood of tears. He hardly ever used my first name, if ever. I would miss this homicide detective. It's a ridiculous thing to think, but it's true.

The sounds of my slobbering must have led the ambulance technicians straight to me. "We've got a cot outside, miss," one said as he helped me to stand.

"I can walk," I said, hoping and whimpering.

"Not on our watch, you can't," the other said, and together, they carried me out of the house and onto the stretcher. A short ride and some powerful pain medication later, I found myself in a hospital bed, quickly succumbing to sleep.

* * *

"You've got some visitors, love," a friendly, vaguely familiar voice cut through my semi-awake fog. "You think you're up for it?"

Opening my eyes, I glanced at the nurse who took care of me the first time I was in this hospital.

"Sure," I grunted, voice hoarse.

"That'll be the pain meds. Parched like the desert," she said, handing me a cup of water with a straw.

"How's my knee?" I asked.

"The doctor will be in shortly, but between you and me, it's just a sprain."

Relief settled over me, but only briefly. "Then why am I in the hospital?" Overkill for a knee injury.

She smiled. "From the looks of you, you've attracted the wrong sort of attention. We treated your burns and cuts, too. And that constable of yours insisted you be looked after properly." She paused, then said, "Although he's in a suit now."

"Detective constable," I said, grinning at her, proud of Edward's new job. "I never thanked you for the makeup before." The last time I'd been admitted, I looked like a skeleton with hair combed by a blender.

"Glad it did the trick, love."

She helped me get presentable, let DI Parikh into the room, and closed the door as she left.

"I'm sorry I've caused you so much trouble since I've been in Bath," I told him.

Parikh removed his glasses, cleaned them, and smiled as he replaced them. "It has been interesting."

A vague response, like too many I've had lately, but the way he said it sounded positive.

"It should be I apologizing to you," he continued. "Our fair city hasn't shown itself in the best light."

"Oh, but it has," I said. "I love it so much."

Now that the immediate and, frankly, long-term dangers were passed, the uncertainty of my future came crashing into me. A tidal wave of questions and doubt yanked me in opposite directions.

Would I be able to stay? If so, where would I work? Would the Baths still want me? Or Dr. Daniels? Or are they sick of the trouble that swirled around me?

Was Lady Vivian counting the days until my departure? She considered me resourceful, but I threw a lot of chaos in her direction, including turning her into a lavender and saffron farmer. The commonness of it must rankle her at some level. The same concerns related to Simon.

And if I obtained a position, could I stay at the Priestlys? They seemed willing before, but then a knife-wielding murderer threatened their beloved rabbit. A tear leaked down my cheek as an image of Roddy dangling at knifepoint flashed in my mind.

Finally, Edward and what to do about him. He seemed to want me here. I thought I wanted to be with him and could picture a future with him. But then what the heck was my brain, or heart, thinking with Gabriel?

"Are you ready?" DI Parikh asked, probably tired of waiting for the turmoil playing across my face to stop.

After blowing my nose and wiping my face, I nodded. "Okay."

"Tell me everything about George Lynch."

I did, including the probably illegal land deals he'd made and the forgery of Jill's recommendation. "If he did one for her, he probably did others. But the most important thing is the second chi stone Jill found in the nymphaeum wall. George was trying to chisel it out to sell it on the black market. You have to find it."

Meticulous as ever, Parikh noted everything I said, asked gentle but probing questions, and occasionally asked me to verify an impressive insight on his part.

Finally, he said, "The brick was discovered in the trunk of Mr. Lynch's car. Along with several texts from rather unscrupulous antiquities dealers on his phone. It will be in evidence, but the National Trust has ensured it's safely stored."

As he stood to leave, I asked, "Can I go home?" My voice caught on the last word. How long could I call the Priestlys' house my home?

"Bailey will be by later to pick you up. He's finishing interviews and paperwork."

Once he left, Roger and Meryl bustled in. Geniuses that they were, they brought my laptop.

"We thought you might be bored, dear," Meryl said.

"The nurse tells us you can go home this evening. We offered to take you now, but apparently, Edward insisted on police protection."

"Boyfriend protection, I call it."

Astonishingly, they didn't seem mad at me. "How's Roderick?"

"Cuddly as ever," Roger said. "Meryl has been spoiling him."

"He deserves it," I said, reliving the experience with a shudder. One thing still bothered me, and I asked Roger about it. "How did you get out of the house?"

"The door in the larder."

Concentrating, I pictured the pantry in the kitchen. "I thought that went to a potting shed."

"It does. And the door in the shed opens onto steps down to the retaining wall, with a narrow path between it and the house."

"You're a literal lifesaver. Thank you."

Criminal for me to have not discovered the space behind the house before. I managed to find a secret gap between walls, but not a back door.

After quick hugs, they left.

Boredom kicked in pretty quickly, so I called Tori.

"You called me at a normal hour. You're on a streak," she answered.

"Considerate, I am."

Squinting into the camera, she said, "Is that a hospital bed?"

"Aye," I answered my observant friend.

"Your constable's Scottishness is rubbing off on you."

Smiling, I said, "Is Scottishness a word?"

"English is fluid. If it's not, it should be. But you're stalling."

After I related my two encounters with George the Druid that landed me in the hospital, Tori said, "I don't recall you being this accident-prone when we were kids."

"I hardly think being attacked by a killer is the same as accident-prone."

A knock on her door interrupted us, and Scott shouted a hello.

"Hi, Scott! Do you need Tori?"

His face appeared on the screen, and he kissed her cheek. "Always."

I marveled at how sweet he'd become. Or how I'd ignored it before. Either way, I was glad for my friend.

Tori's outlook on life soared above mine. She and Scott were committed to one another; her family, including her terrifying abuela, approved of him. Scott planned the weekends to visit her during her internship next semester, which would earn her an awesome and well-deserved career.

Nothing but uncertainty faced me, from relationships to jobs to living situations.

And I needed to figure it out.

Chapter Thirty-Three: Vague Answers

That evening, when Edward picked me up from my afternoon in the hospital, I wanted to get to work. Both literally at the Baths, but they were closed, but also securing my future. Nothing motivated me more than an hour of pouting in a dark room.

Since Edward often dominated my lists of unknowns, I started with him. I needed an answer in the form of concrete commitment. Not long term, not yet, but if everything else came out even, his answer would weigh toward my decision.

As he helped me into the borrowed SmartCar, I started there. "Who is this friend whose mother lets you borrow her car?"

"You've become quite fond of that question," he responded without answering.

"It," I said slowly and clearly to emphasize my point, "is important."

He closed my door and got in behind the wheel but didn't turn it on. "I'm sorry, lassie. You don't like surprises. I dinnae tell you sooner because I was embarrassed that I didn't have a car of my own."

"As I mentioned before, I wouldn't care," I said nonchalantly, rocking back and forth happily because my opinion mattered to him. And you still haven't answered," I added with a smile.

"It's—"

The ringtone on his phone interrupted Edward's confession.

"Parikh," he said, holding the cell to one ear while driving the other.

One series of grunts and okays later, we arrived at Ash Tree Cottage.

"I'm leaving now," he said and hung up. Rather than helping me down the garden path, Edward picked me up and carried me. "Faster," he explained as he deposited me on a bistro chair in the mud room. "I'll be back later if I can," he called as he sprinted up and out the gate.

"Okay, fine," I said to the darkened room. If I couldn't get information out of Edward, the Priestlys would be more forthcoming.

Except, the house stood empty. Christmas music wafted quietly through the downstairs, and lights twinkled, but no one greeted me.

In the kitchen, I found a note and a rabbit. 'Since Edward was with you, we're joining our friends at the Bristol Hippodrome for a show. Roger tells me to add that we will probably have a bit of a lie-in tomorrow morning,' the note said.

Roddy remained quiet but stretched up on his hind legs and set his front paws on me. Gathering him to my chest, I limped to the living room to set up camp by the tree.

Undeterred by the Priestlys' absence, I drew comfort from my furry friend and composed my email to Sam.

Careful not to put an email address in the Send To field until I wanted to send it, I started with overly formal, then too casual, then got the right tone but not the right words. Eventually, I typed, 'HIRE ME!!!' in all caps but quickly erased it.

Everything about this process proved more complicated than expected. But, as Lady Vivian said, about the time I discovered a body floating in the Roman Baths, I am resourceful.

So, I started a new email to her. Formal, grateful, and not pushy, I thanked her for the opportunity and expressed a desire to continue to grow at the Baths.

I read it out loud a couple of times, and it sounded okay, so I put her email address in the field.

And stared at it.

Terrified.

Sending it opened the door not only to success but also to rejection.

I stalled, deciding I needed a good stretch. As I did so, I heard little claws on my laptop keyboard.

When I set the laptop next to me on the couch, Roddy took the opportunity to crawl across it.

"No, no, no," I said to him. "You didn't."

He did. One of his long nails hit the send button.

"Okay, I get it," I said as I picked him up. "No more wavering."

Since one request floated out in the world, nothing remained to keep the others from joining it.

I sent similar messages to Simon and Samantha Niven. With them, I added the information George imparted in the garden about the additional chi stone in the wall. One more discovery I uncovered had to help my case.

Then, I spent more time crafting a request to Dr. Daniels that I be made a part of his team, provided that I remained in school to earn my degree.

After hitting send I hobbled into the kitchen for toast and hot chocolate. One of my favorite meals; I vowed to appreciate it even more when I secured my next year in England.

Positivity stayed with me for about fifteen minutes before doubt reared its soul-sucking force.

Ignoring the time, I called Tori.

"That's better," she said with a yawn, her thick black hair sticking out. "It's not a Maddie conversation unless I'm half asleep."

"I would apologize, but I did it intentionally this time."

"What's up? Did the druid escape?"

"Jeez, no. Why would you even suggest it?"

"Your track record isn't great," Tori reminded me.

"True, yeah, no. This particular disaster is in my mind. I sent out formal requests to extend my stay in England. Well, Roddy sent the first one, but I did the rest."

"Ah," Tori said, using one of my favorite phrases when confronted with confusion.

"Oh, come on. Where are your wise words?"

After a cat-like stretch, she clawed through her hair and said, "You're confusing me with your mother."

"Probably, but I can't call her at this hour. She'd be livid."

"Remind me to have her teach me that."

The penetrating gaze I aimed at her traveled half the world without losing its power.

"Okay, okay, okay," Tori relented. "Who did you send to?"

I told her about my communications and the information I included.

"Wait, go back. You discovered a second chi rho stone? That's huge!"

"To be fair, Jill found it."

"Yeah, but you got to tell everyone. That'll count for something." Pausing, her grin took on a definite impish quality. "So, what was it really like being tied up by Gabriel?"

"Don't go there."

"Come on. It must have been a little exciting."

Holding my wrist up to the camera to show the cut made by the zip tie, I said, "Painful, more like it."

Expression changing to one of fury, my tiny dynamo of a friend exploded in a show of sisterly support. "That rat bastard! He did that to you? Get Edward and DI Parikh and the whole police force after him now! The nerve of—"

"Actually…"

Stopping the tirade, she raised her eyebrows.

"I kind of did this to myself," I admitted, holding up my wrist again. "Gabriel was solicitous for a kidnapper. He let me pick out the chair and location and made sure I had plenty of room as he zipped the ties."

"So," she prompted, her grin returning.

I knew she wanted more about Gabriel, but the secret of his name wasn't mine to share.

"I tried to go all super spy and hop across the room. I got to the table, but he'd taken the SIM card out of my phone."

"Props to you for not damsel-in-distressing. But you know that's not what I meant."

Gabriel's farewell kiss came unbidden to mind.

"I knew it!" Tori said, clapping.

"It's nothing."

"He kissed you, didn't he?"

I waggled my head, noncommittal.

"It's like something out of a pirate movie," she said wistfully.

"Do not dare romanticize this."

Wide-eyed and innocent, she said, "Of course not."

"Moving on. Or backward, more accurately. I haven't seen the stone, so George could have been lying about the chi pointing to the treasure."

"Chi is an X in Greek."

"I know you know your Greek. And Latin. Overachiever," I teased.

"Indiana Jones assured us that X never marked the spot."

"It did in the third movie."

"Point. And you watch too many old movies."

"You watched most of them with me," I reminded her.

"How could I not? You had your own personal TV room, complete with a futon. My brother occupied the spare room in my house." Tori's smile returned. "Seriously, though, what was it like?"

"Having my knee pulled out of joint or almost getting burned alive? Or the knife. Let's not forget about that."

"Don't be dull. Gabriel and his roguish advances."

Like a terrier, she wouldn't let it go. I sighed dramatically and said, "I might have kissed him back."

"Maddie," she said breathlessly, leaning toward the camera.

"And he might have offered that I join him."

"Whoa, no way."

"And he left the coin with me after I told him its value in today's pounds."

Unlike Douglass or Parikh, Tori understood the meaning of the gesture. "Oh wow. He's got it bad." Straightening, she continued, "Well, that seals it then. England loves you. Of course, they'll ask you to stay. And hey, if not—"

"Do not," I interrupted, "suggest that I stay and take up a life of crime."

"You'd be good at it."

"Go back to bed," I told her, then took my advice and curled up on the couch with the rabbit.

* * *

Disoriented, I awoke to unfamiliar surroundings, gasping for breath. Attempting to sit up, I discovered a weight on my chest.

Roddy must have hopped on me at some point, and he slowly cut off my ability to inhale.

Sun shone through the ivory-colored linen curtains, lighting the living room in soft, warm comfort. An extra blanket lay over my feet, my cup and plate gone, and my laptop and phone tucked safely into a nook in the coffee table.

Smiling, I figured Meryl must have checked on me when she and Roger got home from their show. That seemed like the act of someone who would allow me to extend my lease.

Rejuvenated, my positive outlook returned as I got ready for work.

The swelling in my joints dissipated, and with the brace on my knee, I could walk without pain.

After writing a note to the Priestlys, thanking them for their kindness and letting them know I hoped to stay, I walked to the Baths. A cane leaned against the mud room door, which I took as another offering from Meryl. It helped my balance and allowed me to go at a normal speed.

Arriving at the Baths early, I found Sam in the Oversight Office.

"Maddie, me darlin' girl! I've got Simon over at Chedworth this morning, and he's confirmed the second chi rho brick in the nymphaeum. I'm heading over to meet Julie from the National Trust, and we will get it officially recorded.

"I called Dolly in for tours, the dear girl, with all she does at the spa, but she's a trouper that one since I figured your knee wouldn't be up to the uneven surfaces. Down to the crypt for you, but at least you have your padded chair for a break.

"Must be off!"

Without taking a breath or allowing me a word, she fled.

Obviously, she got my email since she sent Simon to Chedworth. But she didn't say a thing about my request to stay on.

Still, sifting in the Undercroft sounded good because it meant working with Dr. Daniels on discoveries.

As I headed to the elevator, I typed a message to Edward that I'd be in the Undercroft with no cell service and put my phone in airplane mode. My sifting table, situated in a utility stairwell, lay ready with the door propped open, a fancy floor lamp turned on, and snacks by my break chair.

Tempting as it was to go in and get to work, I needed to be brave to get answers. And bravery meant finding Dr. Daniels.

Support stick clacking on the cement floor, I marched to the main dig site.

A volunteer said, "You must be our sifter back from Chedworth. I heard you had quite a time out there, ooo yes."

"I did, yes. Some fantastic discoveries." Before she could ask about the other events, I said, "Is Dr. Daniels here?"

"No, not today. Meeting with the museum board, isn't he?"

"Okay. Have fun," I offered before heading back to my ancient dirt.

* * *

Sifting debris from a dig site was an essential job. And I had to keep telling myself that since it is also bone-wearyingly boring. Especially when a tornado of doubt still clouded my brain.

My thoughts took on natural disaster proportions these days. Tidal waves, tornadoes. I'd move onto earthquakes soon, ambiguity creating tectonic shifts in my mind.

As I considered what other catastrophic comparisons I could make, a polite "Ahem" came from an odd direction.

I jumped and maybe squeaked a bit at the appearance of Lady Vivian sitting in the wingback chair I used for my breaks. I had not heard her walk in and had no idea how long she'd been sitting there.

"Hi," I said stupidly.

"Quite."

"Deep in thought," I said, unable to form a complete and interesting sentence.

"Obviously. But not thinking about your job as you have had the same cup of dirt in your hand for quite some time."

I confirmed that, yes, the scoop of debris in my left hand rested on the table, still full, and the screen of my sifting table lay empty. I dumped it and started shaking the table while looking at my guest.

Far from impressing the woman who had such a massive influence on the Roman Baths Museum board, I proved spacey and inept at my job.

Excellent.

"I hear your Boxing Day proved less than pleasant," Lady Vivian said in a stunning understatement.

"Yes, but I did recover one of the lost aurei," I answered, hoping to sound clever and capable. Not that I did anything to get the coin back other than flirting when I shouldn't have.

"Dr. Daniels will be here soon," she said as she stood. "Do try to look productive."

She paced elegantly to the door in a scent of flowers, eyeing me on the way out. I shrank under her scrutiny.

"Next year, it will be easier if you simply join us for Boxing Day."

And she left.

"Wait," I called, but she had gone.

Did that mean I was invited back if I wanted to fly from America, or did it mean she expected me to be in England for the next year?

Either way made sense. I wanted to believe the best, but the disappointment would crush me if I were wrong.

Sifting like the best dirt sifter in the history of excavation sifting, I diligently went through two buckets before Dr. Daniels appeared in the doorway.

I stopped breathing.

"Uh, Maddie, yes, quite right," he said cryptically, then left.

"Sir?" I called, attempting to get up and out from behind the sifting table to pursue him.

Tripping on the cane, I plowed into the table, almost tipping it over. I steadied it just as Dr. Daniels reappeared.

"Yes? Oh, congratulations."

Subtly brushing the cane under the table, I attempted to appear competent. *You can do it, McGuire.*

"Thank you. Did you get my email?"

"Yes," he nodded. "Quite right."

When he strode away this time, I didn't catch him before he disappeared in a sea of assistants.

Except for Simon, Dr. Daniels' non-response covered those I'd emailed about my future. Sam avoided an answer, Lady Vivian offered an invitation that meant nothing or everything, Dr. D. continued his impression of the absent-minded professor, and I still hadn't gotten a straight answer from Edward. Since the Priestlys were seeing shows in another city, at least they weren't looking for a new tenant. At least, I hoped not.

The pub Gabriel mentioned in London started to sound appealing.

Chapter Thirty-Four: New Year's Eve

The Undercroft presented itself the following day, like every morning. Three stories below street level, it remained unaffected by the trivialities of weather, uncaring if I was offered an extension on my internship.

The sifting station in the stairwell housed comforts Simon and his aunt provided, including an elegant floor lamp and a wingback chair for my breaks. The problem at this particular moment was that I didn't want to care. If I couldn't stay, I shouldn't be attached to anything or anyone in England.

On the bright side, the knee brace made it possible for me to move around on my own and not have to call in favors to get to work. Since the most immediate people in my life refused to answer my politely worded queries, I preferred to get around without them.

Arriving to work on time, sifting diligently, and not causing trouble should earn me an excellent reference from the Roman Baths Museum and Dr. Daniels' archaeology team. Other than that, I needed no one.

Including Edward. I mean, what the actual heck was up with him, anyway? I may be out of his life forever in two weeks, and he can't even introduce me to a friend. A good friend. One close enough to borrow a car from his mother. Or hers.

It had to be a girl and a pretty one. Otherwise, why hide them? There was no reason I could think of. And if I go back to the first night we met, Edward was corralling girls out of a bar. Maybe one of them preferred his attention more than I did. He might be keeping her as his safety net girl to go back to once I leave.

Jerk.

My mind whirling, again, this time in new directions, I took a break. A flapjack, the absurd British name for a granola bar, sat on my snack table. Plopping into my chair, I opened the bar.

And what about Simon? I thought we were friends, and he couldn't tell me to my face that I wouldn't be staying. Coward. I mean, I had asked my fair share of questions lately, which no one, not one single solitary friend or colleague, answered, and it wasn't like I'd been a pushy American. I put stuff out there, and had waited patiently, and had that paid off? No, no, it had not. Because there were things I'd liked to…no, cancel that. Things I needed to hear, and all I got were vague responses or no responses at all.

As I nibbled, ranting silently, Sam and Simon came down. "We're off to the pub," Sam said.

"Edward will be joining us," Simon added as a statement instead of a question.

Not about to explain my current levels of angst about everything, I said, "He's at work."

Swallowing my annoyance with everyone, I played nice, asking, "Why are you leaving early?"

Giddy, Sam said, "You can't pretend you Americans don't celebrate New Year's Eve. I've seen Times Square on the telly."

Squinting at her, I recalled the past few days. So much had happened that I couldn't make sense of it. "New Year's? Already?" Days were slipping by, and I'd never get them back.

"Yes, and we're headed to the Huntsman for a pint. Meet us upstairs." Simon said as they left.

How could they not understand my situation? I considered staying at work to prove myself worthy, but I heard the bank of lights near the dig site shut off and realized no one would be here to be impressed.

Half of me wanted to stomp upstairs and make a show of not caring. The other half wanted to sink into earth, hiding until a final decision came through. I compromised by limping to the elevator while grinding my teeth.

The car filled with chattering, excited people discussing their evening plans, making me wonder about mine. Edward might assume we had a date, but he was severely mistaken if he thought he could just show up without making plans.

The Oversight Office overflowed with people, starting the festivities early.

In no mood to join them, I planned to get my answers. Simon would be more accessible, but Samantha Niven held the official post.

"Ms. Niven," I shouted over the din, and she tilted her head at the formality. "May I speak with you about official matters before we depart?"

"What's got into ye, girl?" Sam asked, her eyes twinkling.

"This is important," I told her.

"Alright then. Let's go in the hall."

The museum closed early to tourists readying for a special event that evening. The hallway allowed for a quiet chat.

"I need an answer about the decision of me staying on."

Sam's eyes shifted from side to side. Evasive, she looked behind us, perhaps in hopes of rescue from my penetrating gaze.

Plowing forward, I said as professionally as possible, "I apologize for being pushy, but I must make arrangements either way. I will not hold it against you. My time at the Baths has been invaluable and I'll always consider you a friend in addition to a mentor." My voice caught on the word 'friend,' and I bit the inside of my cheek to keep from crying.

They would have announced it by now if it were good news. But I needed to hear the rejection before I could process it properly.

"But Simon already told you. He said so," she insisted and annoyingly sprinted away back to the Oversight Office.

Before my head exploded, she returned, pushing Simon in front of her. "Tell Maddie what you told me," Sam instructed Simon.

"As you know, Dr. Daniels met with the museum board this week."

As a point, in fact, I did know that. The volunteer at the dig told me. No one else did, though.

I crossed my arms over my chest and said, "No, no one told me that."

"Ah, well. Dr. Daniels confirmed that he went to your stairwell after the meeting and spoke with you."

Taking a deep breath in and out, I explained, "All he said, and I quote, was, 'Yes, quite.' So, yeah, technically, he spoke with me. Conveying information, though, no."

Unable to help herself, Sam laughed. "Better you on his team than me, Maddie, my darlin'. A mad one, he is."

Three words penetrated my brain, cutting through my ennui.

On his team.

I needed to be sure. "Are you saying that the museum board confirmed that I will be a part of Dr. Daniels' team?"

"Yes," Simon said, turning to leave.

Snatching his arm, I stopped his movement. "Say the words. All of them. In order." As an afterthought, I added, "Please."

Simon put his hands on my shoulders and enunciated, "You, Ms. Madeline McGuire of Tempe, Arizona, are to join Dr. Daniels' archaeological dig team at the Roman Baths Museum for a period of two years, reassessed every six months by all parties. The condition that you stipulated about finishing your degree as part of the contract has been accepted, and your workload will be adjusted accordingly."

My jaw clenched shut to keep me from showing undue emotion. "Really?" I squeaked.

"I crafted the communique myself."

With a single motion, I swept his hands from my shoulders and threw my arms around him. Then Sam, and then both of them. Some tears might have leaked out.

"You are excited then?" Sam asked. "I thought you'd changed your mind, you've been so gloomy lately."

"I didn't want to be too disappointed if you all said no."

"And why would we do that?" Sam asked. "You found a piece of a tesserae and gold coins. A dream you are."

Disengaging himself from my overly American display of affection, Simon added, "Aunt Viv invited you over for Christmas next year."

"Boxing Day. But I wasn't sure if she meant I should fly across the pond for it."

"Silly cow," he said and gave me another squeeze.

"Are we ready to celebrate?" Sam asked.

"Oh yeah," I said.

Standing in the alley by the Huntsman, I said, "I should call the Priestlys."

Meryl's voice from around the corner asked, "Call us what?"

I laughed, greeting her and Roger as they neared the door. "To tell you the good news. My contract has been extended." Through my joy, a tiny bit of caution seeped in. I couldn't expect everything to go my way, so I asked my question quickly before another downward spiral took hold. "Would it be possible for me to stay on as your tenant? Or have you rented the room to somebody else already? I totally understand if you want to give a new person the opportunity because it is the most perfect place to stay, but I will still be a student. I'm going to be finishing my degree, somehow. I haven't figured that part out yet. But, again, I understand if you say no, especially after the Roderick incident."

Laughter, joyous and kind, bubbled from both of them. "Yes, of course, my dear. You're part of the family."

I asked Meryl and Roger to confirm it a few more times before I believed them. After offering more hugs, she added, "A box arrived at the house from your father, I think."

They opened the door, and I waved them in before me. I thought about calling my mom, dad, and Tori to tell them the good news but decided to wait for a decent hour.

Staying.

I couldn't believe it.

Inside the pub, a group of employees from the museum and the Pump Room congregated at the back corner, spilling onto two tables.

Lily rushed over to hug me when I came in. "You're staying!" she yelled.

"I am!"

I felt a tap on my shoulder, and Dr. Daniels, pint glass in hand, said, "I thought you two looked alike. Now it's confirmed." Sticking his hand out, he shook mine and said, "Welcome to the team. Let me get you a pint."

"Thank you," I said, almost speechless. I'd never seen the man more coherent.

"If I could have my girl back," a male said, taking Lily's hand.

"Donny. How did you get tonight off from the Boater?"

"Mac said he was miserable anyway, so I might as well have the night."

"All the better for us," I said as Dr. Daniels put a half-pint of beer into my hand.

"Cheers!"

Glasses clinked all around.

A thin arm snaked around my waist, and Dolly hugged me with all her might. "I hear it's settled, then. Perfect. You can help plan our wedding. I don't think I can do it on my own."

"You, Lady Gwendolyn, can do anything, anywhere, with grace and elegance."

Her bell-like laugh filled the room. "And you wonder why I'm glad you're staying."

With Dolly joining us, the evening was almost perfect.

Almost.

An image of Edward came to mind and wrenched my mood sideways. To make matters worse, as I frowned, James sauntered in. Unmistakably brothers, James looked like Edward but thinner and surrounded by a bad boy aura. Tonight, he peeved me more than usual.

Why was he at the pub and not Edward? It was New Year's Flippin' Eve, and the man hadn't bothered to call me.

"Hello, lassie," Edward said, low and intimate in my ear.

Turning around, I almost splashed my beer over him. "What are you doing here?" I asked, somewhat snappishly.

"What's wrong?" Edward asked, his smile falling away.

"Nothing." Okay, yes, it was an invitation to tell him my mind, but if he couldn't suss out how avoiding questions about his friends made me feel, then, well, yeah, childish answers.

"Are you mad at me, lassie?" he asked, demonstrating the thickheadedness of his gender.

"Ya think?"

Sweetly, he launched into a list of apologies about having to abruptly leave on so many occasions. Ending with, "And your phone is still off."

Oops. I put it in airplane mode when I went to the Undercroft and forgot to reactivate it.

Conceding a little, I said, "You never answered my question." There. An opening. He wanted to be a detective, let him detect.

"Yes, I did."

Shaking my head, I asked, "Do you even know which question I mean?"

Somewhat reluctantly, mainly to avoid making a scene, I allowed him to take my hand and lead me outside.

"About the SmartCar. I did answer," he insisted.

"No, you didn't," and at this point, my short, curt answers fell away into a rant, most of which centered around my insecurities. Too many emotions clashed around my system for too many days, and now they bubbled out. "I remember at least two, count them two, and maybe three conversations wherein I asked who owned the car, and you didn't answer. Well, once you said I might have met the person, but that's not precisely an answer because you did some un-constable-like things when you were in Edinburgh and besides which you should have been over with that by the time you first took me to Wookey Hole in the SmartCar. But when I told you explicitly how vital it was to me, you took a call and went to work. And never—"

"Maddie, Maddie, slow down," he said, leaning toward me. You told me the question was important, so I answered it and then took the call."

Blinking rapidly, I thought back to our discussion. He answered his cell with "Parikh." I assumed he was addressing the man, not answering me. But if it were an answer, it meant...

"Are you saying the SmartCar belongs to DI Parikh's mother?"

A glance at his feet, then he nodded.

"Why would you not tell me that?"

His hand raked through his hair. "How would that look to mo leannan that my only friend is a kind super at work? It's bad enough that it's such a wee car. Respecting your mum's wish, that you not ride a motorcycle was the right thing to do. I had to find something."

Ignoring the unfamiliar Gaelic expression, I paused, coming to terms with this confession. He'd said something similar before, but it hadn't sunk in. "You didn't tell me because you wanted to impress me?"

"Ya think?" he said in a great American accent and with a beautiful smile. "Lassie, from the first moment you pretended to ignore me in the bar, I knew."

"You did?" I said, a little uncomfortable about my earlier outburst.

Nodding, he encircled me with his arms, and we kissed.

Tingles erupted from my hair down to my toes as I breathed in his scent. Heart rate accelerating like I was trapped in a burning tunnel, I pressed my body to his.

Raucous laughter erupted as the pub door opened, interrupting our moment. James yelled, "Oi! Come inside."

* * *

After I had another half pint or two while Edward drank soda water, he said, "Come on. I found a spot."

Leaving involved many congratulations and more hugs. The evening confirmed what Meryl said: I was a part of the family, the Baths, and the community. England was my home.

No longer resenting the SmartCar, I gave it a little hug before getting in.

"Where are we going?"

"Beecham Cliffs," Edward answered right away, side-stepping my dislike of surprises.

"Can we stop at the house first? I'll need an extra layer, and I want to open the box from my dad."

Edward threw me a questioning gaze.

"It might have champagne."

The box sat on the white wrought iron table in the mud room. I read the note aloud, "'Congratulations Pumpkin! Viv and I thought this would be the best way to celebrate your extension.'"

Only one other person referred to Lady Vivian as Viv, and that was Simon, her nephew. How my dad managed to make such an impact in such a short time never ceased to amaze me. Putting the note down, I said, "This is great. My dad knew before I did."

"Keep reading," Edward suggested, pulling a puffy jacket from the box. "This'll come in handy tonight."

"He says Natalie, my dorm mate, helped him pack. And here's a note from her."

"Champagne it is!" Edward said, unfolding my down jacket to find a bottle of Cristal. "Wow. Good champagne."

"Only the best from my dad," I said, scanning the note from Natalie.

'Congratulations, girl, I knew you could do it! I'll definitely visit, but the English weather is too cold for these Jamaican bones, LOL.'

Although her parents were native to Jamaica, Natalie was born and raised in Chicago.

'The paperwork you'll need to continue your degree online is in the eight-by-ten envelope. Most of it you can fill out on the internet, but in a stunning display of obtuseness, the university requires real-live paper forms if you're in a different country. Go figure. I'll miss you, but I am so proud of you! Love, Natalie.'

"Ready?" Edward asked as I finished the note.

I smiled and pulled the warm jacket on.

Bouncing, we scampered across the street, over a low fence, and onto the grounds of Beecham Cliff. The city of Bath lay beneath us, spires glowing in the night sky.

Edward opened the Cristal, and we shared sips from the bottle.

Lips tingling from the bubbly, we kissed. After what seemed like forever wrapped in a moment, we broke apart, breathing heavily.

Once I regained some composure, I said, "I wasn't sure if you wanted me to stay. My internship ends in two weeks." My voice got quieter with each word. Any mask of nonchalance I pasted on fled.

"If the archaeologist didn't keep ye on, I would have had MCIT hire you. You're one of the best detectives out there. Anything to get you to stay."

To keep emotion from overtaking me, I asked, "What's mo leannan mean?"

Tucking a piece of my hair behind my ear, a gesture that melted my insides, he whispered, "My sweetheart."

We kissed as bells across town chimed midnight, welcoming in the new year. Fireworks exploded across the sky and in my heart.

Meryl's Cinnamon Rolls

These rolls, made by Meryl, Maddie, and Edward for Christmas, are light and packed with spicy flavor. If you prefer a gentler touch, reduce the cinnamon to 1-1/2 tsp in the filling. Feel free to add frosting of your choice, but Maddie prefers them without.

DOUGH:

- 1 1/2 Cups Milk, scalded (SEE NOTE)
- 7 Tbsp Butter (5 Tbsp butter plus 2 of shortening makes a fluffy dough)
- 2 1/3 oz Sugar, white
- 1 Egg
- 19 oz bread flour (1 lb 3 oz)
- 2 1/4 tsp active dry yeast

FILLING:

- 1/4 Cup butter, melted
- 1/2 Cup Brown Sugar
- 1 Tbsp Cinnamon
- 1/8 tsp salt

INSTRUCTIONS

MAKE DOUGH:

1. Scald the milk: measure out the milk into a pan and set over heat until tiny bubbles form around the edge (180 F).
2. Cut butter into chunks (big is okay).
3. Drop into scalded milk to help it cool.
4. Pour the mixture into the bowl of the bread machine. SEE NOTE if you prefer to mix by hand.
5. Add sugar, egg, flour, and yeast (in that order) into the cooled milk mixture in the bowl of the bread machine.
6. Set bread machine to Dough course.
7. Remove the dough at the end of the course (1 hour 50 minutes)

MIX FILLING:

1. Combine sugar and spices into a small bowl.
2. Gently melt the butter.

ASSEMBLE ROLLS:

1. After the first rise, roll the dough into a rectangle about 12" x 18" 1/2 inch thick. Honestly, Meryl doesn't have time to measure. Eyeball it.
2. Drizzle melted butter over the dough and spread evenly.
3. Sprinkle the cinnamon-sugar mixture over the buttered dough.
4. Roll from the long side and place the seam down.
5. Line two 9x9" pans (round or square or rectangle (9" x 11") with parchment paper.
6. Using a serrated knife or floss, cut one-inch-thick rolls and place them into the pans about one inch apart.
7. Cover and let rise until they are doubled in size, about 25-30 minutes (they should all be touching).
8. Bake at 350 until golden brown, 35-45 minutes.

NOTES:

1. Scalding destroys proteins in the milk that inhibit yeast rising. Do not skip this step!

2. If you do not have a bread machine, bloom the yeast in the milk-butter mixture once it has reached room temperature. Place the milk mixture in a large bowl. Add the dry ingredients. Mix vigorously with a wooden spoon until the dough comes together. Turn out onto a floured surface and knead for 10 minutes. Place in an oiled bowl, cover with a moist towel, and place in a warm area (or use a proofing drawer). Let rise until doubled in bulk. Punch down and knead for another 5 minutes. Allow to rise for 15 minutes, then roll out, fill, cut, and place in pans.

MAKE AHEAD:

Prep up to cutting and placing in pans. Cover with two sheets of plastic wrap and refrigerate for up to 2 days. It works well to make them on Christmas Eve and bake in the morning. Double wrap and refrigerate. In the morning, bring to room temperature (about 30 minutes) until all the rolls have doubled, then bake.

A Note from the Author

A note to clarify artistic license. Several concepts in the novel are true, including that Chedworth Roman Villa is real and has the best-preserved Roman mosaics in Great Britain. It was discovered in the Victorian Era during the Hunting Lodge's construction. As in the novel, the Hunting Lodge holds a museum of important artifacts from the site and has rooms for crew working on the grounds. Chedworth does employ student workers at times to protect, clean, and maintain the Villa, as Maddie and the team do. They might also work on ground-truthing, as mentioned in the novel. The Celts and their priests, the Druids, were chased out of the area centuries prior to the construction of the Roman Villa – Maddie's ire at the inconsistency is valid. The nymphaeum did go through religious changes, starting with nymphs, changing to Christ with the addition of the chi rho stone, and reverting to nymphs with the removal of the stone for use as a building block elsewhere in the Villa. Please see Julie Reynold's fascinating article on the nymphaeum on the National Trust site: (https://www.nationaltrust.or g.uk/visit/gloucestershire-cotswolds/chedworth-roman-villa) In addition to archaeology, Chedworth is home to nature conservation including rare barbastelle bats.

Artistic license comes into play in Maddie's various situations, none of which have occurred at the Villa. Also, while Emperor Aurelian did have a limited run of gold coins, to the best of my knowledge, none has ever been unearthed at Chedworth. However, the time period allows for a guest at the Villa to have carried them. We can always hope one will be found! Finally, there is not a second chi stone at the nymphaeum. My apologies to the National Trust for any additional liberties taken with this magnificent site.

Acknowledgements

My thanks to those in England start with deepest gratitude to Julie Reynolds, Cultural Heritage Curator at the National Trust, who provided me with invaluable information about Roman archaeology in general and the Chedworth Roman Villa specifically (see Author Note). In addition, my thanks to Tim Stuckes, retired Police Inspector formerly of the Avon and Somerset Constabulary, for his insights into the British police force. I also extend my gratitude to Betsy Francis-Mearns, aka @betsyinbath, for her endless recommendations about the elegant city of Bath and for providing me with pictures I could not take myself in the Thermae Spa (no cameras allowed). Also, at the Bath Abbey, my thanks to Tour Guide Toby, who showed me the apotropaic symbol. In America, my thanks go to the wonderful Verena Rose, Shawn Reilly Simmons, and everyone at Level Best Books. Thank you to Sisters in Crime and Mystery Writers of America for their resources and support. Additional thanks go to Kim, Jade, and Alyn for knowing so much that I do not. And finally, my profound appreciation to the Blackbird Writers for their treasured support and wealth of experience.

About the Author

Raised in Arizona, award-winning author Sharon Lynn developed a profound connection to the English countryside during her teenage years in England, a bond that has only strengthened with her frequent returns. This affection vividly colors the pages of A Cotswold Crimes Mystery series. As a professor of theater, film, and writing, she coaches and mentors aspiring artists. Her short stories can be found in anthologies from Malice Domestic and Desert Sleuths. She is a member of the Mystery Writers of America, Sisters in Crime, International Thriller Writers, Crime Writers Association, and Blackbird Writers. Sign up for updates at www.sharonlwrites.com.

AUTHOR WEBSITES:
   www.sharonlwrites.com
   www.blackbirdwriters.com

SOCIAL MEDIA HANDLES:
   https://x.com/SharonLWrites
   https://www.instagram.com/sharonlwrites/
   https://www.facebook.com/SharonLWrites/
   https://www.goodreads.com/author/show/22507717.Sharon_Lynn
   https://www.bookbub.com/authors/sharon-lynn
   https://www.amazon.com/author/sharonlwrites
   http://www.linkedin.com/in/sharonlwrites

Also by Sharon Lynn

Novels:

Death Takes a Fall: A Cotswold Crime Mystery Book 2 by Level Best Books (2023)

Death Takes a Bath: A Cotswold Crime Mystery Book 1 by Level Best Books (2022)

Short Stories:

The Professor's Lesson in *Malice Domestic 16: Mystery Most Diabolical* (2022),

Final Curtain in *Malice Domestic 15: Mystery Most Theatrical* (2020)

Carne Diem in *Malice Domestic 14: Mystery Most Edible* (2019)

Death on Tap in Sisters in Crime Desert Sleuths' anthology *SoWest: Killer Nights* (2017)

Death on Tap and *Carne Diem* are available as standalone short stories on Kindle.

www.ingramcontent.com/pod-product-compliance
Lightning Source LLC
Chambersburg PA
CBHW020609110726
47899CB00002B/438